The years can fly past
like a flock of birds.

—An Amish Proverb

SUGARCREEK AMISH MYSTERIES

Blessings in Disguise
Where Hope Dwells
The Buggy before the Horse
A Season of Secrets
O Little Town of Sugarcreek
Off the Beaten Path
Peace Like a River
Simply Vanished

Simply Vanished

SUGARCREEK Amish MYSTERIES

NANCY MEHL

Guideposts

New York

Many years ago I missed a chance to publicly thank the woman
God used to open a big door for me into publishing.
Now that I can remedy that mistake,
I won't let the moment slip past again.

To Susan Downs
for the second time, God has placed you
in my life. For that I'm incredibly grateful.
Your encouragement and support through the years
has been priceless to me.
I'm so blessed to work with someone
as wonderful as you are.
If I thanked you a thousand times,
it still wouldn't be enough.
But thank you anyway.
You're not only my editor,
you will always be my dear friend.

Chapter One

S ugar and grits." Cheryl Cooper slowly hung up the phone, a frown wrinkling her forehead.

"Is something wrong, my friend?"

Cheryl looked up to see Naomi Miller standing on the other side of the counter. She held a basketful of new goodies for the Swiss Miss.

"No. I mean…" Cheryl paused and smiled at the Amish woman's look of compassion. "It's nothing. That was my mother. She and my dad are coming here. For my birthday."

Naomi's eyebrows shot up. "*Ach*, your birthday? I did not realize…"

Cheryl laughed lightly. "There's no reason you should. I don't really celebrate it anymore. After I moved away from home, it just didn't seem important."

"Birthdays *are* important, Cheryl," Naomi scolded. "They allow us to celebrate *you*."

Cheryl shook her head. "You don't need to celebrate me. You make me feel special every day." She gazed into Naomi's eyes, amazed by the strong friendship they'd developed ever since she'd moved to Sugarcreek, Ohio, and taken over her aunt's gift shop.

Naomi returned Cheryl's smile. "'Friendship is a plant which must often be watered.'"

Another Amish proverb. She was learning that the Amish had a proverb for almost everything. She'd also learned that Naomi didn't need proverbs about friendship. She was a walking proverb.

"You water me often, Naomi. Thank you."

"And you do the same for me, Cheryl." She cocked her head toward the phone sitting on the counter. "Do you wish to tell me why you do not seem pleased that your parents are coming to visit? I remember you telling me how much you missed them."

Cheryl sighed. "You're right. And I meant it. But now that they're actually coming...I don't know. It's complicated." She realized Naomi was still holding the loaded basket. "I'll try to explain it later. First let's see what you brought me."

Naomi put the basket down on the counter. "More cheese, of course. Your customers certainly seem to like it. Especially butter cheese, *ain't so?*"

"My customers love everything you make." Cheryl reached in and began to remove items inside the large woven basket. Besides the cheese, there were jams and jellies and several boxes of Naomi's fudge. "This won't last long," she said, lining up the items on the counter.

"Ach, you speak the truth," Naomi replied. "Levi is bringing some caramel pies and friendship bread later this afternoon. I hope that will hold you for a while."

"Thank you. The new refrigerated cooler should be installed soon. I'm definitely running out of room in my small coolers."

Just then a customer stepped up to the counter, and Naomi moved over to give the woman room. She held two jars of apple butter in her hands and a large jar of honey against her chest. As she set everything down next to the cash register, her eyes locked on Naomi's delivery.

"Oh my," she said softly. "How much is the strawberry jam?"

Cheryl quoted a price, and the woman nodded. "Can I have two jars?"

Cheryl picked up the jam and added it to the woman's order.

"And a box of fudge too, please."

Cheryl glanced at Naomi and winked. Much of Naomi's delivery wouldn't even make it to the shelves. She rang up the woman's purchase and carefully wrapped the jars so they wouldn't break. Then she placed everything into a bag with the shop's name printed on the front. As the woman walked away, Cheryl sighed.

"Maybe I should just keep your food on the counter. That way I could sell it before I have to put price tags on it."

Naomi chuckled. "You certainly keep me busy. I am so happy that *Gott* is blessing you. When He blesses your friend, He blesses you as well."

"Another proverb?"

"Just me this time." The smile slowly slid from her face, and she patted Cheryl's hand. "About your parents?"

Cheryl glanced around the shop. There were only a couple of customers. One was inspecting the shelves, and the other was talking to Esther, Naomi's daughter. Esther usually worked from noon to three every day, but she'd come in early today since

Cheryl's other assistant, Lydia, hadn't shown up for work again. Even though Lydia didn't have a set schedule, Cheryl still counted on her for various tasks. It had been at least three weeks since she'd stopped by to see if Cheryl had any work for her. Frankly, Cheryl was getting worried. Esther and Lydia were both participating in *rumspringa*, an Amish custom that gave young people a period of time to decide if they wanted to be baptized into the church. While Esther seemed happy with her Amish life, Lydia had taken full advantage of her newfound freedom. She'd rejected her Plain clothing, started wearing makeup, and acquired a cell phone. She was also spending more time with some of the young people in town who weren't Amish and less time with Esther who had once been her best friend. Cheryl knew Esther was hurt by Lydia's rejection, but she did her best to maintain a positive attitude, something she'd learned from her mother.

Cheryl waved at Esther to get her attention. Then she motioned toward the office, letting the girl know she'd be away from the counter for a few minutes. Esther smiled and nodded and then turned her attention back to her customer. Cheryl felt blessed to have her helping at the Swiss Miss. She was bright and diligent. She was also completely capable of handling the shop alone if Cheryl wasn't there.

"Let's go into my office," she said to Naomi.

The Amish woman came around the counter and followed Cheryl to the small room at the back of the store. Cheryl closed the door while Naomi sat down in one of the chairs in front of Cheryl's desk.

Wondering just how she could explain her recently strained relationship with her mother to a woman who valued family above everything except God, Cheryl plopped down in her desk chair and took a deep breath. "My parents are great, and we've always been close. But after Lance and I broke up, I could tell they were disappointed. They didn't say it, but it was obvious. I'm turning thirty-one, I'm still not married, and I don't have any prospects. I know they're worried about me, and I understand that. Even so, things seemed fine. They weren't thrilled when I left the bank, but they seemed to understand my decision. They didn't try to talk me out of it. My mother and I have a long-standing habit of talking to each other every Sunday afternoon, but the past few weeks things have been…strained."

"What do you mean by *strained*?" Naomi asked.

Cheryl paused as she tried to find a way to explain something to her friend that she didn't understand herself. "My mother started changing the subject when I brought up the shop…and Sugarcreek. It's as if she doesn't want to hear about my life now. And that's hard because I have so much I want to share. She's rather short with me, which isn't like her. And suddenly she got too busy to talk to me on Sundays." She frowned at Naomi. "Frankly, she's started treating me like Matt, my brother."

"I do not know what you mean by that." Naomi looked as confused as Cheryl felt.

"Matt got into a lot of trouble as a teenager. Since Dad was pastoring a church, I think he and Mom were embarrassed by him. When he was nineteen, he left home." Cheryl shook her head slowly, remembering the day her mother called to tell her Matt had moved out. She was devastated. Cheryl could still hear the pain in her mother's voice. "They don't hear from him that often, but when they do, my mom is pretty cold toward him. She doesn't like talking to him on the phone."

"But I cannot believe any parent would be disappointed in *you*," Naomi said, a look of confusion on her face.

Cheryl felt a rush of affection for her friend. She was an honest woman who didn't say things just to make others feel better. Cheryl was certain her comment was from the heart.

"Thank you," she said. "My dad seems fine, but my mother is definitely upset about something. Lately she's made several negative comments about Sugarcreek. She never understood why my aunt loved this town so much. Now it looks as if I'm following in Aunt Mitzi's footsteps. I don't think this is the life my mother planned for me."

"But your father lived here as a boy, ain't so?"

"Yes, but once my dad left for college in North Carolina, he never really came back. Just for an occasional visit. As few as possible."

"Yet Mitzi never left."

Cheryl nodded. "This was always home to her. I'm sure my father has some good memories, but my mother never really understood its charm." She smiled at Naomi. "I wish they could see this town through our eyes."

Naomi made a clucking sound. "All parents believe they know what is best for their children. It is hard to watch them make their own choices—especially when you believe them to be wrong."

"I guess," Cheryl said. "Maybe I'm blowing things out of proportion. I hope when my mother sees how happy I am, she'll be happy too."

"I will certainly pray that she will. When do they arrive?"

"They'll get to town on Friday. My birthday is Saturday. They're staying at the Village Inn B-and-B. I told them they could bunk with me, but they don't really get along well with Beau."

Naomi frowned. "I do not understand. Your parents do not like animals?"

"They like them in their place. Which is in another room. The idea that I let Beau get on the furniture horrifies my mom. Her house is always picture perfect. Just like her."

"I see. And when do they leave?" There was no judgment in Naomi's voice, but Cheryl knew her friend's heart for animals. Cheryl was certain it was hard for her to understand how her parents could be ambivalent toward them.

"My mother didn't say. Probably after she gets me straightened out. Since it's already Wednesday, I guess I only have two days to prepare myself."

"Oh, Cheryl, perhaps their visit will be a blessing. As you said, perhaps you have misunderstood your mother."

"Maybe you're right. I guess I need an attitude adjustment."

Naomi stood up. "It is not for me to say, but I will pray for all of you. Family is so important." She reached up and adjusted her *kapp*. "How do you intend to celebrate your birthday?"

"I haven't really thought much about it. We'll probably go out to dinner."

"Nonsense," Naomi said huffily. "You will come to our house on Saturday. I will make you a wonderful birthday luncheon. If you still wish to go out to dinner later in the day, you will have plenty of time."

"Oh, Naomi, I don't want you to put yourself out like that. It's too much work and not much notice."

Naomi chuckled. "I believe after all this time we have spent together, you know me better than that, ain't so? I love to cook. It is not drudgery to me." She studied Cheryl for a moment. "If you do not think your parents would be comfortable in our home…"

Cheryl got to her feet. "Oh no. That's not it at all. I'm sure they'll love you."

Naomi nodded, her expression resolute. "Then it is settled. You will bring your parents to our house on Saturday, where we will have lunch and cake as we thank Gott for bringing you into the world—and our lives."

Cheryl was touched by Naomi's offer, but even though she hadn't admitted it, she was a little worried about her mother. She had no problems with the Amish—at a distance. Her father had grown up around the Plain People. He would be gracious and accepting. If there were any problems, they wouldn't come from him. Usually her mom was very careful to follow her husband's lead in public. She saw supporting him as her calling. As Cheryl considered this, she felt a little better. Besides, who wouldn't love the Millers?

"Naomi, I can't thank you enough. I would be so honored to bring them to your home. This will be a wonderful birthday—

because of you." She walked around the desk and gave Naomi a quick hug.

"Ach, I must get on my way," Naomi said when Cheryl released her. "You were only my first delivery today. I have two more stops." She started toward the door but then turned back to look at Cheryl. "I believe you said work would begin this week on your new cooler?"

Cheryl nodded. "Chuck Watson is putting it in. Several people recommended him. Actually, he's coming tonight to tear out the wall. I don't want my customers exposed to all the dust, and the work he's doing tonight will be pretty messy. By tomorrow Chuck said he'd have a plastic sheet hanging up to keep any dust from getting into the shop. Hopefully, it won't be too bad. I'd rather not close if I don't have to."

"What about the food that is back there now? Do you need help moving it?"

"Thanks, but I'll take care of it. Only the food closest to the construction needs to be relocated. I'll do that sometime today. Most of the other food can stay where it is. The sheet should keep it safe."

Naomi nodded. "And how long will the work take?"

"Chuck said it would take less than a week, but I don't know. Knocking out a wall seems like a big deal to me."

"There does not seem to be much space in that corner."

"Chuck says there's a dead space."

Naomi's eyebrows shot up. "A *dead* space?"

"Yeah. An area where drywall extends out a few feet, but he doesn't think there's anything behind it."

"That seems very unusual." Naomi pursed her lips. "I am not experienced in building and renovations like Seth and Levi, but I have not heard of anything called 'dead space' before."

"Me either. But if he's right, with that area opened up and using part of the bathroom"—she pointed to the bathroom connected to her office—"Chuck says we'll have enough room for the new cooler."

Naomi smiled. "I will pray that everything works out the way Chuck says." She squared her shoulders. "Well, I must be on my way. Seth will pick up Esther when her shift is over."

"Thanks again, Naomi. I'm closing at noon on Saturday. We'll head over to your house after that. We should be there a little before twelve thirty. Will that work for you?"

"That will be fine, Cheryl. Do not rush. The food will still be there when you arrive." She grinned. "As long as I can keep Levi away from it."

Cheryl laughed and walked her friend to the front door. Then she got back to work adding the goods Naomi had delivered to the shop's inventory list. After tagging them, she put them on her shelves.

The rest of the day went by quickly. At five, she closed the shop. Beau immediately ran to the back room and stood next to his crate. Cheryl stroked the large Siamese's fur. He had certainly settled in nicely to her routine and her customers. Everyone seemed to love him. "Not yet," she said gently. "We have something else to do first."

A knock on the front door got her attention, and she hurried out into the shop to let Chuck in. He looked relieved when she opened the door. Temperatures were hovering in the low forties, but the wind made it feel much colder.

"It's a little chilly out there," he said as he stepped inside the shop. Chuck was a large man, tall and stout with muscular arms. He wore his graying hair in a style that used to be called a butch cut. Not a hairstyle many men wore anymore. With his deep booming voice and distinctive look, he was certainly unique. He reminded Cheryl of a Marine drill sergeant.

"Yes, it is," Cheryl said with a smile. "But it's nice and warm in here."

Chuck had a large toolbox in one hand and a rolled-up piece of heavy plastic in the other. He headed to the back of the store and set everything down on the floor.

"I haven't moved the food out yet," Cheryl said. "I can do that now."

Chuck nodded. "Might be best. I'm gonna make a pretty big mess at first, but it will be cleaned up before you open tomorrow. I just wanna remove this drywall and get to the studs. I'll hafta do the same to the bathroom. As I told you before, you won't be able to use it for a couple of days."

"I understand." She'd already talked to Kathy Snyder, the owner of the Honey Bee Café across the street. Kathy kindly offered her facilities until the Swiss Miss bathroom was put back together.

Cheryl quickly began unloading cheese, cream cakes, and butter from the cooler closest to the area where Chuck would be working. Once she moved everything, she asked him about the other coolers.

"Nah, they'll be fine. I'll put some extra plastic sheeting over them just in case. After tonight there won't be much dust until the final drywall goes up. Then I'll have to do some sanding, but I'll come back at night and get it done so it won't disturb business." He nodded at her. "A little inconvenient, but in the end, it'll be worth it."

"I believe it will." Cheryl smiled at him, but he didn't smile back. She didn't take offense. Chuck's dour expression never seemed to change. To be honest, he had the kind of face that didn't seem to fit a smile. Kind of like a basset hound having a bad day.

"I'm gonna start tearing out this wall in just a bit," he said. "I'd rather you hang around until I can see what's behind it. I've located all the water pipes and the ductwork for your central air, so I don't expect any surprises, but with these old buildings you just never know what you might find. One time I took down a wall and discovered a stash of drugs and a roll of one-hundred dollar bills."

"In Sugarcreek?" Cheryl knew drugs were everywhere, but Sugarcreek, Ohio, was the last place she expected to see that kind of activity.

Chuck shook his head. "Nah, it was a job in Cincinnati. I've found some odd things here too though. Lotsa old shoes."

Cheryl frowned. "Old shoes? I don't understand."

"Folks used to believe putting shoes inside the wall of a house being built would bring the owners good luck."

"Really? How funny."

"Lots of razor blades too. There used to be a slot in bathrooms where men would dispose of their razor blades when they became dull."

"Sounds kind of dangerous."

"They're usually so dull it's not a big deal." He sighed. "Of course, I've found lots of dead animals, rats and such." He paused for a moment. "Once I found a book and some toys. Obviously belonged to a child. Put there many years before the current owners moved in. Never did find out why they were there. That one still bothers me a bit." He shrugged. "Well, I'd better get to work."

"Thanks, Chuck." His stories about things behind walls left her feeling a little unsettled. As she turned to walk away she realized Beau was sitting a couple of feet away, staring at them. She pointed at him. "You're going in your crate. Trust me. You won't enjoy the noise and the dust."

As if agreeing with her, Beau meowed.

Cheryl picked him up from the floor and took him back to the office. As she worked on the day's receipts, she heard her stomach growl. Lunch had been a long time ago, and she was looking forward to the veggie hummus wrap she'd picked up from the Honey Bee Café earlier in the day. A tiny compact refrigerator in her office allowed her to keep food fresh for lunch and supper.

Suddenly, Cheryl heard loud pounding from inside the store, and the building shook. Even though she'd been expecting the noise, it startled her. Inside his crate, Beau jumped and yowled with surprise.

"It's okay," she said soothingly, not sure if she was trying to console him or herself. Evenings at the Swiss Miss were usually very quiet. After some further pounding, there was a pause in the racket.

"Miss Cooper?" Chuck called out. "Can you come here a moment?"

Hoping he was going to tell her everything was okay and she could leave, Cheryl got up from her desk and headed to the corner where Chuck was working. A large plastic tarp hung from the ceiling. Cheryl pushed it back and found him standing on the other side, an odd look on his face. Cheryl's heart skipped a beat. Uh-oh. Was this going to cost her more than she'd hoped? She coughed at the dust floating in the air. "I found something odd," Chuck said as she came near. "Took me a minute to figure out what it was."

Cheryl prayed he hadn't uncovered something that would have to be moved. It could add significantly to the cost of the project.

He pointed toward the place where drywall had been torn out. Cheryl's eyes followed his finger. Inside the wall was a wooden boxlike structure with a small door. Chuck reached in and pulled the door open. Something was inside the box.

"I don't understand," Cheryl said slowly. "What—"

"It's an old laundry chute," Chuck interjected. "Not unusual for older houses. But it should have been removed before the drywall was put up. And that's not the weirdest thing." He reached inside and pulled out two dusty items that he placed on a nearby sawhorse. "Who puts a woman's purse and a valise in a laundry chute and then covers it up?"

Chapter Two

Cheryl got a rag from under the counter and carefully dusted off the old leather purse and soft satchel.

"These look old," she said.

Chuck nodded. "I'd say they're at least thirty to forty years old." He pointed at the purse. "My mother had a bag like that."

"Can you tell how long they've been in that chute?"

"No, not really." Chuck studied the hole in the wall. "This repair isn't new. The Sheetrock has definitely been here awhile. Someone closed off the bottom of the chute so this stuff wouldn't fall through. I assume it was done around the same time the Sheetrock went up, but I can't say for sure." He stared at the wooden structure for a moment. "Have you ever seen an opening in the ceiling downstairs? You know, where the laundry would fall through?"

Cheryl shook her head. "I think I would have noticed something like that. In fact, we had the ceiling checked when a pipe burst in the bathroom a few months ago. There wasn't any kind of opening."

"Well, I can't tell you much more. Maybe you should ask your aunt. She was the one who turned this old house into a store."

"You're right. I hadn't thought about that."

Cheryl's aunt and uncle had purchased the house twenty years ago, and after extensive renovations, turned it into the Swiss Miss. But why would they hide things in an old laundry chute? It didn't make any sense.

"We try to Skype as often as we can," Cheryl said slowly. "We're supposed to talk Friday evening. I'll ask her about it."

Cheryl slowly opened the old purse. The metal clasp came off in her hand. "Wow, this isn't in very good shape." She reached inside the purse and began to pull out its contents. A thick brown leather wallet, a brush, a compact with rhinestones on the cover, a tube of lipstick, a set of keys, a small coin purse, and an old pen. She carefully placed each item on the sawhorse. She picked up the wallet and looked it over. There was a strip of leather tucked through a loop on the outside. When Cheryl tried to pull the strip through, it fell apart.

"You can't open it without causing damage," Chuck said. "After all this time, I doubt if the owner will care." He frowned. "Could this stuff belong to Mitzi?"

"I don't think so. Aunt Mitzi's not the kind of person to hide things. She's very straightforward. This doesn't seem like something she would do."

Chuck nodded. "I see what you mean."

Mitzi Porter wasn't known for being a passive person. She was talkative and open with everyone. Cheryl's uncle Ralph used to smile at his wife and say, "You know, Mitz, it's okay to have an unexpressed thought now and again." The memory made Cheryl smile.

She carefully pulled the wallet open and found several pockets. Inside one of them was an old driver's license. Although the plastic that covered it was cloudy, it was still readable.

"Ellen Streeter," Cheryl said. "And her address is...here. She lived here." Cheryl gazed up at Chuck. "Have you ever heard of her?"

"Sorry. I knew the Barnes family who owned the house when your aunt bought it, but I'm not sure who lived here before that."

Cheryl stared at the picture on the license, but the plastic was so opaque she couldn't make out the face. Just dark brown hair. Well, at least she knew the purse wasn't her aunt's. But who was Ellen Streeter and why were her personal possessions inside an old laundry chute?

Cheryl looked at some of the other things inside the wallet, but most of it was paper and seemed pretty fragile. She closed the wallet and put it aside. Then she opened the small coin purse. Expecting to find several coins, she was surprised to only find one. She took it out and held it in her hand, palm side up.

"Seems odd to only carry one coin," she said, frowning.

Chuck's quick intake of breath caught her attention. She glanced at him and was surprised by the intense look on his face. "It makes sense if it's what I think it is," he said slowly. He reached over, took the coin from her hand, and studied it carefully, turning it over to look at both sides.

"What do you mean?"

"This is a 1934 S Peace Dollar. It's worth a great deal of money."

"How much?" Cheryl asked.

He handed the coin back to Cheryl. "It's in very good condition. I'd say it's worth somewhere between four to six thousand dollars. In perfect condition it might bring in close to eight thousand."

"How do you know that?" Cheryl asked, startled by his information.

"Coin collecting is my hobby. I don't have anything like this though."

"Wow." Cheryl gazed down at the coin in her hand, wondering what to do with it. "I'd better lock this up. I'll be right back."

She hurried to her office, put the coin in an envelope, and placed it in one of the drawers in her desk that locked. Frankly, it made her nervous to have such a valuable coin in the store. She needed to find this Ellen Streeter, or her relatives, as soon as possible. Maybe they could offer an explanation for this strange turn of events.

She grabbed her purse and Beau's crate and carried them out to the counter. Then she went back and got her dinner out of the fridge before she locked the office door. She set the Styrofoam box from the Honey Bee on top of the crate and then pulled out a large store bag from a shelf. She took it back to where Chuck waited.

"I'm going to take these home and see what else I can find," she told him.

He nodded. "I need to remove the laundry chute so I can move this wall back. Is that okay with you?"

"Sure. If you find something else, will you just put it behind my counter? I'll look it over in the morning."

"Sure, but I think that's it. Whoever put those things inside the chute sealed it up pretty good. They obviously didn't want them found. But before I start dismantling everything, I'll shine a flashlight at the bottom of the chute. Just in case."

"Thanks, Chuck." Cheryl smiled at him. "I'm really excited about my new cooler, and I appreciate your willingness to work at night so I can stay open during the day."

Chuck grunted and patted his stomach. "My concern isn't completely unselfish. I'd hate to miss out on any goodies. Especially Naomi Miller's caramel pie. I think I'm actually addicted to it."

"Believe me, I understand. It's a miracle I don't weigh five hundred pounds."

He nodded and turned back toward the wall.

Cheryl started to walk away but then remembered something and went back. "I'm not going to turn on the alarm," she informed him. "So if you would make sure the front door is locked when you leave, I would appreciate it. Do you still have the key I gave you?"

"Yep. I'll make sure the door's locked tight. Don't worry about it."

Cheryl got Beau, who was obviously a little miffed at being kept so long in his crate. Then she slung her purse over her shoulder. When she reached the front door, she had to put Beau down since her hands were full. She stared at the alarm box next to the door. Frankly, she was glad she didn't have to turn it on tonight. That thing made her nervous. She'd set it off so many times people in town were starting to make jokes about it. She'd never really wanted an alarm, but after a couple of break-ins around town, the need for one had become obvious.

She closed the door behind her and hurried down the steps to her car. The wind cut through her coat and blew her hair around. She laughed when Beau hissed as if the wind were an enemy to be confronted.

"Silly cat," she said softly. She gently set his crate in the backseat and closed the door of her blue Ford Focus. A quick look in her rearview mirror made it clear the wind hadn't messed up her hair much. She ran her hand through her short disheveled locks. "One good thing about hair like mine," she said to herself, "it looks the same no matter what happens to it."

She started the car and began heading home. Even though it was only a little after six o'clock, many of the shops on Main Street were already closed, including the Honey Bee Café and By His Grace, the Christian bookstore. But as she drove down the street, the lights from Yoder's Corner spilled out into the street, bathing it in a soft golden glow. The parking lot was full of cars, and several horses with buggies stood patiently in front of the restaurant, tied to the hitching rail.

It only took a few minutes to reach her house. She was happy to be home, but she was also excited to look more closely through the purse and valise. Maybe there was a clue somewhere inside them that would lead to Ellen Streeter. Cheryl wanted to return her belongings, but she also wanted to uncover the mystery that surrounded their discovery. As she entered the warm and cozy house, she looked forward to her dinner from the Honey Bee along with a cup of hot tea. She'd no sooner closed the front door when drops of rain began to bounce off the front window, sounding like frantic drumbeats. Cheryl found the rain soothing, but Beau wasn't a fan. He yowled with displeasure.

"Perfect night to be inside," she said to him as she opened his crate. He ran straight into the kitchen and sat in front of his food bowl, ignoring the rain for now. Obviously his appetite held first place in his list of likes and dislikes. Cheryl fell into their regular nightly routine. First she fed Beau, then she put the teapot on the stove and took a plate out of the cabinet. She removed the veggie hummus wrap from the Styrofoam box and added two oatmeal walnut chocolate chip cookies to her plate. The cookies were also from the Honey Bee. Although Cheryl liked to bake when she had time, between the cookies at the Honey Bee and all the delicious desserts Naomi made, she just couldn't see the point. In the fridge was some of Naomi's rich, scrumptious cheesecake, along with a box of her fudge. Cheryl tried to limit herself to one piece of fudge a day. It was a special treat, not only because it was the creamiest and most delicious candy she'd ever tasted, but also because it reminded her of her friendship with Naomi.

As she went into the living room, her eyes drifted to an embroidered piece that hung on the wall. *Love Always Finds a Home in the Heart of a Friend.* Cheryl loved the framed artwork. Naomi had made it for Aunt Mitzi, but somehow Cheryl felt as if it also belonged to her now.

She sat down in a large overstuffed chair in the living room, her feet on the matching footstool and a warm comforter over her legs. Beau took up his nightly place, snuggled in a ball on her legs. It didn't take long for him to begin purring contentedly. The rain was much lighter now, so thankfully he'd decided to ignore it.

Cheryl ate her dinner and sipped her tea then picked up the book she'd been reading and settled into a story written by her favorite cozy mystery author. The cold rain outside danced on the roof and slipped down the windows. The sound was so comforting Cheryl didn't realize she'd fallen asleep until she awoke with a start when her book fell off her lap and on to the floor.

Beau raised his head and stared at her accusingly.

"I'm so sorry. Did I disturb your nap?" Cheryl asked.

She could almost swear he winked at her before he put his head down again.

"Sorry, bub," she said, "but I have something to do. You'll have to get up."

Looking slightly offended, Beau jumped down to the floor and waited for Cheryl to get to her feet. Then he leaped back onto the chair, turned around twice, and lay down.

"Well, excuse me," Cheryl said, smiling at his antics. "I guess I'm not the main event. You just want my chair."

She picked up her book, found the place where she'd stopped reading, and slid in her bookmark. Then she carried her dishes to the kitchen. A few minutes later, the dishwasher was loaded and she was ready to find out what she could about Ellen Streeter. She wished she could call Aunt Mitzi right then and ask her about Ellen, but Mitzi spent most of her time away from phones. Being a missionary certainly wasn't a nine-to-five job. As it was, their

Skyping sessions didn't always work out either. Thankfully, Mitzi also sent e-mails and letters, with an uncanny way of timing them so they arrived just when Cheryl needed a word of encouragement. The Lord had been using Mitzi in her life ever since Cheryl was a child. Taking over the Swiss Miss so Mitzi could fulfill the call on her life had also changed Cheryl's life in a very profound way. She'd found contentment living in Sugarcreek. Running the shop brought her a sense of fulfillment no other job ever had. It was as if Mitzi's obedience to God had opened the door to His plan for her niece's life as well. Cheryl had no idea how long she would work at the Swiss Miss, or even stay in Sugarcreek. A lot of those decisions would have to wait until Aunt Mitzi returned. But no matter what, Cheryl had no plans to return to the kind of job she'd had in Columbus. Although some people could be happy being stuck behind a desk, she wasn't one of them.

She took the bag with Ellen's things off the cabinet and sat down at the kitchen table. Then she carefully removed the purse and valise, which she opened slowly, trying not to cause damage to the ancient leather. Inside were clothes, underwear, and shoes. The styles reflected those from perhaps the seventies, but nothing had a "modern" feel to it. Even in the seventies, these clothes would have been considered old-fashioned. A pleated skirt, a plain brown dress, flannel pajamas, brown shoes with metal buckles, some panties, two bras, and several pairs of panty hose. Age had darkened the delicate underthings. There was a small wooden box with a few jewelry items, but nothing valuable. Just some old clip earrings and some blue beads. When Cheryl picked them up, the string that held them together broke, and the beads began bouncing off the table and on to the floor. Almost immediately, Beau came running from the living room and went after them as if Cheryl were playing a game.

"Stop that," she cried out, afraid he might swallow one. Of course, like a typical cat, he totally ignored her. She got down on her knees and quickly scooped up the beads while having to grab Beau and forcibly remove one from his mouth. He wasn't happy about it and retreated under the table to glare at her. "Too bad, you silly old cat," she said. "I'm trying to keep you safe." It was clear he wasn't impressed with her concern for him.

Cheryl returned to her chair, picked up the remaining beads, and put them back inside the box. Then she pushed the valise aside and picked up the purse. Once again she opened it and took out everything, setting all the items in front of her.

"Who are you, Ellen? And why did you need to hide this stuff?"

The wind moaned outside as if in response to her question. The sound made the hairs on the back of Cheryl's neck prickle.

"Don't let your imagination play tricks on you," she whispered to herself. She carefully opened the wallet and began to remove things from it. She checked the driver's license again. It was totally fused to the murky plastic sleeve. If she tried to force it out, she would probably ruin it. She decided to leave it alone.

"Probably got hot in that wall and the plastic melted," she murmured.

She carefully pulled the pocket behind the license open. Thankfully, it wasn't stuck together. Inside Cheryl found an old handkerchief with embroidery. The material had darkened and the colors from the threads had run, so it was hard to tell exactly what the embroidery pattern was supposed to be, but it looked like purple lilacs. There was some money, about eighty dollars, and a piece of paper. Cheryl carefully removed it. At first she was afraid to open it for fear it would fall to pieces, but as she slowly unfolded it, she was surprised to find that the yellowed paper stayed intact. It seemed to be some kind of letter, but the ink had faded and it was hard to read. Cheryl left the letter where it was and went into her bedroom to get her magnifying glass. Although she had good eyesight, sometimes she needed help to make out the small print on medicine bottles and the ingredients on some cans and boxes. Cheryl was convinced some drug companies and food manufacturers hoped consumers would simply ignore the impossibly small print and use their products without question. But Cheryl wasn't that kind of person. She was curious… and somewhat suspicious. Frankly, this attribute had served her well since coming to Sugarcreek, and she had no plans to change her inquisitive nature even though her mother told her a few months ago that maybe Cheryl needed to "mind your own business and start looking for a husband."

Although her mother knew Cheryl's relationship with Lance Wilson, her onetime fiancé, was over, Cheryl hadn't told her that a few months ago he'd visited Sugarcreek. Lance apologized for breaking their engagement and asked her once again to marry him. Cheryl turned him down and sent him on his way. Frankly, she was grateful he was finally out of her life. Ever since coming to Sugarcreek, she'd begun to see things differently. The simple life of the Amish had shown her what was important...and what wasn't. She wanted a man more like... An image of Levi Miller, Naomi's stepson, popped into her head.

"Stop," she chided herself. "That's just ridiculous." Levi had become a good friend, and she had no plans to ruin their relationship with romantic ideas that had no chance of fruition.

Once again seated at the table, Cheryl held the magnifying glass up to the faded letter and stared closely at it. She was finally able to make out some of the handwriting. Small, but perfectly formed, the characters demonstrated beautiful penmanship. Not something that was valued much anymore.

The beginning of the letter was impossible to read. The salutation and first few lines were completely gone. But about a quarter of the way through, Cheryl could discern most of the words:

...in this loveless marriage. I've got to change my life. It's as if I've been living in a prison all these years. You've shown me that there is light beyond the darkness. Even if that life doesn't have you in it. I'm writing this so you'll know that I loved you. Always.

I've decided to leave Sugarcreek. I'm getting on the bus and traveling as far away from here as I can. I have no idea where I'll end up. I have a little money that I've saved down through the years. It's not much, but I can't wait any longer. With God's help, it will be enough to start a new life.

I hope you're reading this letter, my love. Because if you're not...

At this point the writing grew much lighter and hard to read. Cheryl skipped ahead to the signature. She could make out, *I love you... Ellen.*

Ellen Streeter had written this letter, but whoever it was intended for had probably never seen it. Cheryl leaned in closer, trying to make out the last words before the letter ended. Slowly but surely, she deciphered some of the individual letters. She grabbed a nearby pad of paper and a pen and began writing down anything she could make out. When she had done her best, she looked at what she'd written. Adding the missing letters wasn't that hard. As she studied the completed sentences, she gasped. The final line read, *Because if you're not, he's probably murdered me.*

CHAPTER THREE

Cheryl nervously watched the street through the front windows of the shop. It was almost noon. Hopefully Naomi would drop Esther off for work today. Sometimes Seth, Naomi's husband, delivered Esther to work, as did Levi if he was able to get away from their farm.

Although she enjoyed seeing Seth and Levi, Cheryl wanted to talk to Naomi about the letter. She wasn't sure what to do until she knew more about Ellen Streeter. Hopefully, Naomi could give her some information or at least steer her in the right direction. Cheryl didn't feel she could take the letter to the police. It was really old. Anything that might have happened took place a long time ago. Besides, Chief Twitchell was a little irritated with her. She'd set the store's alarm off accidentally so many times, he'd threatened to ignore any calls for help if she didn't get things under control.

The morning had been really slow. Most of the buses that brought tourists to Sugarcreek were on hiatus and wouldn't start up again until next month. Except for the occasional special charter excursions, Cheryl didn't have to deal with the sudden rush of traffic the buses usually produced. Lydia had always been a big help during those really busy times. If she didn't come back to work soon, Cheryl would have to start tracking inventory herself, something Lydia had been trained to do. Cheryl decided that if she didn't hear from Lydia by that afternoon, she'd call her cell phone. She didn't want to pressure the girl, but Lydia hadn't left her much choice.

Movement from outside caught her attention. Naomi's buggy was in front of the shop. Before Cheryl could run out and ask her to come inside, she saw Naomi getting out of the carriage with Esther. They both walked up to the entrance, and Naomi opened the door. Cheryl noticed her friend's pensive expression. She had seen this look before. Something was wrong.

"Hello," Cheryl called out.

Esther looked at her mother, who only nodded her reply. As they came over to the counter where Cheryl waited, she could see that Esther looked as worried as her mother.

"I will watch the store," Esther said, coming around the corner and picking up her apron. "*Maam* would like to speak with you."

"If you have a moment," Naomi said quietly. "But if you are too busy—"

Cheryl waved her hand and gestured toward the empty shop. "I think I can find the time." She caught Esther's eye. "Chuck Watson should be here any minute. He'll be working in the front of the store where our new cooler will be." She pointed to the large plastic tarp Chuck had hung up the night before. "Although it might be a little noisy, it shouldn't be too bad. Also, Polly Barton plans to stop in and pick up some jams and jellies. Her order is under the counter, ready to go."

Esther nodded, but she seemed distracted. Wondering what was bothering the women, Cheryl ushered Naomi into her office. After she closed the door, Naomi immediately sank down into a chair. Rather than sit behind her desk, away from her friend, Cheryl took her place in the other chair next to Naomi.

"What's wrong?" she asked softly.

Naomi's large brown eyes filled with tears. "It is Lydia. She is gone."

"Gone? What do you mean...gone?"

Naomi shook her head. "She has left her family and her friends. She has gone to Toledo to live with her cousin, Gerald. They are not Amish." A tear ran down her cheek. "She has rejected us, Cheryl."

Cheryl reached over and took Naomi's hand. "She hasn't rejected *you*, my friend. I'm sure she thinks she'll be happier living away from her family. Away from any kind of control. She may discover it's not as much fun as she anticipates. There are rules in the world too. Life consists of more than just running around having a good time. There are consequences that she hasn't seen yet." Using her other hand, Cheryl reached over and grabbed a tissue from the box that sat on her desk. She handed it to Naomi who thanked her and dabbed at her wet face. Cheryl was aware that Lydia was underage. Her parents could have her brought back to Sugarcreek if they wanted to. But that wasn't the way it worked with the Amish. They didn't use the world's legal system to control their children. Lydia would be allowed to stay with her non-Amish family if that's what she'd chosen. Although the Amish showed respect toward law enforcement, some things, like the choices given to young people during rumspringa, were kept within the confines of the community.

"Her mother is beside herself," Naomi said. "She shoulders the blame. I tried to console her, but sometimes I wonder." She took a deep breath and let it out slowly. "Why do our children leave? We try to teach them a good way of life. To value Gott and family. To live in a way that honors our wonderful Gott."

Cheryl smiled and squeezed her hand. "You're not the only parent to ask that question, and you won't be the last. We all have to make our own choices, Naomi. And Lydia needs to make hers." She stared into Naomi's eyes. "Are you afraid Esther will follow her lead?"

She shook her head. "Actually, I am not. Esther was very distressed to learn this news. She is afraid for her friend. She does not believe Lydia made a good choice."

"We'll pray for Lydia, okay? And we'll remind ourselves that God loves her even more than we do. More than her family does. He'll watch out for her."

Naomi took a deep, shuddering breath. "Ach, this is the truth. I must trust that Gott will work this out for Lydia's good. But as you can imagine, her parents are very upset."

Nehemiah and Almina Troyer were the parents of nine children. Cheryl thought at least two children were older than Lydia, but she wasn't sure.

"I'm sure they're concerned. I know you'll be a great comfort to them."

Naomi sighed. "I will try, but I must admit that I am worried for her. She has been gone almost three weeks now."

So that was why Lydia hadn't been to work. Cheryl changed her mind about calling. It would be better to leave the girl alone for now. She obviously needed time to decide what she wanted to do with her life.

Naomi started to stand up, but Cheryl gently pulled her back into her chair. "Before you go, I'd like to ask you about something. I hate to bring it up now, but it's important. I need to find someone."

"Of course. Who are you looking for?"

Cheryl got up and went around to the other side of her desk. She pulled her bottom drawer open and took out the bag with Ellen's things. Then she carefully removed them from the bag and put them on top of her desk.

"I do not understand," Naomi said. "These look very old."

Cheryl nodded. "They are." She quickly told Naomi about Chuck finding them inside the old laundry chute.

Naomi nodded. "Many of the old houses in this area had them. I still use mine. My old wringer washer is in the basement. The children drop their dirty clothes down the chute into a large laundry basket. It saves me from rounding up dirty clothes and carrying them down the stairs." She frowned. "But why were these inside the chute? This does not make sense."

"I don't know," Cheryl said. She took out the wallet and showed her the driver's license that belonged to Ellen Streeter. "I realize you probably didn't know this woman. She may have left town either before you were born or when you were a small child. But I wondered if you'd heard of her."

Naomi looked over the license carefully. "She lived in this house?"

"Yes, a long time ago."

"I am sorry, but I do not know of her. The Barnes family lived here for years before your aunt and uncle purchased the house and turned it into this beautiful store. This woman must have been the owner before them." She reached over and picked up Ellen's letter. Cheryl had put it inside a plastic ziplock bag in an attempt to protect it. Naomi quickly read through it. "Oh my," she said when she finished.

"Can you think of anyone who might remember Ellen Streeter?"

"*Ja*. Maybelline Finn would know about her."

Cheryl frowned. "Maybelline Finn? I don't know that name."

"She used to live next door. Until her house burned down."

"You mean where the maze is?"

"*Ja*. The lot was empty for a long time. I think the family wanted to rebuild. But then Maybelline's mother died, and Maybelline did not want to live on the property any longer. She sold it to the Gleasons several years ago, and they built the maze."

"Does she still live in town?" Cheryl asked.

"*Ja*. In fact, I am going to her house this afternoon. I will ask her about this woman."

Cheryl smiled. "Great. Hopefully Maybelline knows something that will lead me to Ellen."

Naomi stood up. "Maybelline is blind from birth and does not spend much time away from her home, but her mother was alive during the time they lived in the house next door. She must have known Ellen."

"Maybelline's blind and lives alone?"

"That is why I go by to check on her from time to time. I am not the only one, of course." She smiled. "Maybelline probably has more company than she would like. But folks in this town look after each other, ain't so?"

Cheryl nodded. Over the last several months she'd experienced firsthand the strong sense of community among those who called Sugarcreek home. She was certain Maybelline was well taken care of.

"I will pick up Esther this afternoon. Hopefully, I will have some information for you."

Cheryl walked Naomi to the front door and said good-bye. She was headed toward the office to work on the books when she noticed Esther's usual smile was missing. Obviously, she was worried about Lydia.

"I'm sorry to hear Lydia is gone," she said gently to the girl.

Esther nodded slowly, not meeting Cheryl's eyes. "I knew she was visiting family, but I did not know she had decided to live in the world." She took a deep, trembling breath. "She was my best friend," she said softly.

Cheryl went over and put her hand on Esther's arm. "She still is," she said. "She didn't leave you, Esther. She's just trying out a different life. And who knows? She may come back."

Mitzi had told her once that many of the young people who left the community during rumspringa returned after facing the realities of life without the support of their friends and family. The idea of freedom sounded good until they were confronted with all the challenges the outside world presented. Amish life was orderly and structured, while life outside the community could be chaotic and confusing for someone brought up in such a different environment.

"I do not know whether to pray she returns or pray that she is successful in her new life," Esther said, her voice trembling. "I do not wish to be selfish."

Cheryl slipped her arm around the young girl. "You're one of the least selfish people I've ever met, Esther. Why don't we both pray that God's will for Lydia's life will be fulfilled? Isn't that what you really want?"

Esther nodded and gave Cheryl a small smile. "Ja, that is what I want. It is what I *should* have prayed for all along. Thank you, Cheryl. Again, you have given me good advice. Your friendship is such a blessing to me."

Cheryl blinked away the quick tears that filled her eyes. "And your friendship blesses me more than I can say." She gave Esther a hug and hurried back to her office where she spent some time praying for Lydia and the Troyer family.

After she finished her prayers, her thoughts drifted to the Millers. They were all so close. Even when they disagreed, they still supported each other. Cheryl hoped that whatever seemed to be bothering her mother would get ironed out while her parents were in town. She missed the closeness they had always shared.

Cheryl heard the bell over the door ring and glanced at her watch. One o'clock. Probably the Vogel brothers arriving to play checkers. The two brothers had spent years apart after Ben left the Amish church. Thankfully, they'd finally reconciled. Meeting for checkers had become a ritual they both enjoyed. Cheryl had grown fond of them and looked forward to their visits. She went out into the store. Sure enough, they'd taken up their seats at the checkers table. She noticed that Chuck had also come in and was working diligently behind the plastic tarp.

"Good afternoon," she said to the brothers who both smiled at her. They looked so similar, yet one was a farmer and the other a retired doctor.

"Good afternoon, Cheryl," Rueben said. "It is cold outside. I hope you are staying warm."

"I am. Thank you." She'd started a fire in the potbellied stove when she came in, and it helped to keep the room warm. It might not be entirely necessary, but Cheryl loved the ambiance of the charming shop. The stove helped to set a cozy mood. She took a box of oatmeal raisin cookies off a shelf, fetched a paper plate, and put the plate on the edge of the checkers table. Then she went to her office and poured two cups of coffee—one black and one with sugar and creamer. She carried the coffees out to the brothers who thanked her for her kindness. Although she didn't provide them with treats every time they came in, she made sure they had coffee. The Vogel brothers were a wonderful reminder that no matter how fractured a family might be, nothing was impossible with God. He was the healer of the breach. The potter who knew how to mend broken pots. Or in this case, broken brothers.

Before going back to her office, she checked with Chuck. He seemed to be making good progress. The laundry chute was gone, and the extra space was already obvious. Even though she couldn't use her bathroom for a few days, it would be worth it.

There were a few customers in the shop, but Esther seemed to be handling everything just fine. Cheryl went back to her office and ate a quick lunch while she finished the books, trying to ignore all the noise Chuck made.

A little after two thirty, she went back into the shop. The brothers were still playing, and Esther was straightening shelves. Outside, a few snowflakes danced around in the air. Thankfully, the weather report had called for light flurries but no significant snow. Cheryl loved the snow, but even though she only lived a few blocks away from the shop, she didn't like driving in it.

A few minutes before three, Naomi pulled up outside in her buggy. Cheryl waited for her to come inside. When she did, she didn't say anything, just headed for the office. Cheryl followed her friend and shut the door once they were both inside.

"Did you find out anything?" Cheryl asked.

Naomi sat down, a frown on her face. "Maybelline remembers Ellen very clearly. She was friends with Maybelline's mother." She looked up at Cheryl. "She also remembers the night she disappeared without a trace."

"What do you mean . . . without a trace?"

Naomi nodded toward the other chair, and Cheryl sat down next to her.

"Ellen Streeter was married to a man named Bill. They only lived in this house for two years. Then Ellen disappeared without telling anyone she was leaving. Supposedly she ran away from Bill, but no one ever heard from her again. A week later, Bill was found dead at the bottom of the basement stairs." Naomi took a deep breath. "Some people in town believed that Ellen Streeter was murdered."

CHAPTER FOUR

Cheryl stared at her friend, not sure she'd heard her correctly. "D...did you say maybe she was *murdered*?"

Naomi nodded, her usual cheery expression replaced by solemnity.

"Was anyone arrested? Who did it?" Cheryl's interest in the mysterious items in the laundry chute had suddenly taken a dark turn.

"According to Maybelline, no one was ever arrested. Some folks believed Bill probably killed her, but he died before they could investigate. There were never any other suspects."

Cheryl shook her head slowly, trying to digest the information Naomi had just delivered. Even though Ellen had mentioned a fear of being murdered in her letter, Cheryl had tried to convince herself the woman was overreacting. "Did the police decide Bill's fall down the stairs was an accident?"

Naomi smoothed her apron, gazing down at her hands, and sighed. "Ja. Maybelline said the police believed his fall was clearly accidental." She looked up at Cheryl, her expression troubled. "It was such a sad story to hear. I love this shop. It is hard to believe there was once so much tragedy here." She managed a small smile. "I am glad the Barnes family lived here after these terrible circumstances. They were a happy group with several rambunctious children. I am certain they filled this house with joy. Then Mitzi came along and turned it into this wonderful place. Thankfully, this building is now full of good memories."

Cheryl nodded absentmindedly. She couldn't quit thinking about Ellen Streeter. Finding her personal belongings hidden inside the laundry chute now had a rather sinister meaning. Was she preparing to leave Bill? Was her valise packed because she was planning to run away? Had Bill stopped her by... Cheryl shuddered. The thought was just too awful.

"Naomi," Cheryl said softly, "did they ever... I mean, was Ellen's... body ever found?"

"No. Ellen never came back to Sugarcreek. Quite a few people, including Maybelline's mother, believed she had left her husband and was living somewhere else. I assume that was one of the reasons there was never a serious investigation."

"Maybe she did," Cheryl said.

The look on Naomi's face was rather guarded. "I suppose you might be right. It is probably best to believe this rather than... the alternative."

Cheryl was painfully aware that Naomi was most likely thinking the same thing she was. That if Ellen had left town, she would have taken her purse and suitcase with her. But Cheryl had no plan to bring this up, and she was certain the mild-mannered Naomi wouldn't give voice to the idea either.

"I do have some better news for you," Naomi said. "Maybelline told me that Bill's brother, Amos, recently moved back to

Sugarcreek from Kansas. His sister, who used to live in Cleveland, recently moved into the Sugarcreek Nursing Home."

"That seems odd. Why would she come here?"

"Her best friend's family, who lives here, moved their ailing mother to the nursing home so they could be near her. Amos's sister, who is also very frail, decided to move here as well so she could be with her friend. Amos came back to Sugarcreek to care for his sister. I am sure it was not a move he wanted to make. I imagine Sugarcreek reminds him of things best forgotten."

"Oh," Cheryl said, "maybe he knows where Ellen is. Even if he doesn't, I could probably turn her things over to him. I mean, if he's the only family left..." Even as she said it, she didn't feel comfortable. If Amos's brother abused Ellen, why should he get her belongings? Hopefully, Cheryl wouldn't have to make that decision. With any luck, Ellen was alive and well, and Amos had stayed in touch with his sister-in-law.

Naomi took a slip of paper out of her pocket and held it out to Cheryl. "Here is their address. They live on Finzer Drive. Do you know where that is?"

"Yes, I've driven down it several times." She looked at the address. "I won't have any trouble finding it." She looked up at Naomi. "I don't suppose you have a phone number?"

Naomi shook her head. "Sorry. Maybelline did not have their number. You might look in a Sugarcreek phone book. Perhaps you will find it there." She frowned. "However, if their move here was after the book was put to press, it may not be listed."

"Thank you, Naomi. I really appreciate your help with this."

"You are very welcome. I am sorry the news is so disturbing. I know it would have been much more enjoyable if I could have told you how to find Ellen."

Cheryl sighed. "Yes, I'd really like to meet her and hear her story. Find out how her things ended up inside the laundry chute."

Naomi stood to her feet. "I understand, my friend, and I hope this will be the case."

"I do too," Cheryl said softly. Although she didn't want to jump to conclusions, there was one question in Cheryl's mind that wouldn't be stilled. If Ellen really was dead, where was her body? The answer to that question filled her with dread.

"Before I leave, is there anything you need help with today?" Naomi asked. "Levi will be in town around four o'clock. He is picking up bales of hay and can stop by if you need him."

Cheryl, whose thoughts had been consumed with Naomi's news, was relieved to hear that Levi would be available. "I'm glad you asked. Do you think Levi could help me move some of the winter gifts downstairs and help me bring the spring gifts upstairs? The quilts are especially heavy, and I don't like to carry them downstairs by myself."

Levi was always willing to assist Cheryl with heavy items, especially when they had to go to or come from the basement where extra supplies were stored. The basement stairs were very steep, and the room itself was a little creepy. It was a wonderful place for storage, but the structure was built in the 1920s, and the cement walls and floors, along with the three very small windows near the tops of the walls, made Cheryl feel slightly claustrophobic. It certainly was her least favorite place in the shop.

"I know he would be more than happy to help. I will leave a message for him at the feed store. I am certain he will be here before you leave."

"Thank you." Cheryl gave her friend a hug. "I want everything to look nice when my parents arrive. It may not look like spring outside, but I want the Swiss Miss to look like it's ready for the season."

"I understand. Hopefully, spring weather will soon replace our cold rainy days with warm sunshine."

As if someone were listening, a crack of thunder made both women jump. Cheryl looked out the window to see the rain beginning again.

"Maybe you shouldn't have said that," Cheryl said, grinning.

Naomi laughed. "Perhaps you are right. From now on I will simply comment on how lovely each day is."

Cheryl accompanied Naomi out into the store where Esther waited for her mother. Cheryl bid the two women good-bye before they hurried outside to the shelter of their buggy.

The rain kept almost everyone away for the rest of the afternoon. A little after four, Chuck started packing up. After taking some things out to his truck, he came back inside the shop.

"I wanted you to know that I called a guy in Akron who's a real expert in rare coins. He confirmed the value I told you, except he thinks that some collectors will pay almost ten thousand dollars for it. He suggested you sell it in an auction."

"I appreciate the information," Cheryl said. "But I can't sell it. It doesn't belong to me."

Chuck shrugged. "Well, at least when you find the owner you can give her some good news."

Cheryl smiled at him. "You're right. Thanks so much, Chuck."

He nodded and walked out.

Janie Henderson, who owned Sunshine Stables, strolled up to the counter with a coconut cake. "Had to run over here and get one of these before you sold out of them again," she said with a smile.

Janie was a single woman with a tremendous talent for training horses. She ran a successful business and was respected by everyone in Sugarcreek, especially Cheryl, who had a great love for horses.

"I'm having a larger cooler put in," Cheryl said. "Hopefully, we can keep some of our most popular items in stock a little longer."

"That sounds like a good thing, but it just might play havoc with my waistline."

Cheryl was amused that someone like Janie was concerned about her weight. If Cheryl could be as thin and fit as Janie, she'd be absolutely thrilled. Cheryl rang up her order and handed her the cake.

"By the way," Janie said, "could you pass the word around that I have a horse that needs a home? He was taken from an abusive situation. The owner ignored him, left him in a dirty stable, and didn't give him much food or water. When Ranger came to me, he was pretty sick, but he's healthy now. A beautiful boy. Very sweet natured. It's amazing since he was treated so poorly."

Cheryl nodded. "Sure. Why don't you talk to Levi Miller? He knows a lot of farmers. Maybe he can hook you up with someone who's looking for a horse."

Janie's eyes lit up. "That's a great idea. I'll corner him the next time I see him. Thanks, Cheryl."

After Janie left, Cheryl checked to see if there were any other customers who needed help, but the only person in the store was a man she didn't know who was looking through the cookbooks. He left a few minutes later without buying anything.

About four thirty, a buggy pulled up in front of the store and Levi got out. Cheryl's hand automatically went to her hair in an attempt to make sure it wasn't messed up.

"Stop that," she whispered to herself.

Why did she find herself reacting that way toward him? Levi would one day marry an Amish woman and settle down in Sugarcreek. It was his destiny, and there was absolutely no reason for Cheryl to imagine it would turn out any other way. Even so, she admired him and was grateful she'd met a man with his qualities. At least now she knew what she wanted. Someone who was strong and gentle at the same time. Who treated everyone with respect. Who was honest and trustworthy.

"For crying out loud, Cheryl. You're describing a Boy Scout," she said under her breath.

Levi hurried up the steps, trying to stay out of the rain. Cheryl smiled when he opened the door. Tall and muscular with longish blond hair that sometimes fell across his face, he really was a good-looking man.

"Maam left a message for me," he said when he saw Cheryl. "She said you have some things that need to be moved downstairs?"

Cheryl nodded. "And other stuff that needs to come up here." She noticed suddenly how weary he looked. "Oh, Levi, this doesn't have to be done now. If you're tired—"

"No, I am fine," he said. "One of our goats gave birth last night, and there were some problems. I must admit that I did not get as much sleep as I would have liked to, but I plan to go to bed early tonight." He laughed at her worried look. "This is normal life on a farm, Cheryl. Trust me, I will be fine."

"Speaking of farms, Janie Henderson was in here earlier. She has an abused horse that needs a home. Can you check around to see if you can find a place for him? I thought maybe some of your farmer friends might need a new horse. Janie says he's a sweetheart, and of course, she's nursed him back to health."

"I would be happy to," he said. "Now, where are these items that need to go downstairs?"

Cheryl quickly began to gather quilts and other fabric crafts together that had dark colors more suitable for winter. She also brought plaques and paintings that reflected cold and snowy scenes to the counter. "These all need to go," she said. She paused a moment, not sure how to frame her next question.

"Is there something else?" he asked, frowning at her.

As Cheryl took a deep breath, she felt her face flush. "When we get down there, I wonder if you'd mind..." She stopped and gazed at him for a moment. "I don't quite know how to ask this."

Looking perplexed, he peered at her through narrowed eyes. "There is nothing you cannot say to me, Cheryl. We are good friends, ain't so?"

She nodded but still hesitated, searching for the right words. Unfortunately, she wasn't sure those words actually existed. "Did your mother get a chance to tell you about her visit with Maybelline Finn?"

"I have not spoken to her today, but I know Maybelline. Maam and *Daed* keep an eye on her, and I have gone to her house several times to fix things. Is something wrong? Is she ill?"

"No, it's not that."

Cheryl was grateful they were alone. Since she would normally close soon anyway and the rain was coming down even harder, she walked over to the front door and turned the Open sign to Closed. Then she went back to the counter, where a very confused-looking Levi stood waiting for her.

"You are beginning to worry me," he said hesitantly.

Cheryl paused a moment, trying to gather her thoughts. Finally she simply launched into the history of Bill and Ellen Streeter, trying not to leave anything out. When she finished, she gazed up at Levi. She was grateful to see he seemed interested in her story. "So you see my problem." She said the words slowly, hoping he'd understand what she was trying to tell him.

"That is a terrible story," he said, his forehead wrinkled in bewilderment. "I am dismayed to hear that Ellen's husband may have taken her life, but I do not see what this has to do with the basement." As soon as the words left his mouth he took a deep intake of breath, and an odd look crossed his face. Cheryl remembered a phrase her aunt used frequently. Levi looked "green around the gills."

"Surely you do not think—"

"How can I not think that?" Cheryl asked in hushed tones. "I wouldn't bring it up, Levi, but I can't stand the thought that Ellen might be..." She took another deep breath, hoping she wouldn't hyperventilate and pass out. That would only add to Levi's distress.

"In the basement?" he said in a near whisper.

"I have to know, Levi," Cheryl said gently. "I can't be comfortable wondering if... Ellen is still here."

She was alarmed to see that Levi's face had now gone pale.

"Just what is it you want me to do?" he asked with hesitation.

"When we go downstairs, just look to see..." She cleared her throat. "You know. If there's any place where the floor looks...odd. Or the wall."

"You mean... you mean..."

Afraid she would spend the next hour listening to him say "You mean" over and over, she held her hand up, gulped, and spit out the words she didn't actually want to say. "I want to know if Ellen Streeter is buried in my basement. I need you to look it over and tell me if there's a place that looks... newer. You know, where the cement was repaired or something."

Cheryl suddenly realized that while she was used to reading mysteries and watching shows on TV that included stories about murders, Levi wasn't. Maybe she shouldn't have broached the subject. "Look, never mind. I'm sorry. I'll ask someone else for help. I guess I turned to you because . . ." Why had she automatically thought of him for the job? She realized it was because he'd come to her rescue before. He was someone she could always count on. But maybe this kind of thing was just too distasteful for an Amish man to confront.

"I am not a coward, Cheryl," he said forcefully. "I will look around downstairs. I will not let you down."

"I didn't say you were a coward," she said soothingly. "I know better than that. But I also know you're not used to things like this."

"Trust me. Being your friend has brought many experiences into my life I would have otherwise missed. This is just one more adventure, I guess. I will carry these quilts down the stairs, and then I will take a look around. Do you have a flashlight handy?"

Cheryl grabbed the flashlight she kept under the counter and handed it to him. "Thanks, Levi. I really appreciate it."

He grabbed the stack of quilts and muttered something that Cheryl couldn't quite make out. However, she decided this might not be a good time to ask him to repeat himself.

She hurried over to the basement door and opened it. Then she followed Levi down the stairs to the cold cement floor in the basement and fumbled for the pull chain to turn on the light. After getting several thick plastic covers, she showed him where he could put the quilts. While she put them into the protective bags, he took the flashlight and began to search the large room. She noticed that her hands shook as she stacked the quilts on the shelves. Although she wanted to know the truth, she prayed Levi wouldn't find anything. Was she being silly? A woman disappears, her purse and valise are hidden inside an old laundry chute and covered up with drywall. Then the husband slips and falls down the stairs a week later. Was it poetic justice? Or was it more than just a strange coincidence?

Something touched her shoulder, and she screamed. When she whirled around, she found Levi standing behind her, his eyebrows raised and his eyes round. "Please do not do that," he scolded. "You frightened me."

Cheryl's mouth dropped open. "I frightened *you*? I think you just took ten years off my life!"

Levi sighed and shook his head. "You are definitely the most unusual woman I have ever known. My life was much more peaceful before you entered it."

Cheryl grinned in spite of herself. "But I'll bet it's more exciting now."

"Unfortunately, I would probably have to agree with you about that." He swept his hand around in a semicircle. "I looked all over the basement. There are small repairs for cracks, but there is nothing that suggests that anything…" He stopped and cleared his throat. "That anything *large* has been buried in the basement. Everything looks original to the 1920s structure."

Cheryl thought for a moment. "So if Bill killed his wife, but he didn't put her in the basement…" Another image popped into her head. "Oh, Levi, maybe he buried her in the yard!"

"I would find that hard to believe, Cheryl. There were houses all around here back then. It would be very difficult to get away with something like that."

"But not impossible."

Levi shrugged. "I suppose it is not impossible."

Cheryl just stared at him. How could she come to work every day, wondering if Ellen's body was buried somewhere on the property?

Levi's eyes narrowed as he returned her gaze. "I beg you. Please do not ask me to dig up the yard."

"We'll talk about it later." She reached over and put her hand on his arm. "Thank you for looking. Maybe we should finish moving everything so we can get out of here. I have a stop to make before I go home."

He nodded and headed back up the stairs. Cheryl stayed behind for a moment and gazed around the basement. The overhead lightbulb cast an eerie yellow glow over the room. She was grateful for all the storage space downstairs, but she'd always felt a little uncomfortable down here. Finding out that Bill had fallen and died in this room didn't help her attitude one bit. She stared at the floor in front of the stairs for a few seconds, trying to wrap her head around the knowledge that a man's life had ended on that very spot. The thought sent a shiver through her body. Taking a deep breath, she followed Levi upstairs, even more determined to find the truth about what happened to Ellen Streeter.

CHAPTER FIVE

Cheryl checked the phone book for Amos Streeter's address, but it wasn't listed. Since she would be busy with her parents for the next few days, she decided to go by his house before she headed home. She carefully packed up Ellen's things, making sure to put the coin back in the small coin purse. If she really was dead, her belongings should go to her family, and right now, that appeared to be Amos.

As she prepared to leave, she glanced at the alarm waiting to be armed. Even though Chuck wasn't supposed to work tonight, she decided to leave it off just in case he changed his mind. In fact, until all of Chuck's work was complete she wouldn't bother to turn it on. Frankly, not having to worry about it was a relief. The last thing she wanted was another lecture from Chief Twitchell.

While attempting to stay dry under her umbrella, Cheryl loaded Beau's crate into the backseat of her car and put the bag with Ellen's belongings on the passenger seat next to her. Then she drove to Finzer Drive. It was hard to see the numbers on the houses. Even though she normally enjoyed the rain, she hoped it would dry out some before her parents arrived. She wanted everything to be perfect for their visit.

Cheryl realized suddenly that she was going the wrong way, so she pulled into a driveway and turned around. Beau was already registering his complaint about being stuck in his crate.

"You'll have to be patient a bit longer," Cheryl said gently, trying to soothe him. The large Siamese meowed loudly, obviously rejecting her attempts to calm him. "Hush," she scolded. "You're just fine, and you know it."

She finally found the right house and pulled into the driveway of an attractive craftsman bungalow. Even though it was getting dark and the rain was making it hard to see, Cheryl could tell that someone had really put effort into enhancing the original style of the 1920s home. She got out of the car, grabbed the bag, and hurried up the porch stairs to the front door. The tree-lined block was quiet, and the rain created a mist that made the street look foggy. Cheryl found it beautiful if not slightly ominous. She shivered, not just from the cold but also from the knowledge that Ellen might be dead and buried somewhere in Sugarcreek. She had no intention of asking Amos Streeter if he believed his brother had killed Ellen. She really hoped he'd tell her Ellen was alive and that he knew where she was.

Cheryl took a deep breath and rang the doorbell. A few seconds later, an attractive older lady opened the door. She flipped on the front porch light, temporarily blinding Cheryl.

"Can I help you?" The woman looked at her rather suspiciously, as if she expected Cheryl's next words to be, "Good evening! Are you the lady of the house? I'm here to tell you about our handy-dandy vacuum sweeper. May I have a few minutes of your time?"

"Hello," Cheryl said, offering a forced smile. "I'm sorry to bother you. I'm Cheryl Cooper. I own the Swiss Miss. The gift shop on Main Street?"

The woman frowned at her. "I know the store. What can I do for you?"

A gust of icy wind suddenly swept across the porch, and Cheryl pulled up the collar of her coat. "I wondered if I could speak to your husband for a few minutes? It's about something I found in the store. I mean, something my contractor found." She held up the bag. "I believe we discovered some items that belonged to Ellen Streeter, your husband's sister-in-law."

The woman's eyes widened. "Just a minute," she said, closing the door.

Surprised to be abandoned and left standing alone on the porch, Cheryl wondered if the woman's next move would be to turn off the porch light. Thankfully, that didn't happen. Instead, about a minute later, the door swung open once again. This time a man stood on the other side. He was tall with wavy white hair. Cheryl assumed he was in his late sixties or early seventies, but he was still a very handsome man.

"I'm Amos Streeter," he said. "My wife said you wanted to talk to me? About Ellen?" He held the door open and motioned for Cheryl to come inside. Stepping into the warm house was a relief, and Cheryl thanked him. She looked around the inviting living room with the fire crackling in a lovely brick fireplace. The woman who answered the door was nowhere to be seen.

Cheryl nodded. "Yes. You see, I own the Swiss Miss on Main Street. The building that used to be your brother's house?"

Amos pointed toward a large couch positioned near the fireplace. "Please have a seat. Can I get you something to drink?"

Cheryl walked over and sat down. The warmth of the fire began to unthaw her, and she could feel her body relax a bit. "I don't suppose you have any coffee."

"Just put on a pot a little while ago. Can I get you a cup?"

"That would be wonderful, thanks."

"How do you take it?"

Cheryl smiled. "Black is fine."

Amos left to get the coffee. Cheryl was grateful to find him much more accommodating than the woman she assumed was his wife. She glanced around the room. Comfortable furniture along with personal touches. Silk flowers arranged in a vase, a beautiful quilt on the arm of the couch, several beautifully embroidered pillows on the couch and the overstuffed chairs. Cheryl found Amos's home extremely cozy and very well designed. She assumed the personal touches had been added by his wife.

"Here you go."

Amos had come back into the room with two coffee cups in his hands. Cheryl wondered if his wife would join them, but she wasn't with him.

He handed her one of the cups and then sat down in a nearby chair. Cheryl took a sip of coffee before setting it on top of a coaster on the coffee table in front of her.

"I'm sorry to just drop by," she said. "I tried to find your telephone number so I could call first, but it wasn't in the phone book."

"We moved here after the book had gone to print," he said. "How did you know where we live?"

"One of your brother's old neighbors told a friend of mine you were here. Maybelline Finn?"

"Sure. I remember Maybelline. How is she?"

"Fine. Her mother passed away a while back, and she lives alone now. People in town keep an eye on her. You know what Sugarcreek is like."

"Yes, I know. Everyone seems to know everyone else's business. One of the reasons I didn't really want to come back here."

Cheryl stared at him, surprised by his comment. "Well, actually I meant that people here take care of each other, but I guess I see your point. There's not much that happens in the morning that most people don't know about by noon."

"That's for sure." He took a drink of coffee and then set his cup down. "Now what can I do for you, Miss...Cooper is it?"

"Yes. But please call me Cheryl." She picked up the bag on the floor next to her and pulled out the purse and small valise. "I'm having some work done in the shop. Moving a wall back so I can add a large cooler. My contractor found these inside an old laundry chute. Someone placed them there years ago and then covered them up in the wall."

Amos inhaled sharply as he stared at the items. "I...I don't understand," he said quickly. "You said these were in the laundry chute?"

"Yes. It seems as if someone wanted to hide them, but I'm not sure why."

As he leaned back in his chair, a muscle in his jaw began to twitch. "I have no idea either," he said sharply. "What does this have to do with me?"

His abrupt change in attitude took Cheryl by surprise. His reaction at seeing Ellen's belongings made it pretty clear that he recognized them.

"They belonged to your sister-in-law."

He arched an eyebrow as if he were surprised. "Oh, really? They don't look familiar. Of course, I didn't know her very well. Bill and Ellen kept to themselves most of the time."

Cheryl hesitated a moment while she tried to figure out what to say next. She was certain Amos Streeter was lying. Did he believe his brother killed Ellen? Was he trying to protect him? But why? Bill was dead, and Ellen was gone.

"Look, Mr. Streeter. I didn't come here to upset you. I just want to get these things into the hands of the person they belong to. Do you know where Ellen is?" She wanted to add, "And just how far we need to dig?" But she restrained herself.

"Ellen left my brother about a week before he died. I have no idea where she is now."

"I guess a lot of people think she's dead," Cheryl said gently. "Is that what you think?"

"Dead? Who told you she was dead?" Amos's voice grew louder. "Like I said, people need to mind their own business."

Taken aback, Cheryl paused a moment to gather her courage. Finally she said, "If you don't know where she is, how do you know she's alive?"

He grunted and abruptly stood to his feet. "I have no idea if she's alive now, but she called me about a week after Bill died. Guess she felt guilty about leaving him, I don't know. That was a long time ago. Have no idea where she is now. Never heard from her again." He gestured toward the door. "Now if you don't mind..."

Cheryl tried to digest this new information. At first she was relieved to hear that Ellen left town alive and that Amos heard from her after her husband's accident. She didn't want to believe Ellen was buried somewhere in Sugarcreek. But Amos's reaction was less than reassuring. Something was wrong, although Cheryl couldn't put her finger on it.

"Why were her things walled up inside the shop? Wouldn't she have wanted to take them with her?" Cheryl leaned over and opened Ellen's purse. "There are some things in the purse you should see."

First she handed him the letter. He opened it carefully and began to read. Cheryl watched as the blood drained from his face.

"Who do you think she wrote this to?" she asked.

His expression grew even stormier, and he handed it back to her. "Obviously, she had someone else in her life. I have no idea who it was. I never trusted her. It's obvious Bill shouldn't have trusted her either."

"But if she almost never left the house—"

"*Miss Cooper*, I understand why you came here, but your questions are...inappropriate. I've told you that I barely knew Ellen, that she's very much alive as far as I know, and that I can't help you. I'm not sure why you think it's your job to stick your nose into my family's affairs, but frankly, I've had enough."

Cheryl folded the letter and slid it back into the wallet. "I wanted to return her things, but I was afraid she was dead—"

"But as I told you, she's not."

Cheryl took out the small change purse. "You see, there's a very valuable coin in here. It's a—"

"A 1934 S Peace Dollar," Amos finished for her. His voice relaxed a little. "You found it. Ellen's father gave that coin to her when she was just a girl. Told her to hang on to it. That it would be worth something someday."

"He was right. A friend tells me it's worth several thousand dollars. Even if I didn't think any of these other things were important, I felt returning this coin to Ellen was my duty."

"I appreciate your honesty," he said quickly, his tone hardening again, "but I really can't help you. If you don't mind..."

Cheryl slowly put everything back into the purse and then returned the purse and the valise into the tote bag. "Thank you for your time. I'm sorry to have bothered you."

Without looking at her, Amos walked over to the front door and held it open. Cheryl had barely stepped out on the front porch when he closed the door behind her. The bright porch light immediately clicked off, and Cheryl stood there in the dark, listening to the rain, feeling confused. Maybe Ellen *was* alive. Cheryl hoped it was true, but her conversation with Amos made her feel unsettled. She felt strongly that he hadn't told her the complete truth. Now she was even more determined to locate Ellen Streeter—alive or dead.

Chapter Six

Friday morning brought clouds, but the forecast called for clearing later in the day. As Cheryl got ready for work, her thoughts went back and forth between her meeting with Amos and her parents' arrival later in the day. She was supposed to Skype with Mitzi tonight at six o'clock and hoped she'd be able to connect with her. Mitzi always had good advice, and Cheryl certainly needed some now.

She dressed, ate a quick breakfast, and headed for the store. Chuck met her at the front door.

"I've got a few things to do today, and then I'll get out of your way," he told her as they entered the store. "Are your parents still visiting over the weekend?"

"Yeah, they're arriving today."

"Well, at least I can get the wallboard up today and get it taped," he said. "Everything will look a lot better. Tonight I'll come back after you close, and sand. Now that will be a mess, but I'll clean everything up really good, and then I'll take the plastic down. By Saturday afternoon I'll be ready to paint. When you arrive Monday morning, my work will be done. When will your new cooler be delivered?"

"The Millers are storing it for me at their farm. They'll bring it by Monday morning."

"Why don't you let me meet them here? That way I can help install it. You'll be up and running before noon."

Cheryl smiled at him. "Thank you so much, Chuck. You've done a wonderful job, and I'm so appreciative."

He shrugged. "No problem. It's my job."

Cheryl watched him carry his toolbox over to the work area. She couldn't help wondering about him. She didn't actually know much about Chuck, but he certainly was an interesting man. Maybe Naomi could fill in the blanks. Was he married? Did he have children? When they first met, she'd asked him how long he'd lived in Sugarcreek. He'd frowned at her like she was asking for his social security number. His reaction kept her from asking any further questions about his life. He was a very nice man, but why was he always so somber?

Cheryl stocked the shelves with the items she'd had Levi bring upstairs the night before. New spring colors brought a festive look to the shop. She got out her duster and ran it over everything, even though Esther had cleaned the day before. Cheryl wanted the Swiss Miss to look its best when her parents arrived. They'd never understood why Mitzi had decided to stay in Sugarcreek. Her father left when he was eighteen and never looked back. She hoped they'd look past their ambivalence for the small town and see it the way she did.

She sighed as she put the duster away. It would be another thirty minutes before she officially opened for business. Cheryl loved the time she spent in the shop before customers came in. The quiet was soothing, and it helped her to gather her thoughts before her day began in earnest. Beau leaned against her leg, and she reached down and rubbed his head. "I'm not the only one who needs to be on their best behavior," she said to the contented cat whose closed eyes and loud purring made it clear he enjoyed the current attention she provided. She scratched his head one more time and went to get the step stool she kept behind the counter. Then she carried it over to the wall where she liked to hang quilts. After choosing one with lovely pastel blocks and colorful tulips around the edges, she added ribbon loops to the back of the quilt and attached the hanger. Then she stepped onto the stool so she could reach the hooks on the wall that would hold the quilt. She was just looping the cord on the dowel over the hooks when a deep voice from behind her said, "This is a holdup. Don't scream."

Ignoring the terse order, she let loose a high-pitched shriek while losing her balance and falling back into the arms of the person who'd issued the frightening warning. She frantically fought to free herself while she twisted around to see who had threatened her. Her mouth dropped open when she found herself looking into the very surprised face of her brother, Matt.

"What in the world?" she sputtered, surprised to see him and furious at the way he'd announced his presence.

He immediately started to laugh, which made her even angrier.

"Are you nuts?" she asked as she slumped against the stool. "You scared the living daylights out of me!"

Matt's amused expression vanished. "Sorry, sis. I just wanted to surprise you."

Cheryl took a deep breath and let it out slowly, trying to calm her jangled nerves. "Well, you certainly managed to do that." She frowned at her brother. "What are you doing here? Mom and Dad never mentioned you were coming."

Matt stepped back, giving Cheryl room to move away from the stool.

"They don't know. I wanted to surprise them too."

As her pounding heart began to beat normally again, Cheryl studied her brother. Frankly, he hadn't changed much at all. Maybe a little more fit, as if he'd been working out.

"When's the last time you talked to them?"

Matt shrugged. "A few months ago. They told me then that they were thinking of coming to see you on your birthday. I tried to tell Dad about my new business venture, but you know how he is."

Cheryl nodded. "Yeah, I know how he is."

Matt's "business ventures" had all been disasters. He'd call home with pleas for money to support some new get-rich-quick scheme that never paid off. A couple of years ago her father had finally declared he was done supporting Matt's sketchy proposals.

"Look, sis, I've got a real job. A great job. In fact, I'm running my own company. I have people working for me."

"Really?" Cheryl sighed. She was really glad to see him, but she didn't have time to listen to some new fantasy he'd dreamed up.

She needed to get the Swiss Miss open. Customers would be showing up soon.

"If you have a minute..."

She shook her head. "I don't. I've got to work. Maybe later." She paused for a moment before giving her younger brother a hug. "I really am happy you're here. It's been too long."

"I know. I'm sorry, Skeeter."

There was that old nickname. Matt had given it to her when they were kids because of her reaction to mosquitoes. She hated mosquito bites with a passion and would run to the house or car to avoid being bitten. She still found them irritating but wasn't as paranoid as she used to be.

"Don't call me Skeeter in front of anyone else, okay?"

He chuckled. "I'll do my best, but don't be surprised if it slips out once in a while."

Except for looking a little older, Matt still reminded her of the mischievous kid she'd grown up with. Dark hair like her father's, a turned-up nose like her mom's, and green eyes just like hers.

"Are you staying at the inn with Mom and Dad?"

He shook his head. "I was hoping to bunk with you... Is that okay?"

"Sure. I told Mom and Dad they could stay at the house, but you know how they are."

"Yeah, I know how they are." He reached over and took her hand. "Look, Cheryl, I want you to know that I intend to be on my best behavior. No meltdowns with the folks. I'm just here to celebrate your birthday, not to get into it with our parents. Please don't worry."

Cheryl sighed. "I hope that's a promise you can keep. I can't remember the last time we all got along when we were together." She motioned for him to follow her and headed over to the counter.

"I know, but when Dad said they might come here for your birthday, I decided it was the perfect time for a reunion. With my new situation, I'm hoping they'll decide I'm not 'frittering my life away,' as Mom likes to say."

Cheryl felt Matt wanted her to ask about his new job, but she just didn't have the time, and frankly, she dreaded having to paste a fake smile on her face while he recited another story about how this was the thing that would finally turn his life around and make him rich. If something went wrong, as it always did, it was always someone else's fault. Cheryl had prayed so many times that Matt would give up all his schemes and search for the path God had for him. So far, he'd never seemed interested in anything except trying to make himself sound important. She knew his problems stemmed from a sense of insecurity, but she'd never been able to find a way to talk honestly to him about it. Anytime she'd tried to broach the subject, he became offended and hurt, claiming no one believed in him.

"Matt, I've got a lot of work to do today since I'm closing early tomorrow. Why don't I give you the key to the house? You can go on over there, unpack, and get some rest. You must be tired from your trip."

He leaned on the counter. "I am. I drove all night from Kansas City, but I'd really like to spend some time with you before the folks get here. Can we have lunch before I head over to Mitzi's?"

"Sure, if you've got the energy."

He grinned. "Can we go to Yoder's? All I could think about on the way here was their fried chicken and that awesome cherry pie I used to get there when we visited Aunt Mitzi."

Cheryl smiled. "Not a problem. Why don't you hang out in my office until noon? After Yoder's we can head over to my house."

He looked confused. "Don't you mean Aunt Mitzi's house?"

Cheryl shook her head. "Yeah. This place feels so much like home sometimes I forget the shop isn't actually mine. Same with Aunt Mitzi's place."

"I understand. I used to think this little town was lame. But when I drove past the big sign on the edge of town, I got a little emotional." He smiled at Cheryl. "We had some great times here, didn't we? Especially when Mom and Dad sent us here during the summer. Aunt Mitzi was great."

Cheryl looked at him with surprise. When they were kids, Matt had taken the news they were coming to Sugarcreek like he'd just been sentenced to prison. After a few days, he'd come around, but being sent to stay with his aunt had never been met with anything but disdain and complaints. Could her brother finally be growing up? Not wanting to be disappointed like she'd been so many times before, Cheryl decided not to get her hopes up.

"We did have fun. Mitzi was always great to us. She's still wonderful. I miss her."

"Sometimes it's hard to believe she and Dad are brother and sister."

"Dad's a good man, Matt. And a great father."

"I know, but Mitzi's so...relaxed. Dad expects a lot from himself and from everyone else. I swear, sometimes he looks at me like he's convinced he got the wrong baby at the hospital."

Cheryl nodded. "He does the same thing to me sometimes, but it's only because he wants us to make good choices in life."

Matt didn't respond, just shrugged and stared at her.

"Come on back, and I'll set you up in my office," Cheryl said, glancing at her watch. She really was falling behind in her schedule.

"Let me get my laptop out of the truck first," Matt replied. "I can get some work done while I wait."

Cheryl watched as he went out the door to a nice black truck parked in front of the store. It looked brand new. She prayed he hadn't gotten in over his head again. Matt's list of repossessed vehicles was long. She hoped this truck wouldn't end up with the same fate.

When he came back with a laptop case in his hand, Cheryl led him into her office and got him set up at her desk. She pointed out the coffeepot and the small fridge, telling him to help himself to coffee or one of the cans of pop she kept cold.

"Thanks, sis," he said. "Is there a restaurant nearby that serves breakfast? I'm really hungry."

"No need to go out. I can take care of you." She hurried into the shop and took a package of croissants out of one of the small coolers. Then she got a jar of Naomi's strawberry jam and headed back to her office. After taking a paper plate and some plastic utensils out of the coffee cart, Cheryl plopped a couple of croissants on the plate and opened the jam. Matt had already poured himself a cup of coffee.

"Try these. I think you'll like them," she told her brother with a smile.

"Wow, this looks awesome. He slathered some jam on one of the croissants. Then he raised it to his mouth and took a big bite. His eyes widened, and he quickly scarfed down the rest of it. "Oh, Skeeter, it's delicious. I'm surprised you're not humongous."

"Believe me, watching my weight around here is tougher than you can imagine. Now I've got to get to work. If you need anything, let me know."

Matt pointed toward the closed bathroom door. "Why is that locked?"

"Sorry." Cheryl quickly explained the work Chuck was doing on the wall. "We had to close the bathroom for a couple of days. But my friend Kathy Snyder who owns the Honey Bee Café across the street will let you use her bathroom if you need to. Just tell her you're my brother."

Matt cocked his head to the side and raised his eyebrows. "Let me get this straight. If I have to...use the facilities...I have to walk into a public place and declare out loud who I am and what I'm there to do?" He shook his head. "Thanks. I'll wait."

The look on his face made Cheryl giggle. "I forgot about your bathroom phobia."

"It is *not* a phobia," Matt declared huffily. "I'm just a very private person."

"It's up to you, but if you end up outside in the bushes there's a good chance you'll make a much more permanent impression in this town. At least at the Honey Bee only a few people will know your business."

He shook his head and took another bite of his croissant, indicating he was finished with the conversation. Biting her lip to keep from laughing, Cheryl left the office, closing the door behind her.

The morning passed by quickly and was busy due to people picking up what they needed for weekend guests and special dinners. Esther's father, Seth, dropped her off for work at twelve and took off as soon as Esther got out of the buggy. Cheryl was hoping to see Naomi so she could tell her about her visit with Amos Streeter. The unusual meeting still bothered her, and she wanted Naomi's take on it.

After getting Esther squared away, Cheryl went back to her office to get Matt and go to lunch. When she opened the door, she was shocked to see her brother sitting in her office chair with Ellen Streeter's belongings strewn across her desk.

CHAPTER SEVEN

What are you doing?" Cheryl snapped. She hadn't meant to sound defensive, but finding her brother going through Ellen's things upset her.

"I...I'm sorry," he stammered. "I was bored, and there was a big sack sitting behind your desk. I was just curious."

Cheryl had meant to put the tote bag in her large desk drawer and lock it, but she'd forgotten. She closed the door, plopped herself down in one of the chairs in front of her desk, and sighed. "No, I'm the one who's sorry, Matt. I didn't mean to sound so..." She let her voice trail off. How had she sounded? Accusatory? As if Matt was trying to what...steal something? She instantly felt ashamed of herself. "I'm a little sensitive about that stuff. You just got in the way." She began to tell Matt about finding the purse and valise in the laundry chute. She recounted the information Naomi had given her, as well as the uncomfortable visit with Amos the night before. "I'm just a little worried about it. I really want to find Ellen. Amos swears she's alive, but I'm not so sure."

Matt frowned. "So this Ellen disappears and then her husband falls down the stairs and dies? Very convenient."

"I honestly don't know what to think," Cheryl replied. "But I have to find out. First of all, if Amos is lying, Ellen might be...might be—"

"Closer than you'd like to think?"

"Unfortunately, yes. And I'm wondering if Amos might be involved somehow. I just need to find the truth."

"Well, I'd say from what I could read of that letter, Ellen had a boyfriend."

"It sounds like that, doesn't it?" She sighed. "Look, let's talk about this later, okay? I've got too much to do right now." Cheryl pointed at Matt. "Please don't mention any of this to Mom or Dad, okay? It would freak them out, and they might start pushing me to leave Sugarcreek."

Matt snorted. "I don't know. Just to see the looks on their faces..." Seeing his sister's expression, he laughed. "I won't say anything, Skeeter. You have my word." He put everything back inside the purse and then slid it and the valise into the large bag. Then he held it out to Cheryl. "No more snooping. Feel better now?"

"Again, sorry. You didn't do anything wrong. I'm just...jumpy."

Matt stood up and grabbed his laptop bag. "I'd be jumpy too if I thought a body was buried on my property."

Cheryl took the bag and carefully placed it in her large desk drawer—what she should have done in the first place. "So are you ready?"

"For some reason those croissants just made me hungrier," he said, grinning. "I can't wait for Yoder's fried chicken and cherry pie à la mode."

"Sounds good. Let's go."

Cheryl ushered her brother into the main shop. Esther was behind the counter and turned around when they came out of the office.

Cheryl smiled at her. "Esther, this is my brother, Matthew. We call him Matt."

"I did not know your brother was here for a visit. I am very happy to meet you."

"I'm glad to meet you too," Matt said. "Cheryl didn't know I was coming, but I'm here to celebrate her birthday."

"Oh, then you will join us for lunch tomorrow?"

Matt swung his gaze to Cheryl. "I don't know. This is the first I've heard about it."

"I was so surprised to see you I haven't had time to think about anything else. Esther's mother, Naomi, is a close friend. She's asked all of us over to her house on Saturday to celebrate my birthday." She frowned at Esther. "Are you sure your mom has room for one more?"

Esther grinned. "You know my mother better than that, ain't so? The more the merrier as far as Maam is concerned."

Cheryl laughed. "I guess I do know her better than that." She turned her attention back to Matt. "Before you say anything else, I must tell you that the croissants and jam you had for breakfast this morning were made by Naomi."

"I was going to say yes anyway, but that information seals the deal." Matt nodded at Esther. "I would love to come. Thank you so much for including me."

"Ach, you bless us with your presence. I will let Maam know. It will give her an excuse to bake an extra pie."

"Okay, now I'm really, really hungry, sis," Matt said. "You need to get me to food. Now. I'm not sure how much longer I can make it." He put his hand on his forehead in a dramatic gesture.

Esther giggled at his antics. "I believe you must attend to your brother immediately, Cheryl. I do not wish to see him faint from lack of sustenance."

"Trust me, when Matt gets hungry, he finds food. No matter where he is." She grabbed her purse and put her arm through Matt's. "Let's get going little brother, while Yoder's still has enough food to satisfy your enormous appetite." As she walked toward the door, Cheryl glanced back at Esther. "You might want to tell your mother to bake two extra pies."

Cheryl waved good-bye before they stepped outside. The clouds had finally moved away from Sugarcreek, and the sun was finally out.

"I'll just follow you," Matt said. "That way I can drive straight to Mitzi's after lunch."

Cheryl nodded, but her attention was on Matt's truck. It looked even fancier up close. Brand new, in fact. Probably cost three times what she'd paid for her Focus.

She got into her car, pulled out into the street, and waited for Matt to get behind her. Then she drove the short distance to the restaurant. Yoder's was busy as usual, but it was a large building with lots of seating. She'd never had to wait long for a table.

Cheryl and Matt parked in the lot to the north of the building. The horses and buggies were in one area and cars and trucks in another. She looked for one of the Millers' buggies but didn't see one.

When they went inside, there was only one couple ahead of them. Within a few minutes, Greta Yoder came over to seat them. When she saw Matt, a big smile lit up her face. "Ach, Cheryl. Is this who I think it is? Your little brother?"

Cheryl nodded. "It's been so long, I'm surprised you remember him."

Greta chuckled. "Remember him? Of course I remember Matthew. No one loved our fried chicken more than he did. Besides, he looks exactly the same. Just bigger. A good-looking boy is now a good-looking man."

Matthew beamed at her praise. "And you are as beautiful as ever, Greta. I always had a crush on you."

Cheryl grinned. Greta was a wonderful woman, but she was far from beautiful.

The restaurant owner burst out laughing. "Ach, you are still the same rascal. You always used your charm so I would give you extra pieces of chicken when you came here to eat with your aunt."

"Well, it worked, didn't it?"

She nodded and winked at him. "Ja, it did. And it is working now."

Matt turned to smile at Cheryl. "I'll bet I get more chicken than you do."

"I have a feeling you're right."

Greta picked up two menus from the stack near the cash register. "You are both incorrigible, but I am so glad you are together again. August will be pleased to see you, Matthew."

Cheryl and Matt followed her to a table in the corner of the large room. Several people greeted Cheryl as she walked past them. Lisa Troyer from Heini's Cheese Chalet waved at her. Lisa's family had been in the cheese business for a long time. A lot of the cheese Cheryl sold in the store came from Heini's. Lisa was an exuberant woman who loved her family, their business, and Sugarcreek with all her heart. She was also a very kind woman who did many things to help others in her community. Cheryl really liked her. She smiled and waved back.

She passed by Sandy Schlesman from the Sugarcreek Sisters Quilt Shoppe. Sandy called her over to say hello, and Cheryl introduced her to Matt. Greta waited patiently as Matt shook Sandy's hand.

As Cheryl and Matt started once again toward their table, someone else called Cheryl's name. She turned to see Laura and Frank Early waving at her. The owners of the Little Switzerland Bed-and-Breakfast, they were a very nice couple who bought a lot of items from Cheryl for their scrumptious morning breakfasts. Laura particularly liked the apple butter Cheryl sold in the shop.

As she passed by another table, Roxanna Velandria, the owner of Artistic License, a new art gallery that opened up after Bye Bye Blue closed, grabbed her arm. "I have some new things in the shop," she said with a smile. "You must stop in. I think you'll love the new watercolors." Roxanna and Cheryl had similar tastes in artwork, and Cheryl enjoyed spending time in the gallery. Since it was actually located in the basement of the building that housed the Honey Bee, it was simple for Cheryl to pop in after lunch.

"Thanks," Cheryl said with a smile. "I'll come by as soon as I can."

Cheryl said hello to several other people before they were finally seated. When Greta left, Matt said, "Wow. You seem to be very popular here. What are you? Sugarcreek's rock star?"

She shrugged. "It's a wonderful town. Most of these people shop in the store, and some of them go to my church."

"What church do you attend?" Matt asked, clearly interested.

His reaction surprised her. Matt had sworn off church years ago because churches were "filled with hypocrites."

"I attend Silo Church in Dover. It's not far from here."

Matt snorted. "Don't tell me you actually meet in a silo."

"Of course not. They have a great building. Lots of people, young and old, attend. I love it. The members are really on fire for the Lord, and they do so much to reach out to the community and the world. It's awesome."

Matt nodded and picked up his menu. "Sounds like one of those happy clappy churches, as Dad would say."

"I guess the people are happy. Dad's church has contemporary worship too, Matt."

Her brother looked up in surprise. "I thought he hated the new stuff."

"Things change. Their worship leader uses some of the newer songs, but they've also kept several of the old hymns. I'm glad. I don't think we have to have just one or the other. The idea is to praise God, and some of the old hymns are wonderful. 'Amazing Grace,' 'How Great Thou Art,' 'Nothing But the Blood'—"

"I know," Matt said, interrupting her. "We grew up on those songs, and I like them too. But I really love some of the newer songs. They really speak to me."

Cheryl's mouth dropped open as she tried to digest what her brother had just said. "Are you telling me you go to church?"

He stared at her over the top of his menu, his eyebrows knit together in a frown. "Why is that such a shock?"

"I... I don't know. I mean, you told me you'd sworn off church."

"That was years ago, Cheryl. As you say, things change. If Dad can allow contemporary worship in his services, I guess I can start going to church. Right?"

Cheryl studied him for a moment. Was he telling the truth? What good would it do to lie to her? She was about to ask him about his church when the waitress came up to their table. She took their drink order and told them she'd be right back.

Before Cheryl could frame her next question, Matt put his menu down. "Look, sis, a lot has changed in my life. I have a great job, and yes, I'm going to church. I attend every week...with my girlfriend."

So that was it. He was going to church because of some girl. As soon as the thought struck her, Cheryl realized that as far as she knew, it was the first time her brother had dated a woman who went to church. Even Matt wouldn't use religion as a way to attract a girlfriend. This was actually very good news.

"That's great, Matt. I'm really glad. Are you two serious?"

He smiled. "Yes, we are. Nicki is just wonderful, Skeeter. I really want you to meet her."

Cheryl was surprised by the tone in his voice and the glow on his face. Was her playboy brother finally ready to settle down?

A few minutes later, the waitress came back to take their orders. Cheryl decided to get the chicken too. It really was delicious even if it wasn't good for her waistline. Of course, it wouldn't help her to lose that fifteen pounds she seemed to always struggle with. Naomi had scolded her when she'd mentioned it once.

"Ach, Cheryl," she'd said. "You do not want to be a skinny scarecrow. You are a woman who enjoys life and appreciates food. You are lovely and perfect. Do not let negative voices get into your head."

Cheryl wasn't sure what negative voice she'd been talking about, but she was pretty sure the voice she heard from time to time had a Southern accent. Her mother was slim and beautiful. She never criticized Cheryl for her extra weight. It was just the way she looked at her sometimes and the occasional comment about "wearing the right kind of clothes for her body type." Cheryl was pretty sure that meant wearing something designed to hide those pesky extra pounds.

Cheryl wanted to learn more about Matt's job and his new girlfriend, but as they waited for their food, he began to ask her about the shop and about living in Sugarcreek. They chatted amicably until their lunch was served. Sure enough, Matt got an extra piece of chicken. Greta came by and patted him on the back, and even August came out of the kitchen to say hello. By the time they got ready to leave, Cheryl was almost convinced her brother had finally grown up. But she'd been fooled before. Was this change real? Or was Matt after something? Only time would tell.

Cheryl enjoyed telling Matt about some of her experiences in Sugarcreek, but for some reason, August's cherry pie tasted a little sour in her mouth. She was pretty sure it had nothing to do with his recipe and everything to do with the apprehension she just couldn't seem to shake.

CHAPTER EIGHT

After getting Matt settled in the guest room, Cheryl went back to the shop. It was almost three when her father called.

"Sorry it took us so long, honey, but your mother had to stop along the way. You know how she loves antique stores."

"I'm so glad to hear from you, Daddy. So you and Momma are in town?"

"We just checked in. Give us a few minutes to unpack, and we'll head over to the store, okay?"

Although she was excited to see them, Cheryl glanced around the shop with a critical eye. She'd cleaned and straightened so many times everything looked almost perfect. Almost. Cheryl felt she'd added her own touch to the Swiss Miss. Would they see it? Would they even care?

"Sure. I'll see you when you get here."

After she hung up, Cheryl hurried around the store, checking shelves and displays one more time, trying to make certain the Swiss Miss looked its best.

After checking out a couple of customers, Esther joined her as she rearranged a shelf of jellies and jams. Some of the jars had been put back with the labels facing the wrong way.

Esther put her hand on Cheryl's shoulder. "You seem nervous. Is something wrong? Can I help?"

Cheryl took a deep, cleansing breath, trying to calm herself down. "It's my parents. They'll be here any minute. I just want everything to look…good."

"Cheryl, the shop is beautiful. They will be so impressed." Esther took Cheryl's arm and led her away from the display. "You wait for your folks. I will finish straightening up, ja?"

"All right. Thanks."

As she waited for her dad's car to come down the street, Cheryl remembered Aunt Mitzi's words to her when she'd first taken over the shop. Cheryl was feeling inadequate and worried that she wasn't up to the challenge.

"Honey, if we rely on ourselves to accomplish anything, we're making a big mistake. But if we rely on God, nothing is impossible. God brought you here, and He will equip you for whatever is ahead." Then she'd taken Cheryl's hands in hers. "I think you're incredible. So unique and so gifted. And God sees you the same way. He says you are the apple of His eye. His precious daughter. But you must make a decision, Cheryl. Will you believe God? Or will you believe people? If you believe people, you will never be good enough. Life will knock you around and beat you up. But if you believe God, nothing can keep you from your destiny."

"I believe You, God," Cheryl whispered, wiping away a tear that escaped from her eye. "I believe You." Why was she worrying so much about what her parents might think? They had always been supportive. Maybe her life wasn't going the way they'd planned, but that didn't mean they wouldn't understand why living and working in Sugarcreek was so important to her.

At that moment, she saw a silver sedan pull up in front of the store. She watched as her father got out and walked around to the passenger door to open it for his wife. Cheryl took a deep breath as he helped her mother exit the car. She stood up and stared toward the Swiss Miss.

"I am loved by God," Cheryl whispered to herself. "I'm good enough for Him." She prayed their visit would go well. She dreaded telling them that Matt was in town, but it was probably better to rip the bandage off quickly rather than to pull it slowly. The pain wouldn't last as long.

Cheryl walked out on to the porch and waited as her parents approached. Her father saw her and smiled, but Momma was busy looking up and down the street. Cheryl saw her shake her head. Cheryl's heart fell. What was that about?

She hurried down the stairs toward her father who held out his arms. As soon as she reached him, he wrapped her up in a big hug.

"Hi there, Snicklefritz. I've missed you so much."

Although Cheryl disliked the nickname Skeeter, she loved it when her father called her Snicklefritz. It was actually a Dutch word used to describe mischievous or talkative children. And Cheryl had been an excessively verbal child, always asking questions. The first person to use the term in reference to her was her great-uncle Dave. Married to her father's aunt late in life, he'd been one of Cheryl's favorite relatives. He'd been very close to her father as a boy. Her dad began calling her Snicklefritz after Uncle Dave passed away. It made her feel as if her uncle were still with them.

"I've missed you too, Daddy." She let go of him and turned to her mother. "Hi, Momma," she said. "Glad you're here."

She hugged her mother, taking in a whiff of the perfume she always wore. Cheryl's mother never seemed to age. Although she shared the same coloring as her daughter, red hair and green eyes, Ginny Cooper always looked perfectly groomed and put together. Cheryl was lucky if she remembered to check her flyaway hair more than once a day. After Cheryl stepped back, her mother's gaze swept over the Swiss Miss. "Well, it certainly looks the same. Nothing ever changes in this town."

Cheryl swallowed the retort that immediately jumped into her mind and forced herself to smile. "We have some new shops on Main Street, and the Swiss Miss has been repainted. Other than that, you're right. Sugarcreek is just as charming as it's always been."

Before her mom could respond, Cheryl quickly turned away from her. "Why don't you two come in for a while? I'll show you around, and then we can discuss our plans for the time you're here."

"That sounds great," her father said. They followed her up the steps and into the shop. Esther stood near the counter with a smile on her face.

"Daddy and Momma, this is Esther Miller. She works here in the afternoons. I couldn't run this place without her."

Her father immediately stretched out his hand, and Esther shook it. "I'm so glad to meet you, Esther. Thank you for being such a blessing in my daughter's life."

Esther blushed. "Ach, she is more of a blessing to me—and to our family. We were sad to say good-bye to Mitzi, but Gott is good. He has sent Cheryl to us, and we love her more than tongue can tell."

Cheryl felt tears spring to her eyes at the girl's sweet words. "I feel the same way, Esther," she said in a choked voice.

Esther looked at Cheryl's mother and extended her hand. "I am blessed to meet you too."

"Thank you, Esther," she said with a smile. "It's comforting to know our daughter has people in her life who care about her."

At that moment, the bell over the front door tinkled, and Cheryl saw Naomi come in. She introduced her to her parents, and they greeted her as cordially as they had Esther.

"We look forward to having you come to our home tomorrow," Naomi said with a smile. "It is an honor to share in Cheryl's birthday celebration."

Cheryl's mother frowned. "I don't understand."

"I haven't had the chance to tell you," Cheryl said. "Naomi has invited us over to her house tomorrow for lunch. As a way to celebrate my birthday."

Naomi nodded. "Cheryl has become a dear friend. It is a privilege for us to open our home to you. And to your son."

Ginny's eyes widened. "Our son?" She swung her gaze to Cheryl. "What does she mean? Is Matthew here?"

"Yes, Momma. He showed up this morning. I had no warning that he was coming."

Her mother turned toward Naomi. "Thank you for your invitation, Naomi, but right now I'm feeling somewhat ambushed. If you don't mind, I'd like to talk to my daughter before we completely change our plans. We came to town believing we would be spending our time with Cheryl, and now we're told about this party...and that our son is in town. He didn't even bother to let us know. I hope you won't think I'm being rude, but I need some time to...process this information."

"Of course," Naomi said. "Please forgive me. I should have considered your feelings. It was not my intention to interfere." She nodded at Esther. "We must leave, Daughter. Please gather your things."

The look on Naomi's face made Cheryl's stomach turn over. She reached out and grabbed her arm before she could make a getaway. She turned to confront her mother while trying to control the rush of anger coursing through her.

"As I understand it, Momma, the person with the birthday should be able to have a say-so in how her day is celebrated. I'm glad you and Daddy are here. It means a lot to me. But tomorrow I will be having lunch with my best friend, Naomi, and her family. Of course you're welcome. In fact, this woman specifically asked us to her home to make it easier on you, so you wouldn't have to plan anything. I hope you and Daddy will join me and Matt tomorrow. If you choose not to attend, I'll see you as soon as I return from my party."

Her mother's face turned red, a reaction she shared with her daughter when she was embarrassed or upset. Before she could respond, Cheryl's father put his hand on his wife's arm. "Naomi," he said, addressing the flustered Amish woman, "I'm grateful you've given us a chance to celebrate our daughter's birthday in style. Of course we'll be there. And thank you for your graciousness." He turned to smile at Cheryl. "I take it we can all go together? You and Matt and your mother and me?"

Trying to push back her irritation, Cheryl nodded. "I think that would work. I'll talk to Matt. He's staying at Mitzi's with me."

"Wonderful. I guess we'll see you tomorrow, Naomi." He turned to smile at Esther. "And you too, Esther. We're looking forward to it."

Esther, who looked slightly confused, managed a small smile. "We will be pleased to have you in our home." She hurried over to the counter, took off her apron, and placed it on the shelf underneath. Then she joined Naomi who quickly guided her daughter out the door.

As soon as the door swung shut, Cheryl's mother swung around to face her husband. "I don't appreciate being embarrassed in front of strangers, George."

"I wasn't trying to embarrass you, Ginny. I think you're tired from our trip and didn't realize you sounded a little impolite."

At that moment, the bell over the front door rang. Delores Delgado, the receptionist from the Sugarcreek Police Department, came in. Cheryl waved at her and whispered to her mother. "I need to take care of these customers. Why don't you and Daddy wait in the office until I'm finished? The door's unlocked."

Without saying another word, Cheryl went over to help Delores pick out cheese. She came in regularly for butter cheese, croissants, and apple butter. Three of the store's best sellers. After helping Delores with her order and ringing her up, Cheryl stood at the counter, trying to rein in her jumbled emotions. Her mother was hardly ever rude, and Cheryl couldn't understand why she'd reacted so strongly about the birthday luncheon. Was it because Matt was in town? When she felt calm enough, she went back to her office where her parents waited. She could hear her mother's high-pitched voice and thick Southern drawl. When she was upset, her Southern roots showed. She was obviously irritated.

"...think about our feelings."

"Ginny, this is *her* birthday," her father said soothingly. "Let her celebrate it the way she wants. Besides, I'd like to meet her friends. If Cheryl's determined to stay here, we might as well accept it. There's not much we can do about it, is there?"

A pause in the discussion gave Cheryl a chance to open her office door. Although she acted as if she hadn't overheard them, she was bothered by her father's comment. On the one hand she was grateful he'd stepped up to support her, but on the other hand, he sounded resigned. As if he'd given up on her. It was becoming clear that Cheryl's suspicions were correct. Her mother was upset because she was still living in Sugarcreek.

"Why don't you go back to your hotel and rest for a while?" she told them as she walked through the door. "I'll pick up Matt, and we'll meet you at the Canal Tavern at six o'clock." The Canal Tavern of Zoar was a landmark, originally opened in 1829. It was located in Bolivar, a small town about twenty miles away from Sugarcreek.

Her father smiled. "That sounds wonderful. I love that place. Best steak I ever had." He frowned. "It's been a while though. Remind me how to get there?"

Cheryl gave him directions, which she wrote down on a piece of paper she took from the notepad on her desk. After she handed it to him, she held the door open, expecting her folks to leave, but her father hesitated.

"Look, Cheryl. I'm sorry about what happened before." He ran a hand through his salt-and-pepper hair. Her father was a handsome man. Tall and angular, but with a presence and a deep voice that reminded people of the late Gregory Peck. He still turned heads to the chagrin of Cheryl's mother. "We were just taken off guard. We came here to see you. It's been a while, and at first the idea of spending our time around other people seemed…inconvenient. But after talking about it, we realize that you have your own life now. And your own friends. Having lunch with the Millers, people who obviously care about you, is our pleasure. I hope you'll forgive us."

Her mother nodded. "Your father's right, Cheryl. It was a long trip, and I'm tired. I'm very sorry for what I said. I think part of it was finding out Matt was here. I want to see him, I'm just…" She shook her head. Her mother didn't need to finish her thought. Cheryl understood her concern completely. "I'll apologize to Naomi and Esther tomorrow," she continued. Then she offered Cheryl a small smile.

"Thanks, Momma. I really am glad you're here. I've really missed you." Cheryl felt her body relax a bit. Maybe everything would be all right after all.

"We've missed you too," her father said.

"So are the plans for tonight okay with you?" Cheryl asked her mother.

"It sounds fine," her mother replied. "We'll see you at six."

With that she got up and walked out of Cheryl's office, waiting by the front door for her husband.

Cheryl's father came over and gave her a hug. "Don't worry, Snicklefritz. Everything will be okay. Your mother loves you. Unfortunately, she worries about you too much. We thought you planned to be in Sugarcreek temporarily. Just to help your aunt. We just don't want you to make a decision you'll regret later."

Cheryl gazed up into her father's face. "Look, Daddy, I don't know how long I'll be here. I know when you sent me to college you didn't imagine I'd end up a shopkeeper in a small Amish town. And I realize you thought I'd be married by now, but I just couldn't marry Lance. He wasn't the right man for me. This life might not look the way you imagined it, but I hope you'll see that I'm happy. Really happy. Can't that be enough?"

Her father took a step back. "Of course happiness is important, honey. Maybe you don't want the things we've wanted for you. But this?" He motioned toward the shop. "We're afraid you're hiding out in this small town as a way to protect yourself from life. And we don't want that for you."

"But that's not true. I've found more *life* here than I ever had before. I get up every day looking forward to what's ahead. When I worked for the bank, I couldn't wait to finish the day and get home." She grabbed his hand. "Please try to see this place through my eyes while you're here, okay?"

He frowned at her. "I grew up in Sugarcreek, Cheryl. I left for a reason. Because I couldn't see a future here. Even your aunt left. She ran off to...wherever she is."

"Papua New Guinea, Daddy. Don't you keep in touch with her?"

"We write each other, Cheryl. Maybe not as much as we should, but we're both very busy. I just forget where she is sometimes."

"She wasn't running away from anything, Daddy. She was running *to* something."

He smiled. "I know. You're right, of course. I'm very proud of my sister. She's doing the Lord's work."

"I'm proud of her too, Daddy. And I'm proud I could help her live her dream. Yes, this might be temporary, but if it is, I'll figure out what's next when she comes back. For now, I'm just happy to keep the shop going."

He nodded and gave her a tentative smile. "All right. I understand. Look, just cut your mother a little slack. She's just worried, honey. She loves you so much, and all she sees is that you're still alone. She thought by now you'd have your own family, and we'd be grandparents. Coming to Sugarcreek, a small town with even fewer prospects than you had in Columbus, was a shock to her. When you started talking as if living here might be permanent, I think it frightened her."

"Is that why she shut down our Sunday phone calls?"

"Probably." He sighed deeply. "We doubt Matthew will ever settle down and get married." He brushed a strand of Cheryl's wayward red hair from her forehead. "We so wanted grandchildren. You were our only hope."

"Don't give up on me yet, Daddy," Cheryl said softly. "I want those things too. But I believe if I'm in God's will, He'll bring me the right husband—in His timing."

"I won't give up, Snicklefritz, but I'm pretty sure your mother will have a harder time of it."

"I know. But I'm turning thirty-one years old. Don't I have the right to pick my own path?"

He chuckled. "It probably should work that way, but your mother believes every year you grow older your options decrease. I think your birthday got her stirred up. She'll come around. You know that, right?"

"I hope so. I've never seen her like this." Cheryl shook her head. "Will you help me to make this an enjoyable visit, Daddy? I know Matt being here adds some pressure, but he seems... different. He says he's changed."

Her father rolled his eyes.

"I know. I felt the same way when he told me, but what if it's finally true?" She grabbed his hand.

The smile slipped from his face. "I pray it is, but if he asks us for money, our answer is still no. We love him, but he's got to take some responsibility for his life. He's never paid us back a penny he owes us. We don't care about money, but we care that he's never made an attempt to keep his word."

Cheryl slumped against her desk. "You and Momma made the right decision to cut him off financially. He says he has a good job now. And that he's going to church."

"He's always got a job on the line, Cheryl."

"I know, but he's never mentioned church before." Cheryl released her father's hand. "Please, Daddy. Listen to Matt. Give him a chance."

"I will, Snicklefritz." He leaned over and kissed her forehead. "My sister has told me many times that Matt would turn out okay. Maybe she was right. I'll try to keep the faith."

Mentioning Mitzi suddenly reminded Cheryl that she was scheduled to Skype with her aunt at six o'clock. "Daddy, can we meet at seven instead of six? I forgot about something I'm supposed to do after work."

He nodded. "Not a problem. It will give us a little more time to rest." He looked out into the shop where Cheryl's mom stood next to the front door. "Your mother's tired."

"Travelling can be exhausting. You guys had a big trip today. How were your flights?" Cheryl asked.

"They were fine. We flew into Columbus and rented a car. Your mother wanted to do some shopping along the way. Lots of antique stores and small shops in Ohio. You know how much she loves that."

Cheryl just looked at him. Her mother hadn't even given the Swiss Miss a second glance.

Her father obviously got the irony of his statement. "Give her time, honey. I think the shop is charming. You've done a great job." He gave her another quick hug and then went out to meet her mother, who opened the door when she saw him coming. Her father waved before he got into the car and drove away.

Although Cheryl felt better after talking to her dad, the butterflies in her stomach hadn't gone away. All she could do was trust God and pray He'd make everything turn out okay. She wanted her family back. The way they used to be before Matt left home. Was that even possible?

CHAPTER NINE

That night Cheryl hurried home from work. After a quick shower she changed her clothes, and then she positioned herself in front of her computer. After signing into Skype, she waited patiently, hoping to see Mitzi come online. It wasn't always possible for her aunt to know where she'd be, so even though she tried to pick a time that should work, there were occasions when she just couldn't make it back to the house where she stayed with a missionary couple who'd spent many years in Papua New Guinea. Cheryl would get an e-mail later explaining why she couldn't keep their Skype appointment.

As she waited, she tried to sort out all the conflicting thoughts in her head. With her family in town, she hadn't had time to think much about her visit with Amos Streeter. It still bothered her. From talking to him, she still wasn't sure if Ellen was alive or dead. She wanted to believe that he'd talked to her after Bill's death, but something about his attitude confused her. She couldn't shake the feeling that he wasn't completely honest. She was conflicted about what to do now. If she dropped it and Ellen was dead, it was possible someone in Sugarcreek had gotten away with murder. Unfortunately, she would probably have to put the situation with Ellen on hold until her family left town.

Tonight would be the first time they'd *all* been together in a very long time. She'd visited her parents in Seattle a few times in the last several years, and they'd come to Columbus more than once, but Matt was never there. He didn't even show up at her uncle Ralph's funeral. Although his absence didn't seem to bother Mitzi, it still upset Cheryl. Mitzi was like a second mother to both of them. Surely there wasn't anything more important than being with their aunt during a time of great loss.

"God, I could sure use Your help," she prayed quietly. "You know I have a temper. Even though I try to control it, I almost lost that battle this afternoon. I came so close to saying things to my mother I shouldn't say. I'm trying to be respectful, but I'm finding it hard to control my tongue. Help me to walk in love and stay peaceful. I've got to commit this thing to You. If I try to fix it, I'll just mess it up more. Would You do something wonderful for us? Bring reconciliation, Lord. I really love my family. Help us build bridges and learn to love each other the right way. And please, God, help us to accept each other for who we are." She thought for a moment before saying, "None of us can fix Matt. You're the only one who can really change people. I want to believe he's different, but how can I do that when he's let me down so many times?"

Beau rubbed up against her leg, and she had just reached down to pet him when her computer made a little whirring sound, an indication that someone had signed on to Skype. Sure enough it was Mitzi. Cheryl clicked on her profile picture, and the screen popped up. Mitzi was looking at her through the computer.

"Hey there, beautiful girl," her aunt said with a big smile. "I'm so blessed to see your gorgeous face."

"Hi, Mitzi," Cheryl said. "I'm really glad we're able to talk this evening." Surprisingly, her voice broke with emotion. For some reason, every time she talked to Mitzi, her real feelings seemed to come out. She couldn't hide much from her aunt.

"Oh, honey, what's going on?" Mitzi asked.

"I should be asking you about your adventures," Cheryl replied, trying to control her emotions. "What you're doing is so important. My problems are silly compared to the incredible things you're accomplishing there."

"Oh, honey, God doesn't see it that way. Everyone has their own calling, and one is not more important than the other. Why, I know people who can lead large meetings where a thousand people come forward to receive Christ. But in their personal lives they're nasty and spiteful. Even their own families don't want to be around them. I sure don't know everything, but on that day when we stand before God, I think He's going to care more about the people closest to us than anything else. You might be surprised to see the famous evangelist get a shack while the men and women who worked hard all their lives and brought their children up in the admonition of the Lord move into big, beautiful mansions." She pointed her finger at her computer screen. "You just do what God puts in front of you, dear girl. And He didn't put Papua New Guinea in your path. He put it on mine."

"Well, normally that might make me feel better, Aunt Mitzi, but Momma and Daddy are here. And so is Matt. They came to celebrate my birthday."

"Oh my." Even Mitzi seemed a little taken aback by this news. "And how's that going?"

Cheryl sighed. "Momma isn't herself. She's upset. And Matt? He's hiding here at your house. Until this evening that is. We're all going for dinner at the Canal Tavern. You remember how much Daddy likes it."

Mitzi chuckled. "My brother loves a good steak." She paused for a moment before saying, "And how is he handling all this?"

"He's trying to bring peace without taking sides. He says Momma's not really mad at me. She's worried I'm making bad choices and that I'll never get married and give her grandchildren."

"And what have they said about Sugarcreek? About the shop?"

Cheryl shook her head. "Momma didn't say a word. Daddy said the store is charming. I cleaned and straightened like a crazy person, and they didn't even bother to look around."

Mitzi smiled into her camera. "Honey, your contentment needs to come from God, not from people. If you rely on people to bring you affirmation, you'll never find satisfaction. But you know that, don't you?"

"Yeah, I know it. I was remembering something similar you told me about that same thing right before my folks got here. Now I just have to *act* like I know it."

Mitzi laughed. "You'll all be fine, you know. I have faith in every single one of you. Your mother loves you. If she sees how happy you are, she'll come around. More than anything, parents want their children to be happy."

"Even Matthew?"

"Yes, even Matthew. Cheryl, Matthew is a good man, and he's going to come out just fine. But do something for me, will you? Give him some room to change? Let him know you believe in him? We all need someone to encourage us. To see the good in us. Will you do that for me, please? It's important."

"Okay, Aunt Mitzi. I'll try."

"Good. That makes me feel much better." Her aunt laughed as something pushed at her. A little goat looked into the camera. His walleyed stare made Cheryl giggle.

"Have a new friend?" she asked her aunt.

"This is Georgie. He's adopted us. We've taken him in as our mascot. Quite a little character."

Cheryl snorted. "You named him after my father? Your brother?"

Mitzi grinned. "Don't you tell him."

"Oh, I wouldn't dare."

Mitzi turned and leaned away from the camera. "Shoo, Georgie. I'll be done in a bit, okay?" She turned back to the computer screen. "How are things at the shop? Is the new cooler in yet?"

Cheryl took this as her cue to tell Mitzi about the laundry chute and what she'd discovered about Ellen Streeter. She recounted everything that had happened since Chuck had opened up the wall.

"So did you know anything about this?" she asked her aunt when she finished.

"I didn't know the Streeters," Mitzi said, "but Maybelline Finn and her mother knew them. They told me a few stories." She frowned. "According to them, Bill wasn't a very nice man. Kept

Ellen a virtual prisoner in her own home. Then she left town, and a short time later Bill died. Maybelline's mother, Doris, told me some people thought Bill killed Ellen. But he didn't. Doris was certain Ellen left Sugarcreek before Bill's accident." She shook her head. "I'm sorry, honey. That's all I know. The person to talk to is Maybelline. You should visit her."

"I intend to, but it looks like I might have to wait until my parents and Matt leave."

"You know, there was something else. Something odd that Maybelline told me about the night Ellen left, but I just can't remember it. I guess it wasn't really important to me at the time. But you might ask her about it. Maybelline and her mother were quite worried about Ellen." Cheryl wanted to talk to her more about Ellen, but at that moment, she heard Matt coming out of the bathroom after finishing his shower. She turned to see him coming up behind her as she sat at her kitchen table.

"Aunt Mitzi, I have someone here who'd like to say hi to you," she said.

Cheryl scooted over so Matt could grab another chair and pull it in front of the computer.

"Hi, Aunt Mitzi," Matt said. He was rewarded with a huge smile from his aunt.

"Oh, Matthew, it's so good to see you. How wonderful of you to come to Sugarcreek for your sister's birthday. You always were such a thoughtful boy."

Cheryl watched Matt's face light up at his aunt's kind words, but something inside her rebelled. Thoughtful? Matt was anything but thoughtful. But suddenly, memories of Matt as a young boy flooded her mind. Picking flowers and bringing them to Mitzi. Asking her constantly if he could do anything to help her. He even mowed her yard when they came to visit in the summer. His generosity didn't stop there. He'd use his limited allowance money to take Cheryl for ice cream. Then there was the time he pushed Mitzi's mower around Sugarcreek, cutting lawns so he could earn money to buy Cheryl a necklace with a gemstone set in a silver heart. Cheryl had seen it in a local store and fallen in love with it. And Matthew's kindness to her hadn't been limited to Sugarcreek. He'd done many nice things for her at home as well. Why had she forgotten them? She suddenly felt ashamed.

"Yes, he is thoughtful," Cheryl said, wrapping her arm through her brother's. She turned to see him staring at her with a surprised look on his face, which only made her feel worse. "And I'm really glad he's here."

Matt's slow smile warmed Cheryl's heart. Mitzi was right. Her brother needed encouragement, and she was determined to give it to him no matter what her parents said or did.

"I wish I could be with you on your special day," Mitzi said. "I sent you a small gift, but it may not get there by tomorrow. If not, be looking for it."

"You've already given me the best gift I could ever get," Cheryl said, her eyes misting. "Your love and the opportunity to come to Sugarcreek. I'm very happy here, Aunt Mitzi. I honestly don't remember ever being as content as I am now."

Mitzi smiled. "That's because you're in God's will, honey. Some people think I've lost my mind, living in conditions they consider untenable, but I love every second of my life now. Paul said 'I know what it is to be in need, and I know what it is to have plenty. I have learned the secret of being content in any and every situation, whether well fed or hungry, whether living in plenty or in want. I can do all this through Him who gives me strength.' That's how I feel. God helps me in every situation. I'm never alone, but I am shepherded by the One who loves me with an unfailing love. And it's a wonderful place to be."

"Thank you for being such a good example to us," Cheryl said. "You're such a blessing."

Instead of reacting positively to her comment, Cheryl was surprised to see her aunt frown.

"Your parents are excellent examples of God's love, Cheryl. Maybe their dreams for you and Matt aren't necessarily *your* dreams, but have you ever considered that their concerns are out of love? There are parents who don't care enough about their children to interject themselves in their lives at all. Your parents love you both so much. They have been through many trials. Some you don't know anything about. But they have never turned their backs on God—or on their calling. And Matt"—Mitzi pointed at the computer screen—"what you see as your father's unwillingness to help you is actually his attempt to make your life better. It's easy to say yes to our children. But saying no is hard. A real test of love. God says no to us sometimes too, but not because He doesn't love us. It's because He does."

At one time Matt would have been angry at Mitzi's admonition, but to Cheryl's surprise, he just nodded. "I know, Aunt Mitzi. I think I finally figured that out."

"Not a surprise to me, dear boy. I always knew you would."

A voice from behind her caused Mitzi to turn her head. She said something in a language Cheryl didn't understand and then turned back to the camera.

"I have to go, dear ones. We are traveling a long way today and must get started." She reached up and put her hand near the computer screen. "I love you both very much, and I will be praying for you. Please respect each other, and remember that love is something you give, not something you take. Always give each other the benefit of the doubt, okay?"

Cheryl put her hand close to her aunt's. "Okay, Aunt Mitzi. We love you too."

"Yes, we do," Matt said softly. "We'll be praying for you, Aunt Mitzi."

"I know you will. Good-bye, my loves."

With that, the Skype program closed. Matt went back to his bedroom to finish getting ready, but Cheryl sat at the computer for a few minutes, just staring at the screen. Mitzi's words echoed in her head. *Please respect each other, and remember that love is something you give, not something you take. Always give each other the benefit of the doubt, okay?*

Could she do what her aunt had asked her to do? Could God mend their broken family? Cheryl prayed it wasn't already too late.

Chapter Ten

Cheryl offered to drive to the restaurant. Matt seemed nervous and kept tapping his fingers on his knees. Although he wasn't making any actual sound, it began to get on Cheryl's nerves. At one point she started to tell him to stop it, but she realized her reaction came from her own trepidation.

She made a quick stop at the shop to check on Chuck. Sure enough, he was working hard. When he stepped out from behind the plastic tarp, he was covered with dust. Thankfully, most of it was contained to the area where he worked.

After taking off his dust mask and goggles, he assured her that everything was on track and that he would clean up any mess before he left. Feeling relieved, Cheryl allowed him to get back to work. Before she left, she went into her office to get an extra house key she kept in her middle desk drawer. She wasn't sure how long Matt would be staying, but she realized he might need to let himself in when she wasn't there.

When she got back in the car, one look at her brother made it clear he hadn't calmed down. She put the key in the ignition but didn't start the car.

"You look like you're getting ready to be thrown into the lion's den," she said. "You need to relax. We're your family, and we love you. Can you focus on that?"

He shook his head. "I know I'm being ridiculous, but I really miss Mom and Dad." He looked at Cheryl. "And you. It's my fault for walking away. Now I just want to make things right, but I'm not sure I can."

Cheryl reached over and put her hand on his shoulder. "Matt, everyone makes mistakes. I've made them too. I agree with Aunt Mitzi. Our parents love us even if we're not living the lives they wanted for us. Momma and I have always gotten along, but lately it's like we're strangers. It seems we've both disappointed them in some way. That doesn't mean they've given up on us. Let's give them a chance before we assume the worst, okay?"

He took a deep breath and let it out slowly. "Okay. You're right. It's just…" He looked silently out the window for a few seconds before continuing. "It's just that I want them to see I've changed." He turned toward her. "I really do have a good job now, Cheryl. My life is finally on track."

"Then tell them that," Cheryl said gently. "They'll believe you."

"Will they? Or will they look at me the same way you did when I told you I was running my own business?"

Cheryl shook her head. "I'm sorry, Matt. It's just that—"

"I've said it so many times before." He gave her a small smile. "I know. I'm like the boy who cried wolf. Now that it's true, no one believes me."

"Well, I believe you."

He sighed. "Thank you, sis. Now if Mom and Dad could just do the same."

Cheryl started the engine. "You may have to be patient with them. Don't be upset if their first reaction isn't what you want."

He nodded. "You're right. I shouldn't be angry with them because of a situation I caused." He smiled at her. "I'm so glad you're with me. If you and Mitzi believe in me, I can make it through anything."

"Good." Cheryl got back on the road and drove to the restaurant, not sure if Matt's confidence in her wasn't misplaced. She was trying to believe he'd finally grown up. His interest in church was the thing that really gave her hope. She'd never forget the argument he'd had with their parents before he walked out. "If you're an example of God's love, I can live without Him," he'd said. Cheryl could still see the looks on their faces. Matt's anger and her parents' hurt. They didn't talk much about Matt after that, except when he called to ask for financial help. After a few years, her father finally delivered an ultimatum. Either Matt could come home and start looking for a job, or he'd have to quit asking for money. After that Matt cut off almost all contact with his family. Although he'd call Cheryl or send a card from time to time, their relationship suffered too. Then her father accepted the position in Seattle, and the family was separated even more. The last time they were together was a disastrous Christmas several years ago. That experience made things even worse.

The restaurant finally came into view, and Cheryl pulled into the parking lot. Her parents' car was a few spots down. As they got out of her car, Cheryl caught Matt's eye.

"It's going to be fine," she said, trying to reassure them both.

"'Once more into the breach,'" he muttered.

Cheryl grinned at him. "I hardly think Shakespeare will help us now."

Her comment made Matt laugh nervously as he followed her into the restaurant. The Canal Tavern looked like a big white farmhouse on the outside. Inside, the walls were brick, and the tables and chairs were dark wood. Cheryl had forgotten how charming and cozy it was. She looked around but didn't see her parents. Then the hostess motioned them over.

"Are you meeting the Coopers?" she asked.

After confirming they were, she led them to a table in a corner where their parents waited.

"We went ahead and got a table," her father said as they approached. He stood up and smiled at them. "I hope that was all right."

"Absolutely," Cheryl said.

"So good to see you, son," he said to Matt. He walked over and gave Matt a hug.

"I'm glad to see you too, Dad."

As her father went back to his chair, Matt sat down next to his mother. "Hi, Mom," he said. "You look beautiful this evening."

She smiled. "Why thank you, Matt. You look wonderful too. We're so glad you found the time to come here for your sister."

Although most people wouldn't have caught the small dig hidden within her mother's words, Cheryl noticed it. Her mother was accusing Matt of coming for Cheryl's benefit but not for theirs.

"I came to see you and Dad too," he said gently. "I've missed you both very much."

Her mother sniffed. "We've been in the same place for a long time, Matthew. Were we really that hard to find?"

"Ginny," her father said. "That's enough. We talked about this, didn't we? Being accusatory won't help anything."

Although she didn't respond, Cheryl's mother stayed quiet as she perused her menu.

"How was your trip?" Matt asked, obviously trying to lighten the mood.

"Fine," his father said. "All in all, everything went well."

Cheryl's mother shot her husband a look that said something different. "It was a long trip, and the plane ride was awful. The man across the aisle from us complained during the entire trip." She sighed. "I was certainly glad when we landed."

"I'm sorry, Momma," Cheryl said.

"It's all right. Not your fault. I'm just happy to have time with you." She looked over at Matt. "With both of you."

"I agree," her father said. He gazed down at his menu. "So what looks good to you, Cheryl?"

"The fillet sounds great," she said. Like her father, she enjoyed a good steak, and the Canal Tavern had some of the best she'd ever tasted.

"Good choice," her father said with a smile. "I've got to have the strip steak. It's been on my mind all day." He turned his attention to Matt. "How about you, son? What are you hungry for?"

"I'll go along with you, Dad," Matt said. "The strip sounds super."

"Of course," his mother said softly. "The most expensive thing on the menu."

Matt turned red and stared at his mother. "All right, Mom. I'll just have a house salad." He shut his menu with a snap and picked up his water.

"Don't be silly, Matt," his father said. "You'll have the strip steak." He put his menu on the table and stood up. "I'd like to talk to you, Ginny. Will you come with me, please?"

Even though it was obvious she was embarrassed and didn't want to go with him, Cheryl's mother got up slowly and followed him out of the room.

"This is going well, don't you think?" Matt said, making a face.

"Yeah, great." Cheryl shook her head. "What are we going to do, Matt?" Cheryl reached over and put her hand on her brother's arm. "I'm really sorry."

He shrugged. "Look, Cheryl. I know you don't want to hear this, but our mother has no use for me. She never did. You were always her favorite. I don't think she even wanted a boy."

Cheryl pulled her hand back quickly. "Don't say that. It isn't true. She loves you, Matt. She's just hurt. Give her some time. She'll come around."

"You don't understand," he replied. "I found something a long time ago that proves she never wanted me."

She frowned at him. "What are you talking about?"

"I was snooping in their room when I was a kid. Looking for hidden Christmas presents. I came across...a box."

Cheryl glanced toward the patio where her father had taken her mother. They were standing a few feet away from a large window, having a very animated conversation. Cheryl swung her gaze back to Matt. "A box? A box of what?"

Matt leaned forward and lowered his voice. "A box of baby things. All pink. A little sweater, some booties, a few other clothes, and a baby blanket with the name *Maddy* embroidered on it."

Cheryl frowned. "Maddy? Wasn't Mom's grandmother's name Madeline? Seems like she told me the family called her Maddy."

Matt leaned back in his chair. "See? They thought I was going to be a girl. When I showed up, Mom was disappointed. And she still is. That's never changed."

"Oh, Matt, I just don't believe that." She frowned. "I never saw that box. Maybe it didn't even belong to our mother. Could it have been a gift for someone else?"

"Hidden in the back of the closet? No. Cheryl, there's no denying it." He pasted a smile on his face. "I've accepted it, but I realize now that's when I started rebelling. I was so . . . hurt. I guess it turned into anger."

"Why didn't you tell me?"

"You were away at college, and I guess I wanted to just forget about it."

"Obviously, you didn't."

Matt shook his head slowly. "No, it seems I didn't. I think Dad and I will be all right. I'll never be the son he wanted, but I still believe we can have a good relationship. But Mom?" He shook his head. "That ship sailed the day I was born."

"I can't believe that." Cheryl grabbed a roll from the basket on the table and began to butter it. She was starving, and it looked as if they wouldn't be eating for a while. "You forget that I'm five years older than you. I watched our mother with you when you were little. She doted on you, Matt. It's not my imagination." She took a bite of her roll and then put it on a small plate near her water. "Do you remember picking dandelions from the yard and bringing them in to her? She would put them in a small vase and set them on the mantel. It was like you'd given her a dozen roses. She certainly didn't act like a mother who was disappointed in her son."

Matt raised his head to study his sister, but he didn't say anything.

"Once you asked her to wait for you to grow up so you could marry her. I saw her cry over that." Cheryl shook her head. "You're wrong. She loves you, Matt. I know it in my heart."

"Maybe she did once," he said in a whisper. "But not now."

"Real love is forever, Matt. Nothing can destroy it. That's how God loves us."

Cheryl was surprised to see tears in her brother's eyes. "I know how much I love her," he said in a choked voice. "That's why it hurts so much."

Cheryl looked up to see her parents coming back. She cocked her head toward them to warn Matt. He picked up his napkin and dabbed at his eyes before they reached the table.

"Everything okay, Daddy?" Cheryl asked.

He held out his wife's chair while she sat down. Then he smiled at Cheryl. "Everything is fine, Snicklefritz."

Once Cheryl's mother was seated, he went over and sat down in his own chair. He'd just started to say something when the waitress came up to the table.

"I'm sorry," her dad said to the young woman with the order pad. "Could you give us a few more minutes?"

She nodded and walked away. Cheryl took another bite of her roll and wondered just how long it would be before they ate.

"Listen, children," her father said in a low voice. "It isn't a secret that your mother and I are concerned about some of your...choices. And Matt, walking away from us hurt. A lot. But we both want to make things better. We realize we can't fix everything in one visit, but we want to try. We love you both. Very much."

"We feel the same way, Daddy," Cheryl said. "Matt and I love you and Momma. We're a family. If we all try, we can get along. In fact, maybe we could even enjoy being together. We certainly used to."

"I didn't come here just for Cheryl's birthday," Matt said softly. "I also came because I wanted to make things better. I've made a lot of mistakes, and I'm sorry for them. But my life is better now, and I hope you'll be proud of some of the things I've accomplished."

At that moment, the waitress came back, so all conversation ceased. As they ordered, Cheryl looked around the table. She thought about the last time she'd eaten with the Millers. As they'd gathered around their table, there had been laughter, love, and harmony. The Millers seemed to find loving each other easy. Why did it seem to be so hard for the Coopers?

Chapter Eleven

Cheryl woke to a rainy Saturday morning. She'd hoped the rain would stay away today, but it was clear that hadn't happened. She got out of bed, went to the kitchen, and ate a quick breakfast. Then she got ready for work. After being fed, Beau walked over to his crate.

"Not today, boy," she said. "You stay here with Matt."

The night before she'd talked to her brother about leaving Beau with him since the store would only be open until noon. Matt planned to drive over to the store, then they'd swing by and pick up their folks. That way they'd only have to take one car to the Millers'.

Cheryl wanted to look forward to her birthday celebration, but she was worried something would happen that might embarrass her in front of her Amish friends.

"This may turn out to be the worst birthday ever," she said to Beau, who just stared at her accusingly. "Yes, I know you want to go to the store, but you'll be happier here, trust me."

She tiptoed over to the guest room and opened it a crack. Beau immediately slipped in, jumped up on the bed, and then turned around a few times before settling in to sleep near Matt's feet. Her brother had stayed up late last night, attributing his restlessness to the dinner with their parents.

About an hour after Cheryl had gone to bed, she woke up, thinking she'd heard his truck pull out of the driveway. She fell asleep again, and when she got up a couple of hours later to go to the bathroom, Matt was in bed. A few of the houses on her street didn't have garages, and many times people who owned those homes pulled into her driveway to turn around so they could park on the street. As far as she knew, that was what she'd heard. In the end, it didn't really matter. Cheryl was just relieved he hadn't run away. It had been a pattern with him when things got tough. Her family had no chance of working things out if he took off again before they were able to reconcile completely.

Cheryl grabbed her raincoat, her umbrella, and her purse and headed to work. She was excited to see the finished wall. It would look even better after Chuck painted it this afternoon. She hoped the rain wouldn't put that on hold. She didn't want anything to delay the cooler being installed Monday morning.

When she pulled up to the shop, she got out of her car, opened her umbrella, and ran up the steps. Once inside, she hurried back to the place where Chuck had been working. Sure enough, the wall was up and the plastic sheet was gone. The area was spotless, and there was no dust anywhere. Cheryl was thrilled with the results. Now there was plenty of room for the new cooler.

Smiling, she went to her office. As she opened the door she realized it wasn't locked. She must have forgotten to lock it after she picked up the key for Matt yesterday. She wasn't really concerned about it. Chuck had been in the shop last night, so it wasn't as if the store was unprotected.

Cheryl opened the door to her bathroom and was pleased to see the wall was up in there as well. It also needed to be painted, but Cheryl had told Chuck not to worry about it. She planned to paint the small room herself. She wanted to add some color and a little decoration, but she hadn't settled on the exact changes she wanted to bring. At least now she and Esther wouldn't have to go across the street to the Honey Bee if they wanted to use the bathroom.

Cheryl busied herself with adding money to the cash register and getting everything ready for opening. As she checked the shelves, she realized that all the Amish dolls had been sold. She hesitated a moment, not really wanting to go down to the basement. A sudden crack of thunder made her jump.

"Don't be so silly," she scolded herself. "So a man tripped on the stairs forty years ago. What does that have to do with you? Nothing. Grow up."

She walked slowly over to the door that led to the basement and opened it. Then she made her way down the stairs, one step at a time, and reached for the pull chain to turn on the lights. Even though she didn't want to think about Bill Streeter, it was almost impossible to keep unwelcome images out of her head.

She quickly found the shelf with the Amish dolls and removed several of them. As she headed back toward the stairs, she thought she heard something. Stopping, she looked around, but nothing seemed out of place. She waited a few moments, but there weren't any other noises. When she reached for the stair railing with one hand, the other arm wrapped around the faceless dolls, there was another clap of thunder and the lights went out.

"Oh, perfect," Cheryl said, her voice higher than it should be. She took a deep breath and began to feel her way up the stairs. It was still early, and with the clouds and rain, she was surrounded by darkness. Determined not to be afraid, she kept moving forward, talking softly to herself.

"Lightning knocked out the electricity," she said in a near whisper. "It will come back on in a minute. Quit being such a baby."

When she finally reached the top of the stairs, she sighed with relief. Although the shop was dark, at least there was some illumination. The early morning sun was hidden behind clouds, but enough light filtered through that Cheryl could make out her surroundings. She carried the dolls to the shelf and placed them in a row. She was looking them over when she felt a hand on her shoulder. She screamed and whirled around, finding herself staring up into the face of a very surprised Levi Miller.

"Levi!" she said, gasping for breath. "You frightened me. Wh...what are you doing here?"

"I...I'm sorry," he said, his eyes wide. "I came in the shop looking for you, but I could not find you. Then the lights went out."

Cheryl put hands on her hips and glared at him. "So your response was to sneak up on me and scare me within an inch of my life? Why didn't you say something?"

He sighed and shook his head. "Because I was afraid I would startle you, Cheryl. I see my choice was not a good one."

Cheryl sighed in frustration. "No, it wasn't."

"So would you have felt better if I had simply said your name?"

She thought about his question. A man's voice saying her name in a darkened room? Not much better than her brother's bad joke. That was two frightening situations in a row. Hopefully, there wouldn't be any more.

"Okay, maybe I wouldn't have reacted well to that either. Let's just forget it. Why are you here?" She looked over at the front door. "I thought I locked that."

"No. That is why I was concerned. The door was unlocked, and you were nowhere to be seen."

"I guess I can understand why you were worried."

He pointed toward the counter. "You asked Maam for more cheese. I brought it."

She nodded. "Oh yeah. I'd forgotten all about that." Cheryl walked over to the counter and found a large basket filled with different kinds of cheese. "Although the harder cheese will keep, if the electricity doesn't come back on, I might not be able to sell the softer varieties. I'm only open a half day today."

"Whatever you do not sell, bring with you this afternoon. Maam will serve it at lunch."

Suddenly, the lights flickered and then came back on.

"Thank goodness," Cheryl said. "The last thing I wanted to do today was spend time trying to figure out how to move all my perishable goods someplace where they'd be safe."

Levi grinned. "If you had a propane refrigerator as we do, you would not have these kinds of worries."

Even though he was teasing her, Cheryl knew he was right. She'd actually thought about putting a large propane fridge in the garage at home. That way if the shop and the house both lost electricity, she would have a place to store things. Although it would be handier to add it to the store's basement, Cheryl was concerned about improper venting. People she'd talked to were divided. Some said it wouldn't cause any problems while others weren't sure it was safe—or even allowed under city code. Not wanting to make a mistake, she'd settled on the garage at home. But before she actually made any major purchase, she wanted to get Mitzi's permission. Even though the shop and house were beginning to feel more like hers every day, she had to keep reminding herself that she was just the tenant. Mitzi was the boss. However, when she'd asked about moving the wall and putting in the new cooler, Mitzi had said, "Run the Swiss Miss like it's yours, Cheryl. Do you think you need a new cooler?" She'd probably say the same thing about the propane refrigerator, but still, Cheryl felt better about running it past her first.

"Maybe I should load everything up and bring it to your house then," she said.

Levi smiled. "And you would be welcome to do so. You are family as far as we are concerned."

"Thank you, Levi. I feel the same way. Frankly, right now I feel more comfortable with your family than I do my own."

He frowned as he began helping her take the cheese out of the large woven basket. "Maam mentioned something about your parents. Are you certain they want to come to our home today? If they are not comfortable, perhaps you should make other arrangements."

Cheryl paused and stared out the window at the rain. "To be honest, I thought about it, but not because I was concerned about them. I'm more worried about all of you. My father will be...my father. Gracious and friendly. But my mother..." Her voice trailed off as she tried to find the words to explain to Levi why she was afraid her mom would say something unkind and hurt their feelings. "She's always been so supportive, and even though it might not look like it, we're very close. Lately she's been different. And with Matt here...well, it's been even worse."

Levi reached over and put his hand on her shoulder. "Cheryl, you must do what is best for you. But we will not be offended by anything your mother says. Our Lord instructed us to love one another. Even in Sugarcreek, sometimes the Amish are not treated with kindness. We have thicker skin than you might imagine."

Cheryl had an urge to put her hand on his, but she resisted it. Levi went back to working on the cheese. Cheryl's face felt hot, and she hoped she wasn't blushing. Even though she tried hard not to react to him in an improper way, she couldn't help the feelings that came over her when she was near him.

"I appreciate that, Levi," she said, trying to focus on what he'd said and not the dimples in his cheeks. "But I don't want to be someone who puts you in that situation. Your mother is my very best friend, and the rest of you mean the world to me."

Levi took out the last block of wrapped cheese and put it on the counter. Then he picked up the basket and set it on the floor next to him. "I am certain everything will be fine. We hope you will enjoy yourself today. Maam has been cooking up a storm, and all of us have been working on gifts for you."

Cheryl's eyes flushed with tears. "You didn't have to do that. I don't need gifts."

"Oh, my friend," he said, obviously noticing her reaction. "We do not do this out of obligation. We do it out of love."

His voice softened when he spoke the last sentence, and for just a moment Cheryl thought she felt something pass between them. But she quickly chalked it up to her imagination. Of course Levi meant the kind of love taught in the Bible. Godly love. She couldn't allow herself to think it was anything else and ruin their friendship.

"I know that, Levi," she said, looking away. "We're good friends. I love giving your family gifts. Frankly, accepting attention from others has always been a little hard for me. It's something I need to get over."

He laughed lightly. "Ach, then I think you must 'get over it' rather quickly. Before this afternoon."

Cheryl chuckled. "I'll do my best."

"I must go," he said. "We will see all of you around noon?"

"Actually, I'm closing the store at twelve. Then Matt and I will pick up my folks and drive straight to your house. We should be there before twelve thirty."

"I look forward to your visit. Good-bye, Cheryl." He started toward the front door and then stopped and turned around. "And happy birthday. I meant to say that when I first arrived, but my concern for your safety made me forget. I am sorry."

"You shouldn't be. You're the very first one to wish me a happy birthday. Thank you."

He gave her a wide smile and left.

Cheryl went back to her preparations to open the store. When she was ready, she headed back to her office to get her apron and pour herself a cup of coffee. Realizing she wouldn't have time to count the day's receipts and money before she left, she decided she'd have to put everything in an envelope and reconcile it on Monday. She sighed as she remembered she'd done the same thing last night because she was worried she'd be late for her session with Mitzi. Now she'd have two days to reconcile. She slid her key into the lock on her large desk drawer and turned it, but to her surprise, the drawer wasn't locked. When she pulled it out, her mouth dropped open.

Ellen Streeter's purse and valise had simply vanished.

CHAPTER TWELVE

For several seconds Cheryl just stared at the open desk drawer. Maybe she hadn't put Ellen's things there after all. Could she have made a mistake? Had she moved them somewhere else? Racking her brain, trying to remember the last time she'd seen them, she got up and thoroughly searched the office. When her frantic hunt didn't reveal anything, she sat down again. She was absolutely sure she hadn't taken them home. She must have put them in the drawer, but when? As she tried to remember, a sick feeling rose in the pit of her stomach. It was right after she caught Matt with the purse and valise on her desk.

She noticed the envelope with Friday's receipts and cash. Try as she might, she couldn't remember seeing the bags in the drawer when she put the envelope inside. If they were already gone, she hadn't noticed, but it seemed odd that she would have missed that. The other thing that seemed strange was that the envelope full of money was still there. Wouldn't an ordinary thief grab something like that? The answer was yes, unless they were only interested in Ellen's belongings.

Although she tried to push the thought out of her mind, there was no way she could ignore the suspicion that whispered in her head. Did Matt have something to do with this? He knew about the coin. But Cheryl just couldn't accept that. Matt may have been irresponsible with money in the past, but he wasn't a thief. Besides, he knew where the coin was. Why would he take both the bags? Why not just slip the coin out of the change purse? Cheryl probably wouldn't have even noticed the theft for quite a while. It wasn't Matt. She refused to believe he was involved.

She slowly closed the drawer and tried to figure out what to do. Should she contact Chief Twitchell? Or should she keep this to herself and try to find out what happened on her own? The chief would probably want to know who knew about the coin. Wouldn't she have to be honest and mention her brother? She realized that bringing in the police could be a big mistake. It might bring about consequences that could hurt her brother—and her family. She wished she could talk to Naomi. Maybe this afternoon they could slip away so Cheryl could tell her what had happened. For now, however, she decided to keep quiet.

She checked her watch. Maybe there was still time to reconcile the cash and receipts and put them in the safe. She did the work quickly, also taking the change she needed for the cash register. Since someone had broken in, she would have to make sure the money was always locked up from now on. Of course, even though the small safe was bolted to the floor, if someone really wanted it, they could probably pry it up. Checking to make sure her office door was locked and using the alarm was something she would have to always remember in the future. Someone had gotten in, and she had no idea how.

She left her office and went out into the store. Around nine she unlocked the front door but didn't turn the Closed sign over.

She regularly opened an hour early for local residents who wanted to stop in for something before tourists hit town. Although business was slower now than it would be in the summer, Cheryl kept up the habit since many residents were used to it. Around nine fifteen, Chuck came through the front door.

"Just stopped by to see how you like your new wall," he said, his usual dour expression firmly in place.

"It looks great, Chuck," Cheryl said. She left the counter and followed the big man over to the corner of the store.

"I'll paint this afternoon, and then we'll be done with that part. As I said, I'll be back Monday morning to help move the cooler in."

"Thanks."

Cheryl heard the bell over the door ring and turned around to see Molly Bakker, one of the owners of the Village Inn Bed-and-Breakfast, head for the shelf where they kept the jams and jellies. Cheryl waved at her then took Chuck's arm, gently guiding him a few feet away so she wouldn't be overheard.

"Chuck, there's something missing from my office, and I'm trying to figure out when it might have been taken. I know it was there yesterday afternoon. Did anyone come into the store while you were here?"

He frowned. "No, but I wouldn't have let anyone inside when you were closed." He looked decidedly uncomfortable and refused to meet Cheryl's gaze.

"Okay. Look, Chuck, I trust you. I really do, but if there's anything you need to tell me..."

He grunted and shook his head. "Last night I thought I heard something. I'd been sanding, but when I turned the sander off, there was a noise."

"What kind of noise?" Cheryl asked.

"I...I don't know. Like a door closing. I went to check but no one was here." He crossed his arms and frowned at her. "I checked your office door, and it was unlocked. Maybe you don't usually lock it, but you should, you know. I looked around but no one was there. Then I checked the front door."

He hesitated and stared down at his shoes.

"Yes?"

Chuck cleared his throat. "It wasn't locked either." He swung his gaze up to Cheryl. "I was certain I'd locked it when I came in, Cheryl. But maybe I didn't. I just don't know now."

Even though she should be upset with him, she couldn't hold back a smile.

"It's not really funny," Chuck said, his basset hound expression deepening.

"I know it's not funny," Cheryl replied. "But if I told you how many times I've forgotten to lock that door, you'd think there was something wrong with me. I can't even use the alarm system without setting it off. Of course you should have locked the door, but I'm the last one to get upset if you forgot. Besides, we don't know if that's what happened. Maybe someone broke in or had a key. I have no idea how many keys are floating around this town. Mitzi trusted everyone."

"Well, I appreciate that, but if I messed up, I'll take the consequences. Can I ask what was taken? Can I replace it?"

She paused before answering. Chuck knew the value of the coin in Ellen's purse. She didn't want him to feel as if it were his job to reimburse her that much money. Besides, the coin didn't even belong to her. Unfortunately, her hesitation gave him time to anticipate her answer.

"Is it the coin?" he asked. His eyes widened with alarm.

"Not just the coin, but everything. The purse and the satchel too. They're both gone, along with everything inside them."

Chuck's usually stoic expression softened. "If it's my fault…"

Cheryl reached out and touched his arm, trying to reassure him. "Look, the fault lies with whoever broke in here. Not you. If you left the door unlocked, and we have no proof that you did, it was just a mistake. Besides, I still haven't been able to locate Ellen Streeter. If I can't return her belongings to her anyway, then no one has lost anything."

He cleared his throat. "Still—"

"Chuck, you're an honorable man, and I don't want you to worry about this anymore. I mean it."

He didn't say anything, but he slowly nodded his head. Cheryl hoped it meant he'd accepted her admonition.

"So all you heard was a noise," Cheryl said slowly. She pulled her arm back. "Did you see anything? Anything at all?"

He rubbed his chin and stared past her as if trying to remember. Finally, he shrugged. "I didn't. Except for cars driving by." He took a quick breath. "I'd forgotten about it until now, but at one point I went out to my truck to get some tools. There was a big dark-colored truck that drove by kind of slow. I can't say I know all the cars and trucks in town, but I'd never seen this one before. It looked brand new. I guess I noticed it because it was pretty late. You know almost everything on Main Street is closed at night, and there's not much traffic after ten o'clock. Just seemed kinda strange."

"Did you notice what kind of truck it was?"

"No, sorry. I don't spend much time looking at new truck models. I've driven my old faithful Ford for many years and have no use for anything else."

"That's okay." She smiled at him. "Hey, once again, the wall looks great. I can hardly wait until it's painted. Were you able to match the color to the rest of the shop?"

Chuck actually came close to smiling, although he reminded Cheryl more of a baby with gas. "Your aunt made such a fuss about wanting the walls painted a 'robin's egg blue' that everyone in town knows the right paint color. Randy over at the paint store wrote down the exact way he mixed it for her in case she ever needed to paint again."

Cheryl laughed. "That sounds like Mitzi, all right. The nicest person in the world, but when her mind is set on something—"

"That's the way it has to be," Chuck finished for her. "Well, I'd better get going." Instead of walking away, he stood where he was for a moment. Taking a deep breath, he said, "As kind a lady as your aunt is, I'm not sure I'd call her the nicest person in the world. You'd certainly be in the running for that title." With that he turned around and walked out of the store. Cheryl watched him leave, confused by what had just happened. Had the taciturn, unemotional contractor actually paid her a compliment? She couldn't help smiling as she went back to the front of the store where Molly waited to check out.

"We had some Coopers check in yesterday," she said as Cheryl rang up her order. "Any relation?" Molly was a petite woman with dark hair and eyes. Her small size supported a large personality. Molly was the kind of woman who knew how to liven up any gathering. Gregarious and fun, she was in the perfect profession. People loved to be around her.

"My parents. I haven't seen them in quite a while."

"Oh." Molly looked a little confused. "They didn't want to stay with you?"

Cheryl smiled. "My mother isn't fond of cats. Besides, my brother's already camped out in my spare room."

"Oh. A family reunion?"

Cheryl nodded. "Kind of. Impromptu." She wrapped up the jams and jellies and then put them in a bag and handed them to Molly.

"Well, I hope you all have a great time. We'll treat your folks like they're family."

"Thank you, Molly. I appreciate that."

After Molly left, Cheryl got a cup of coffee from the back room and turned the conversation she'd had with Chuck over in her mind. Frankly, she didn't know anything more than she had before she'd talked to him. He *might* have left the door unlocked. He *might* have heard someone come in or go out of the shop. He noticed a dark-colored truck, but he didn't know the make or model.

Cheryl realized there were a lot of dark-colored trucks in Sugarcreek. Of course, Matt's truck immediately came to mind when Chuck mentioned it. "Stop it," she said to herself. "It wasn't Matt." Cheryl could feel the beginnings of a tension headache tickling her temples. She had the party to get through, so this situation would have to go on the back burner for now.

She kept busy the rest of the morning. About eleven forty-five, Matt's truck pulled up in front of the shop and he got out. Cheryl had no plans to mention the robbery. The last thing she wanted right now was for Matt to think she didn't trust him.

"How long until we leave?" Matt asked when he came in.

Cheryl checked the clock on the wall behind her. "Give me a few minutes to close up."

She'd already posted a note on the door telling her customers she would be closed for the afternoon, but she still needed to clear out the cash register and put the proceeds in the safe. She'd just taken the money to her office when she heard the bell over the front door ring. Wishing she'd locked up first, she quickly slid the receipts and cash into an envelope and put it into the safe. Before she left, she also checked her desk drawer to be sure it was locked tightly. Maybe there wasn't anything valuable in it now, but she still felt the need to make sure it was secure. Then she grabbed her purse and jacket and left the office, careful to lock the door behind her. She felt a little funny cutting off Chuck's only entrance to the bathroom, but he'd told her early on that he either went down the street to the filling station or to the Honey Bee when he needed to use the restroom. "Contractors shouldn't be using the customers' facilities," he'd told her. "Besides, you have things that need to be protected in there. Lock it up and don't worry about me."

As she pulled the door shut, she realized that if Chuck had wanted to take Ellen's belongings, he could have done it when he first started her project. Since moving the wall had provided access to the bathroom, he could have slipped into her office without a problem. It wasn't until the wall was up that the items disappeared. Another reason it didn't make sense for Chuck to be a suspect. Unless he planned it that way so he wouldn't look guilty. The thought slipped in before she had a chance to push it away. She hated suspecting people she cared about. When she turned around, she found Chuck standing near the front door, paint cans in his hands. "Thought I'd get in before you left," he said.

A feeling of guilt washed over her before she reminded herself that Chuck couldn't read her thoughts.

"Sure, that makes sense," Cheryl said quickly, trying to look innocent even though she didn't feel that way. She smiled at him. "Chuck, I don't think you've met my brother, Matt." She motioned toward Matt who came over and held out his hand.

"Glad to meet you," he said.

Chuck set one of the cans of paint down and shook Matt's hand. "Good to meet you too. I didn't know Cheryl had a brother."

Matt chuckled. "I don't think she likes to admit it."

"That's not true," Cheryl said. "This is his first visit in a long time," she said to Chuck. "You see, he lives in Kansas City, but my birthday is today, and he came to celebrate it with me. Along with my mother and father. They're here from Seattle. My father's a pastor." Cheryl realized she was babbling and forced her lips together. She could feel herself flush with embarrassment. Suspicion was making her crazy.

"Okay." Chuck's one-word response made her nonsensical stream of gibberish seem even more absurd.

She turned to see Matt staring at her as if she had cucumbers growing out of her ears. After a quick shake of his head, he swung his gaze to Chuck. "Can I help you carry anything?" he asked.

Chuck hesitated a moment before saying, "There's a can of primer and a bag of brushes and stuff in the back of my truck. If you really want to help—"

"Not a problem. I'll get them." Matt pushed open the front door and headed out to Chuck's truck. Cheryl wondered if he was just thankful to get away from his crazy sister.

"Cheryl, I..." Chuck paused and cleared his throat. "Look, I'm sure it's just a coincidence, but I think you should know..."

Cheryl frowned at him. "Know what, Chuck?"

"The truck parked out front. Is it your brother's?"

Cheryl nodded, but she didn't respond. She already knew what he was going to say.

"That's the same truck that drove by here last night. I just thought you should know."

CHAPTER THIRTEEN

Cheryl and Matt drove to the inn. When they pulled up, her folks were waiting on the porch. The storm seemed to have moved on, but clouds still covered the sky. The weather mirrored Cheryl's mood. She usually looked forward to going to the Millers', but today she almost dreaded it. So many things were swirling in her mind, not the least of which was the worry that her mother would be rude to Naomi and her family.

Cheryl got out of her car and opened the trunk so her parents could unload the gifts they held in their arms.

"Good morning," she called out.

"Happy birthday, Snicklefritz," her father said, giving her a hug. "I'm so glad we're here to share this day with you." He smiled. "Thirty-one years ago today was one of the best days of my life."

"Thanks, Daddy," Cheryl said.

"Yes, happy birthday," her mother said. She gave Cheryl a quick kiss on the cheek.

"Thanks, Momma," she said.

She waited as her parents unloaded their packages and then closed the trunk.

The front passenger side door opened, and Matt got out. "Do you need any help?" he asked.

"As you can see, we've already put our things in the trunk," his mother responded, shaking her head.

"Oh, sorry. Guess I was a little too slow." Matt held open the door to the backseat.

Cheryl's father smiled at him. "That's okay, Matt. Thanks for the offer." He looked back and forth between his children. "I feel so blessed that we all get to celebrate this wonderful day together."

Ginny gave her husband a tight smile. "Yes, it's very nice." With that she walked past Matt and slid into the backseat. Her father walked around the car to the other side and opened the door. "Guess we'd better get going."

Matt shot Cheryl a look and rolled his eyes. She forced a smile. Chuck's information about Matt's truck had confirmed her fears. Was she wrong to trust her brother? She didn't want to think he'd steal from her, but how could she deny that he had the perfect opportunity? He could have easily gotten inside the shop last night and taken her things without Chuck noticing. He had access to her keys, so he could have unlocked the door.

As Cheryl pulled her car into the street, her mother started complaining about how little room there was in her backseat.

"Now, Ginny," her father said, "it's just fine. Besides, I don't think we have far to go, do we, honey?"

"No, not long at all." She wanted to whisper "thank goodness" under her breath, but she held her tongue. This certainly wasn't the time to test her mother's auditory skills.

When Cheryl made the turn that would lead to their destination, her father mentioned the signs with directions to the Millers' petting zoo and corn maze.

Cheryl described the zoo and the animals usually on display. "I love it. The Millers treat their animals with respect."

"The Amish used to see animals in a completely different way," her mother said. "They were only around to help with farm work."

"Aunt Mitzi mentioned that," Cheryl said. "I think a lot of things have changed over the years, but they still hold fast to many of their traditions and to the idea of keeping life simple."

"As long as grace isn't replaced by legalism, I don't see any problem with simplifying life," her father said. "Sometimes I wish my life were simpler."

The wistful sound in his voice surprised Cheryl. Her father had always thrived on being busy, accomplishing goals he set for himself.

Cheryl's mother sniffed. "Well, I think it's sad. Putting themselves through hardship because they think it's what God wants. To be honest, I'm not sure they're even saved."

Cheryl pulled the car over to the side of the road and stopped. She turned around to meet her mother's surprised gaze.

"Look, Momma, you're entitled to your opinion, and I even understand why you might say that, but these people are...very special to me. And I can guarantee you they're saved. As saved as anyone I've ever met. Maybe they do things and believe things that aren't really necessary, but every Amish person I've met understands salvation."

"I'm not sure that's true," her father said slowly.

"And how many Amish friends do you have?" Cheryl shot back.

Her father didn't respond, just stared at her.

"Look, I don't mean to upset you, Daddy, but I must insist that you and Momma treat the Millers with consideration. I ... love them. Naomi is my best friend."

"For crying out loud, Cheryl," her mother snapped. "Your father's a pastor, and I'm a pastor's wife. You wouldn't believe some of the people we've had to deal with over the years. We do know how to act." She sighed dramatically. "Honestly."

Cheryl had to bite her tongue to keep from saying something that would upset her mother even more. She struggled to calm herself. "I'm sure you're right. I just want to be very clear about how important this is to me."

"You don't need to worry about us, Cheryl," her father said. "Everything will be fine. This is your day, and we won't cause any problems with your friends. Besides, maybe you're right. I grew up around the Amish, but that was a long time ago. There were some people who wanted nothing to do with us *Englischers*, but we also knew some wonderful Amish families. In fact, I was friends with a boy who moved away when I was ten. His parents treated me like part of their family."

"Thanks, Daddy. We can disagree with doctrine, but we shouldn't judge the heart. Trust me, the Millers know Christ." She put the car in gear again and continued the drive toward the Millers' farm.

She couldn't help but remember how much she'd been missing her parents. Now she just wanted them to go home. But as soon as the thought came, she realized that wasn't true. What she really wanted was to work things out with her mom and see her parents reconcile with Matt. It was a tall order, but she had to believe it was possible.

"Well, this is just beautiful," her father said as they drove across the covered bridge that led to the farm.

"Yes, it is," Cheryl agreed. As she pulled up in front of the house, the Millers' dog, Rover, came running up to the car. Rover was an abandoned pup, dropped off in the country by cruel owners who didn't want to be bothered with him. The Millers took him in, and Levi had been training him. A collie mix, he had ears that stuck straight up as if he were listening intently to everything around him. Black and white, with brown eyebrows, he had a white streak down the middle of his face that spread out and covered his snout. His body was a mixture of black-and-white patches and spots without any kind of logical pattern. Although Rover was responding to Levi's patient lessons, he still had the boisterous spirit of a young dog. When he saw Cheryl, he began to leap up and down with joy. Cheryl loved the little dog, and when she got out of the car, he jumped up on her. Unfortunately, the ground was still wet from the rain, and Rover got mud on her slacks.

"Rover, down!" Levi came out of the barn and jogged over. "I am so sorry, Cheryl. He gets excited and forgets what I have tried to teach him."

Cheryl smiled. "It's only mud, Levi. Naomi will help me wash it out."

"I am sure she will. Maam has a way of getting dirt and stains out like no one else." He took a thin piece of rope out of his pocket and tied it around Rover's neck. The dog knew he'd done something wrong and looked so miserable, Cheryl had to laugh.

She squatted down and hugged him. "It's okay, boy. We're still friends." A few thumps of his tail told her he would recover from his faux pas. Cheryl stood to her feet and turned toward her family as they waited next to the car. "Levi, I'd like you to meet my parents, George and Ginny Cooper. And this is my brother, Matt." She nodded at her family. "This is Levi Miller, Naomi and Seth's oldest son."

Her father stepped up next to Levi and extended his hand. "Glad to meet you, Levi. You have a beautiful farm."

Levi shook his hand. "Thank you. We like it, but it takes a lot of work to keep it running."

"I'm sure it does," her father said. "Maybe after lunch you could show me around?"

Levi smiled. "I would be happy to do that."

"I'd love to come with you," Matt said. "If it's all right."

"Of course," Levi said. "You're welcome too, Mrs. Cooper."

Cheryl's mother smiled at him. "I would love to, Levi, but I'm afraid I wore the wrong shoes today. Maybe I could just stay in the house and get to know your mother a little better. And please, we're Ginny and George, okay?"

He nodded. "Thank you." He looked at Cheryl. "If you would take your family into the house, I will put Rover in the barn."

"Sure."

"Let me get your presents out of the car first, honey," her father said.

While Cheryl and her mother waited, her dad and Matt got the gifts out of the trunk. Cheryl watched Levi as he walked toward the barn, Rover trailing behind and pulling against the rope, obviously wanting to stay and visit with the Millers' guests.

"He seems nice."

Cheryl turned to find her mother staring at her strangely. "Yes, he is. Very nice. I really value his friendship."

"As long as it never goes any further," her mother said quietly. "He's Amish, Cheryl."

She felt her cheeks flush. "Don't be ridiculous, Momma. He's just a good friend."

Her dad and Matt joined them, their arms full of packages. "We're ready," Matt said.

Cheryl turned and began walking toward the big front porch of the Millers' two-story farmhouse, trying to get her mother's comment out of her head. Had Cheryl done something to make her mother think she had feelings for Levi?

With effort, she pushed the troubling thoughts away. She was determined to enjoy this afternoon. She loved spending time with the Millers, and she adored their wonderful house, not only because of its simple, friendly architecture, but also because of all the love contained inside its walls. She felt so comfortable here.

They'd just reached the steps when the front door flew open, and Naomi stepped out on to the porch.

"Happy birthday, my dear friend," she called out, a wide smile on her beaming face. "I am so glad to see you."

Cheryl introduced her to Matt. She greeted him and welcomed Cheryl's family to their home. As they entered the house, Cheryl kept an eye on her mother. Thankfully, she was friendly to Naomi and complimented her farm and house. She also made a point to thank her for putting on a birthday dinner for her daughter. Cheryl breathed a sigh of relief.

Seth introduced himself and his family to her parents and to Matt while Naomi took Cheryl in the back washroom so she could clean off the mud Rover had gotten on her clothes.

"I am so sorry about that dog," Naomi said, frowning. "Levi is trying to train him, but I am afraid it will take Rover a while to learn. Dogs have their own minds, ain't so?"

"Oh, Naomi, you know I don't care about a little mud. I love Rover."

"That is because you have a good heart. That is also why Rover loves you so much. Too much, I think." She dampened a washcloth and knelt down to wipe off Cheryl's slacks. Cheryl would have told Naomi she could do it herself, but she knew her friend well enough to know that she wouldn't pay any attention.

"I need to tell you something," Cheryl said, keeping her voice low. She quickly told Naomi about the purse and valise. Then she shared what Chuck had said about Matt's truck.

Naomi was quiet. When she got up to rinse out the washcloth in the sink, Cheryl could see the concern on her face.

"What are you thinking?" Cheryl asked.

"Sometimes we must believe the best about family even when everything tells us we might be wrong," Naomi said softly.

"In my heart I really don't believe he did it, Naomi," Cheryl said. "My brother has his faults, but he's not a thief. Besides, he seems so different now. He insists he has a good job, a girlfriend, and that he's back in church." She slowly shook her head. "I just can't accept that he was involved in any way. No matter what Chuck said."

Naomi knelt down once again and continued to work on Cheryl's pants. "Then you must stick by him, Cheryl. You might think I am being naïve, but many times our loved ones see themselves through our eyes. If we believe in them, they will believe in themselves. I think Matthew needs you to believe in him now."

Cheryl realized Naomi was echoing the same sentiment expressed by Mitzi. "You're right," she said. "I can do that." She thought for a moment. "But who could have slipped past Chuck last night and taken Ellen's things? Hardly anyone knew about them." She looked down at Naomi. "Do you think Chuck could have stolen them? I really hate to think he would do something like that."

Finally satisfied with her efforts, Naomi stood up. "You are wet, but the spots will dry soon. I do not believe anyone will be able to notice Rover's enthusiastic greeting."

"You're not going to answer me, are you?"

"Ach, Cheryl, it is not my job to judge." Naomi frowned at her. "Something valuable has been taken. What is the proper procedure to follow?"

"Report it to the police," Cheryl said. "But how can I bring Chief Twitchell in on this?"

"But if the chief looks for the truth, it will actually keep you from casting aspersions on friends and family members, ain't so?"

Cheryl immediately saw the wisdom behind Naomi's advice. Maybe she'd contact the police after all. Let them investigate. That way Cheryl wouldn't be in a position to accuse anyone. She smiled. "As usual, you've given me the perfect solution. The one thing I can't understand—"

"What is that, my friend?" Naomi rung out the washcloth one last time and laid it on the side of the sink.

"Why did they take the bags? If the thief knew about the coin, why not just find that and remove it? It would have been a while before I would have discovered the theft. Given them more time to dispose of the coin. At first I thought it was because they didn't have time to find the coin and remove it. But even if that were true, why not just take the purse? A quick look would have made it clear the coin was inside it. Why would they want that old valise? And why leave the money from the store in the drawer?" Cheryl shook her head. "It just doesn't add up."

Naomi shrugged. "I cannot say, but it does seem a little strange." She cocked her head to the side. "The chief will probably ask you who knew about Ellen's belongings. Are you willing to bring up Matthew's name?"

Cheryl sighed. "I don't know. If I do, I'll tell him I don't believe Matt had anything to do with this."

Naomi nodded. "I believe you have a good plan." She clapped her hands together. "Now, are you ready to begin your party?"

Cheryl smiled. "Thanks again for doing this. I really appreciate it."

"It is a privilege. Thank you for allowing us to celebrate the day of your birth."

Naomi reached for the door handle, but Cheryl stopped her. "I'd like to meet Maybelline," she said. "I have some questions about the night Ellen left. It might not help, but I want to know I did everything I could to find the truth. Do you think we could see her on Monday during my lunch hour?"

"Of course. I can drop Esther off at noon, and we can go to her house together. Would that work for you?"

Cheryl nodded. "I'll see the chief first thing Monday morning. I suspect whoever has the coin will probably try to sell it. When it shows up we'll know the truth."

Naomi reached over and gave her a hug. "Everything will turn out fine," she said. "Gott has a plan, and He loves Matthew even more than you do. You must trust Him."

"I know you're right." She smiled at Naomi. "You go ahead. I'll be there in a minute."

When Naomi closed the door behind her, Cheryl slumped against it. Although she kept insisting Matt was innocent, there was a seed of doubt in her mind. A small whisper that wouldn't be still. She had to trust God to help her because without Him, the cost she might have to pay to learn the truth about Ellen Streeter was just too high.

Chapter Fourteen

As the Millers and Coopers gathered around the large kitchen table for lunch, Cheryl pulled her father aside and quickly reminded him about the Amish way of praying. He hadn't forgotten, but he decided it would be best to inform her mother and Matt about their silent prayer. Even though Cheryl doubted her mother or Matt would have suddenly launched into a hearty prayer, she wanted to avoid anything that might cause awkwardness.

As the family passed around a large platter of sliced roast beef and bowls of mashed potatoes, gravy, creamed spinach, and homemade applesauce, her parents exchanged small talk with the Millers. Cheryl had just started to relax when Naomi addressed Cheryl.

"We have heard something from Lydia," she said. "She called Marion Berryhill."

Cheryl frowned. Marion and her husband owned the Christian bookstore where Lydia and Esther bought books. "I wasn't aware she was that close to Marion," she said slowly. She was a little hurt Lydia hadn't called her. After all, Lydia worked for her. Cheryl spent more time with Lydia than Marion did.

"Lydia probably called her because she was not comfortable talking to anyone she thought might urge her to come home."

Cheryl nodded, feeling a little better. "And what did she have to say?"

"She says she is happy living in her cousin's home, but Marion told me she heard something in Lydia's voice that did not support her words. She did not sound happy."

"I'm sorry," Cheryl's mother said, "but did this girl run away?"

"Yes," Cheryl said.

"How old is she?"

"She is only sixteen," Naomi said. "And very immature. I am concerned for her."

"Why don't her parents call the police?" her mother asked. "Isn't sixteen too young for her to legally take off?"

An uncomfortable silence filled the room. Cheryl caught her mother's eye and shook her head slightly.

"Does this have something to do with rumspringa?" her mother asked.

"Yes, Momma," Cheryl said quickly. "It's something the Amish take very seriously. I don't think we should talk about it—"

"Cheryl," Naomi interjected, "we do not mind talking about rumspringa. You worry too much about our feelings." She swung her gaze to Cheryl's mom. "I am happy to answer your questions, Ginny."

Her mother hesitated a moment, and Cheryl prayed silently that she'd decide to change the subject.

Cheryl's mother clasped her hands together and frowned at Naomi. "I just don't understand how you can actually encourage your children to sin. In our church, we teach them that sin is something to stay away from."

"Mother..."

Matt's warning was ignored.

"I'm sorry, but as a mother I feel it's my job to make sure my children grow up knowing right from wrong. I wouldn't send them out into a busy street to let them learn it's dangerous. I *teach* them that it's a bad idea."

Cheryl could feel sweat break out on her hairline. This was exactly what she'd been dreading. But strangely, as she glanced around the table, she realized that not one person in the Miller family looked ill at ease. In fact, most of them seemed to be quite interested in the conversation. How could this be?

"I completely understand your concerns," Naomi said, "but we look at it a little differently." She put down her fork and smiled. "There are so many children who join churches because their parents are members. Because it is expected. But when they are older, they fall away. We want our children to join the church because they want to. Because their commitment to Gott is real, and it is a true decision they make with their whole hearts." She paused and stared down at the table a moment before speaking again. "It does not always work the way we would like. Some children decide to follow the ways of the world. Some still join the church for the wrong reasons, but many take this time to really think about Gott—who He is and what His will is for them. And when they decide to join the church, it is a heart choice, not a head choice."

"That makes perfect sense," Matt said. "Since my parents are pastors, I always felt as if I was *expected* to follow in their footsteps.

It wasn't until I got out in the world and made my own mistakes that I began to realize why I needed the Savior. When I finally gave my life to Christ, it was real. As you said, Naomi, a heart choice."

Cheryl felt her eyes fill with tears. She'd never heard her brother talk about God like that.

"Do most of them stay in the church?" her father asked. "I mean, after they join?"

"Ja, they do," Seth said. "And we believe it is because they were given the right to choose."

Cheryl's mother cleared her throat. "Of course, if they do decide to leave later, after they've been baptized, they're shunned, aren't they? I guess their right to choose goes away once they're part of the church." She seemed to study Naomi for several seconds before saying, "Thankfully, God doesn't kick us out even when we walk away. Just like the prodigal son, He always waits for us to come home. With His arms open wide."

Naomi nodded, her eyes shiny with tears. "I completely agree with you, Ginny. Thankfully, shunning is becoming less prevalent in the church. Our church does not shun unless there is serious sin and the member is not repentant. Instead we try to bring reconciliation. I have not seen anyone shunned in many years." She picked up her napkin and wiped away a tear that rolled down her cheek. "Please forgive me. I had a dear friend who was shunned when she was in her twenties. The pain of her rejection stays with me."

Cheryl's mouth dropped open as she watched her mother reach over and take Naomi's hand.

"I'm so sorry," she said softly. "Rejection hurts. I hope your friend turned out all right."

Naomi nodded and smiled through her tears. "Thankfully, she did. She found a wonderful Christian church in Cleveland that took her in and became her family. I imagine it was much like your church."

"No church is perfect because they're made up of imperfect people. But if we can manage to walk in love and forgiveness, we can certainly touch more lives for Christ."

"I believe that as well," Naomi said softly.

Ginny scooted her chair closer to Naomi's, and the two women hugged. Cheryl felt ashamed for doubting her mother. Maybe she was worried about her daughter's choices, but she was a good woman. Cheryl's heart swelled with love and pride for her mother.

"I believe I'd like another slice of your delicious roast, Naomi," George said with a smile.

Naomi wiped her eyes with her napkin and passed the plate down to him. As her father helped himself to the roast, he asked Seth how long the farm had been in their family. The rest of the meal was spent in friendly, relaxed chitchat. Although Cheryl joined in, she was still touched by what had transpired between Naomi and her mother. It made her more determined than ever to work things out with her mother.

When everyone finished eating, Naomi got up from the table and motioned to Esther. They both went into the pantry while Elizabeth, Eli, and Caleb began to clear the table.

"Let me help," Cheryl said, pushing her chair back.

"No, Cheryl," Levi said forcefully. "The birthday girl must stay seated."

Cheryl raised her eyebrows at him, and Levi smiled.

"Please," he said. "You will understand in a moment."

She scooted her chair back toward the table. "What are you up to?"

Her father chuckled. "My daughter is nothing if not suspicious, Levi," he said. "She's been that way ever since she was a little girl. I think it comes from reading too many Nancy Drew mysteries. She thinks there's a mystery around every corner."

Levi snorted. "She has certainly proven this to be true," he said. "Your daughter has made our lives much more interesting." He looked over at her and smiled. There was something in his eyes that caused her breath to catch in her throat.

Suddenly Naomi and Esther came out of the pantry carrying a huge cake ablaze with lit candles. Naomi began to sing, and everyone joined in. Cheryl was a little surprised to hear the same song that Englischers sang when celebrating birthdays. Although some of the Amish customs were very foreign to outsiders, many of them weren't very different at all. It seemed a birthday party was a birthday party, *Englisch* or Amish. Naomi and Esther carefully lowered the big cake down to the table in front of her as the song came to an end.

Eli added, "And many more" at the end, and everyone laughed.

"Now you must blow out the candles and make a wish," Naomi said with a smile.

Cheryl stood up. "I don't know. It looks like you stuck a hundred candles on this cake. Just how old do you think I am?"

Naomi shrugged. "The scripture says, 'Those that be planted in the house of the Lord shall flourish in the courts of our God. They shall still bring forth fruit in old age.'"

As Elizabeth and Esther snickered, Cheryl shook her finger at her friend. "I'll remember this on your birthday, you know. The scriptures also say we will reap what we sow."

As laughter once again broke out around the room, Naomi gave Cheryl a big hug. When Naomi let her go, Cheryl dabbed at her eyes with the back of her hand. "I am so blessed to have such good friends. I don't know what I did to deserve all of you, but thank you. This is a wonderful birthday."

"We are all pleased that you are happy," Seth said, his expression serious. "But will you please blow out your candles before my house burns down?"

Cheryl giggled and bent over the cake. She blew as hard and as long as she could, but the candles wouldn't go out. After taking a deep breath and giving it another try, she straightened up. "Very funny. These are the kind of candles that can't be blown out."

"You are actually claiming that a devout Amish woman would pull a trick on her friend?" Naomi asked innocently.

Naomi's expression made Cheryl giggle. "That's exactly what I'm saying."

"Maam, the cake will be ruined if we do not remove these candles soon," Esther said.

"You are right, Daughter." Naomi grabbed a nearby plate, and the women quickly picked the candles off the cake. Then Esther ran them over to the sink and put the plate under running water to make sure the flames were finally out.

"I believe you will still get your wish, Cheryl," Levi said. "Even though my 'devout' mother tricked you."

Cheryl smiled at him. "Actually, I can't think of anything I'd wish for, Levi," she said. "I seem to have everything I've ever wanted."

He returned her smile. "That makes me very happy."

"Everyone gets cake and ice cream, and then we will go to the living room and open presents," Esther said impatiently. Obviously she was more excited about the gifts than she was the cake.

Cheryl looked around the table. "I hope you haven't gone to too much trouble. This is more than any one woman could ask for."

"*Pshaw*," Naomi said. "When people love you, nothing is ever too much trouble." She began to slice the cake and hand pieces to the people gathered around the table. Caleb retrieved a large container of vanilla ice cream from the freezer and followed the slices of cake, adding a big scoop of ice cream to the plate of anyone who asked for it.

Cheryl took a bite of her cake. It was the richest chocolate cake she'd ever tasted. "Oh, Naomi, this is wonderful. We need to sell this in the store."

Naomi shook her head. "This is one thing I will not sell. It is a recipe passed down through my family and is baked only for birthdays."

"That's a lovely tradition." Cheryl's mother got a dreamy look on her face. "I used to make a special coffee cake for Christmas morning when the children lived at home. No matter how much they begged me to make it other times during the year, I never did. It was only for Christmas."

"See, your mother understands," Naomi said. "Mothers must keep some things to themselves. It helps them to be...special. And we know you will remember these traditions when we are gone. Just as I remembered this cake, my mother remembered it from her mother, and her mother before her." She looked at Esther and Elizabeth. "Someday my girls will make this cake for their families." Naomi looked over at Cheryl's mother. "This is one of the ways we live on in our children's lives."

She watched the two women exchange knowing looks.

"Exactly," her mother said.

As Cheryl quietly ate her cake, she watched her best friend and her mother bond in a way she'd never anticipated. Her parents seemed so comfortable with the Millers, and her Amish friends appeared to enjoy the company of her family. Levi and Matt were talking and laughing about something as if they'd known each other for years. For the first time since her parents and brother arrived in Sugarcreek, Cheryl began to relax. Maybe everything would turn out all right after all. Rather than being a disaster, today was turning out to be the best birthday of her life. Even so, she couldn't completely quiet the voice inside her that kept whispering Ellen's name.

CHAPTER FIFTEEN

After everyone finished their cake, the Millers and Coopers relocated to the living room.

"You must sit in your favorite chair," Naomi said, motioning toward a lovely carved rocking chair made out of mahogany. After she took her seat, Elizabeth walked up to her and took something from behind her back.

"Eli and I made this for you," she said. A tendril of dark hair had worked its way out of her bun and peeked out from her kapp. Her brown eyes sparkled with happiness as she put a crown made out of yellow construction paper on Cheryl's head. Jewels had been drawn on the paper with multicolored markers. "You are now the birthday queen."

Cheryl laughed. "Thank you. I never anticipated being a queen." She gazed around the room at her amused friends and family and then raised her right hand and wiggled it back and forth in a queenly salute. Although Matt laughed, Cheryl noticed the Millers looked at her with confused expressions. She blushed as she realized they'd never seen the queen of England wave—or anyone who made fun of her royal gestures. She quickly dropped her hand. "The queen is ready," she said, trying to move things along.

"Please, Ginny and George," Naomi said. "You are Cheryl's parents. Give her your gifts first."

"Thank you." Cheryl's father got up and walked over to the corner where two gift bags and a large wrapped box waited. He picked them up and carried them over to Cheryl. "These are from your mother and me," he said, setting them down on the floor in front of her.

"Thanks, Daddy." Cheryl picked up one of the bags and found a darling pair of designer sandals. "Oh, I love them," she said. "I needed new sandals so badly. Thank you."

"Look in the next bag before you open the box," her mother said.

"Okay." Cheryl put the sandals back in the bag and moved it to the side. Then she grabbed the other bag. Inside she discovered an engraved sterling silver bookmark that read: *The Light of God surrounds me; the love of God enfolds me; the power of God protects me; the presence of God watches over me. Wherever I am, God is!* "Oh, it's just beautiful." She held it up so everyone could see it.

"That *is* lovely," Naomi said.

"Your maam and daed care about your safety when you are gone from them," Esther said. "It is wonderful."

Cheryl looked at her parents and nodded. "Yes. Yes, it is," she said softly.

She moved to the box and found it to be very heavy. Matt came over to help her lift it. When she tore it open, she found several books.

"You can use your other gift with this one," her father said.

"Dickens!" she squealed. Cheryl had read every book written by Charles Dickens before she was thirteen. Some of her favorite stories were in the box. After she'd left home, her mother had donated many of her books to the local school library, including her set of Dickens novels. She hadn't realized Cheryl planned to keep them. Her mother had always felt bad about her mistake.

Esther got up and came over to look at the volumes as Cheryl began to remove them from the box.

"Oh, Charles Dickens," she said, her eyes wide. "I love his books."

"I didn't know you read Dickens," Cheryl said. "I thought you and Lydia were into bonnet books."

Esther smiled. "Marion loaned me some of her personal volumes." She turned to look at her mother. "With Maam's permission, of course."

Naomi nodded. "Although my parents encouraged us to make the Bible our most important book, my daed loved Charles Dickens and allowed me to read his novels. Seth and I could not see anything wrong with Esther reading his works. He wrote from a Christian perspective, and his words touched me as a young girl."

Cheryl shook her head. Just when she thought she had the Amish figured out, something happened that proved no group of people can be confined by stereotypes or titles.

"You can borrow any of these books you want to," she told Esther.

The young girl's face lit up. "Ach, Cheryl. Thank you. I have read *A Tale of Two Cities* and *Oliver Twist*. But I have not yet read *David Copperfield*."

Cheryl reached into the box and pulled out a beautifully hardbound copy of *David Copperfield*. She handed it to Esther. "Here you go. Just bring it to work when you're finished. And no rush."

"Oh, thank you so much." Esther leaned over and gave Cheryl a hug. "Now I feel as if this is *my* birthday."

"And speaking of birthdays, we have some presents for you as well," Naomi said.

One by one, family members brought their gifts to Cheryl. Elizabeth's present, a beautifully woven basket filled with fruit, had a large bow on the handle. Elizabeth had painted small flowers on the ribbons. Eli and Caleb had carved a gorgeous quilt rack made from dark oak.

"The boys' gift hints at our present," Naomi said. She got up and grabbed a large box that was behind the couch and handed it to Cheryl. When she opened it, she found an incredible patchwork quilt done in the colors used in the Swiss Miss.

Cheryl gasped. "Oh, Naomi, it's gorgeous."

"I am so glad you like it," Naomi said.

"My part was the most difficult," Seth said with a smile.

Naomi laughed. "My husband took care of many of my duties while I worked on your quilt."

Eli snorted. "Ach, seeing Daed in an apron cooking in the kitchen will stay with me for many years."

Naomi pointed her finger at her son. "Real men are willing to help their wives without worrying about what anyone thinks. I hope you remember this when you are married."

"Your mother's right," Cheryl's mother said. "Last month I led a women's meeting at church that stretched over several days. The last night I came home just exhausted. When I walked into the house, I found a lovely dinner waiting for me. The house was cleaned, and all the laundry had been done." A smile lit up her face. "It was my husband's way of telling me he loved me without one word being spoken."

Naomi nodded. "You do understand."

Cheryl's mother reached for her husband's hand. "Yes, I do," she said softly.

"I have something for you as well," Esther said. "I hope you will like it."

"I'm sure I will," Cheryl said with a smile.

Esther reached next to her and picked up a rather large square package. It was thin like a picture. Since the Amish didn't believe in taking pictures, Cheryl couldn't imagine what it could be. Esther carried it over and handed it to her.

"I want to tell you how grateful I am for my job. I love working for you. You have taught me so much."

"Thank you, Esther," Cheryl said, touched by the young girl's words. She slowly tore off the wrapping paper. Inside was a beautifully crafted and framed cross-stitched picture of the Swiss Miss. Every detail of the structure was added, from the chairs on the front porch to the flowers that grew along the front of the shop. "I...I don't know what to say," she said, stuttering. "This must have taken you hours and hours to finish."

"It did," Naomi interjected. "She started it some time ago, but she rushed to complete it for your birthday. I would find her up late, working away, but I did not tell her to go to bed. This was truly a labor of love."

"Thank you, Esther," Cheryl said, her voice choked with emotion. "This will go up in the shop. I will treasure it forever."

Esther, lightly blushing from the attention being shown to her, smiled. "I am honored." She went back to sit down while Cheryl continued to stare at the image of the store she'd come to love so much.

"I haven't given you my gift yet," Matt said, breaking the silence.

Cheryl looked at him with surprise. It had been years since Matt had given her or her parents a birthday gift. Sometimes he managed cards, but with his lack of funds, Cheryl had gotten used to never receiving more than an occasional call or a random greeting card.

"I'm sorry," she said, carefully putting the picture down next to her. "I just assumed—"

"I didn't bring you anything?" He shook his head. "It's been a while, hasn't it? I'm sorry about that. Maybe this will make up for it." He got up and walked over to the coat rack where Esther had hung up their coats and jackets when they came into the house. He pulled a small box out of the inside pocket. He walked over and handed it to Cheryl.

"Thank you," she said. As he went back to sit down, she removed the lid on the box. Inside was a beautiful silver bracelet. She removed it from the box and looked at it carefully.

"It's a charm bracelet," Matt said. "I only added a few charms to start it. That way you can pick your own or tell me what other charms you want. Down through the years, we can add to it."

"Oh, Matt, it's beautiful."

Cheryl looked up to see him grinning. "There's an angel. It's called the Angel of Hope. It's to remind you that with God nothing is impossible. And there are ballet slippers. I still remember your ballet lessons. When you danced, it amazed me."

Cheryl laughed. "You made fun of me constantly when I took ballet. You called me Twinkle Toes."

He nodded. "That's a brother's job. But secretly I thought you were incredible."

"And what's this last one? The heart?"

"That one's called Always in My Heart. Because you are."

Cheryl choked back a sob. "I'm going to be absolutely dried out by the end of this day." She looked at Matt. "Thank you so much." She slipped the bracelet on to her wrist. "It's absolutely beautiful."

"You're welcome. Happy birthday, sis."

"Thank you, everyone," she said, smiling. "I'll never, ever forget this birthday."

Naomi stood up. "We have fresh lemonade and *kaffee*. And there are cookies if anyone has room for them."

As almost everyone headed toward the kitchen, Levi came over and stood in front of Cheryl.

"I have not given you my gift yet," he said.

"Oh, Levi, you don't need to give me anything. You already gave me that beautiful Bible cover."

"That was not a birthday present." He turned to look behind him. No one was left in the living room. "Will you come with me?" He motioned for her to follow him.

As they went out the front door, Cheryl was confused. What in the world could he have for her that couldn't be brought into the house? She followed him over to the corral area where Samson and Methuselah stood, watching them. The other horses were probably in the stable. As Levi opened the gate and went into the enclosure, he instructed Cheryl to stay where she was. She ran her hand down the horses' faces as they tried to nuzzle her.

"You two are so silly," she whispered. "I love you both to pieces."

Suddenly the stable door opened and Levi came out leading a beautiful black horse. As he came closer, she realized it looked like the horse Janie Henderson had described to her, the one she'd rescued. "Is that Ranger?" Cheryl asked.

Levi nodded.

"What are you doing with him?" Even before he answered, Cheryl realized that he was Levi's gift. "You...you got him...for me?"

Levi brought the beautiful horse over and opened the gate, directing Cheryl to come inside. Once she closed the gate behind her, he handed her the reins. "You love horses and told me you had always wanted one. When I spoke to Janie about Ranger, she gave him to me. So actually the gift is from her. You can come and ride him, spend time with him, whenever you want. I will board him, feed him, and take care of his needs. That is my gift to you." He frowned down at her. "You are crying again? I am becoming concerned for your health."

Cheryl quickly wiped her face on her sleeve. "It's not my fault. You are all too good to me. I don't deserve—"

Levi hushed her before she could finish her sentence. "Do not be foolish. Your friends and family do not bless you because you deserve anything. They do it because they love you."

Cheryl felt her face flush, and she looked away from him.

Levi cleared his throat. "I do not mean . . . I meant to say—"

"I understand," she said softly. "Please don't be embarrassed. There's nothing wrong with loving our friends. Jesus instructed us to love each other." For just a moment, she wrestled with the desire to tell him she loved him too, but she couldn't do it. It felt too heavy and important to say. So she kept quiet.

"That is true," Levi said. "Thank you."

Cheryl reached over and began to stroke Ranger's face. "No, thank *you*." She gazed up into Levi's dark blue eyes. "I don't have the words to tell you how much it means to me."

"That makes me very happy," he said softly. For a few seconds they continued to stare at each other until Levi looked away, his face flushed for some reason. "I must get back inside. Please spend as much time with Ranger as you wish. I will remove his reins and put him away later."

With that, he turned away, left the corral, and began walking toward the house. Cheryl stroked Ranger's neck, wondering if the happiness she felt was only from her joy at finally getting a horse.

CHAPTER SIXTEEN

Saturday night Cheryl and her family had dinner at Yoder's. Although she was happy her family was back together, she kept wondering if her mother would use the time to criticize Naomi or her family in an attempt to discourage her from staying in Sugarcreek. Even though she seemed to like Naomi, Cheryl couldn't help but worry that the other shoe was about to drop. But she needn't have worried. Her mother had nothing but positive things to say about the Millers. Eventually, Cheryl relaxed. It seemed that her mom and Naomi had bonded as mothers. She found that a little odd since their styles were so different, but at this point, Cheryl was just grateful everyone had gotten along so well.

After agreeing to meet for church in the morning, Cheryl and Matt drove back to the house.

"How about a cup of hot chocolate?" Cheryl said after they got inside and hung up their coats.

"Sounds great," Matt said. He patted his pockets and then went back over to his jacket and began to search through it.

"What are you looking for?" Cheryl asked.

"My cell phone. I got a text from one of the guys in my office, and after I texted him back, I think I put the phone on the table." He glanced at his watch. "Yoder's should still be open. Go ahead and make the chocolate. I'll be right back."

"Okay." Cheryl watched as he threw his jacket on and hurried out the front door. She waited to hear his truck start and peeked through the window as he pulled out and turned into the street. Not sure of how much time she had, she quickly jogged to the guest room. Even though she felt ashamed of herself, she wanted to drive away any doubt she had about Matt. Not sure how long it would take him to get to the restaurant, retrieve his phone, and come back, she began to quickly go through his things.

After looking through the closet, checking under the bed and the mattress, she'd just opened the top drawer of the dresser when she heard a noise behind her. She turned to find Matt standing in the doorway, staring at her.

"Can I ask what you're doing?"

The angry look on his face stopped Cheryl in her tracks. She suddenly felt guilty.

"I'm just...I mean, I..." Shaking her head, she sat down on the edge of the bed. "I'm sorry, Matt. But Ellen Streeter's stuff is gone. Someone broke into my office and took everything."

Matt's eyes widened. "You think I did it?"

"No, I'm sure you didn't. It's just that..."

As he leaned against the doorframe, his expression turned to something else. Sadness. To Cheryl, it was worse than anger. "It seems like something I would do?"

Cheryl looked away from him, regretting her rash decision to search his room. "I'm sorry. I should have just talked to you about it.

But when you left, the idea popped into my head to go through your room. I didn't think it through, and I shouldn't have done it. I'm truly sorry." She turned her face toward him. "You didn't have enough time to go to the restaurant and come back. What are you doing here?"

Matt snorted. "Wait a minute. Are you mad because I came back too soon and caught you?"

Cheryl sighed. "I don't know. Maybe."

"I was on my way to the restaurant when I saw the phone on the floor of the truck, so I turned around and came back." He walked over and sat down next to her. "I didn't take that stuff, Cheryl. Even at my worst, I wouldn't steal from you. I thought you knew that."

She reached over and grasped his hand. "I do, but I guess I wanted to chase away any last doubt so I wouldn't have to even consider the possibility. Does that make sense?"

He paused a moment. "I guess so. Maybe I'm asking too much from you. And from the folks. I want all of you to see that I've changed, but it seems I'll have to prove it."

"I can't speak for them, Matt, but you don't have to prove anything to me." She squeezed his hand. "You're not a thief. I know that. As far as the past is concerned, trust is a choice, and I choose to trust you, okay?"

He nodded slowly. "Okay. Thanks." He took a deep breath and turned his head to meet her gaze. "You know, I've been here a day and a half and no one has asked me about my new job. I've mentioned it more than once, yet Mom and Dad...and you...seem completely uninterested. May I ask why?"

"I think it's because you used to spin these wild stories about jobs you supposedly had—or were going to have—when you asked for money. After a while we got tired of hearing it. And we quit believing the stories."

Matt was silent for a moment. "I guess I deserve that. And you're partially right. Sometimes it was just manipulation. I wanted Dad to think I only needed help one more time. Sometimes I was telling the truth, or at least I thought I was. I guess I was a little too optimistic. Jobs I thought I had didn't turn out for me."

"You always made them sound more important than they were anyway. I don't care what kind of job you have, Matt. You don't have to have some kind of impressive title. I just want you to be responsible. And happy."

"I am. And I'm sorry too." He let go of her hand and ran his fingers through his dark wavy hair. "You know, when I was a teenager, I just couldn't seem to live up to Mom and Dad's expectations. I got so tired of seeing the disappointment in their eyes. It was when I started to see the same thing from you that I left."

Cheryl leaned her head on his shoulder. "Oh, Matt, I'm so sorry. I hate that you thought I was disappointed in you. I wasn't. Really." She sighed. "We have great parents, but they've had plans for both of us that didn't turn out the way they wanted. Mom wanted me to marry Lance. Or someone. And even though I didn't follow them into the ministry, she could stomach my job at the bank. Coming here, taking over Aunt Mitzi's shop in Sugarcreek, is something she may never understand. But I'm so happy, Matt. Happier than I've been in a long time. This is where I want to be.

Even more importantly, I believe this is where God wants me to be. At least for now."

He smiled. "I see how satisfied you are, and I'm glad. I hope you'll feel the same way about me."

Cheryl stood up and held out her hands. "Let's get that hot chocolate, and you can tell me about your new job."

Matt took her hands and let her pull him to his feet. "What are you going to do about the theft, Cheryl? Have you contacted the police?"

"Not yet. I've been afraid—"

"It was me?" Matt pointed at the dresser. "Please finish looking. I don't want there to be any doubt."

Cheryl walked over and firmly closed the drawer. "There's no doubt, Matt. I don't have to look."

"Well, I definitely think you should talk to the police. Right away. Whoever did it will probably try to sell the coin as quickly as possible. What if Ellen shows up someday? I think she'll want her coin—and her other belongings. Besides, someone gained access to your store. What if they decide to come back for something else? You need to find out who's behind this."

Cheryl leaned against the chest-of-drawers. "I need to ask a question, Matt. Not because I have any suspicions, but just because I'm curious. Chuck thinks he saw your truck out in the street the night we think the thief got in. Was he right?"

"You mean last night?"

Cheryl nodded.

"No, he's right. I just went for a drive. Wanted time to think, I guess. Seeing my family again has been wonderful...but stressful. I slowed down in front of the shop because I saw a man there, taking things out and putting them in a truck. As strange as it sounds, I was afraid someone was breaking in. Once I got close enough, I remembered you said Chuck would be working Friday night, so I didn't stop."

"That's what I figured, but if I call the police, they may ask you about that. Chuck will probably be questioned, and I'm sure he'll bring it up."

Matt shrugged. "That's fine. I don't care." He frowned at his sister. "Could Chuck have taken those things?"

Cheryl shook her head. "I thought about it, but I don't believe so, although he knows about the coin. He's the one who told me how much it was worth." She couldn't help worrying that Chief Twitchell would see both Matt and Chuck as suspects. That wasn't something she wanted.

As if he could read her mind, Matt said, "Cheryl, the outcome isn't your responsibility. You can tell the police you don't think Chuck or I would take anything. After that, you have to walk away. Leave it to the police to find the truth."

"You're right. I just hate—"

"Confrontation?" Matt grinned. "It's something neither one of us like, but I saw how you defended your friend Naomi. You're willing to stick up for ideas and people you care about, Skeeter. You're just not great at defending yourself."

"Right back atcha," Cheryl said. "Maybe we both need to change that."

He nodded slowly. "Maybe we do."

Matt followed Cheryl into the kitchen and sat at the table while Cheryl began to pull out all the ingredients for hot chocolate. She liked to make it the old-fashioned way with milk, cocoa powder, and sugar. In her opinion, microwave cocoa couldn't hold a candle to the real thing.

"Whipped cream or marshmallows?" she asked her brother.

"Marshmallows," he said with a grin. "Just like when we were little."

Usually Cheryl used whipped cream, but tonight she added marshmallows to both cups. When they were kids, their mother always made hot chocolate with marshmallows. Thinking about those times made Cheryl feel a little nostalgic. When she and Matt were younger, their family was close. It wasn't until they were older that cracks in their relationships began to appear. Even though their parents never put any real pressure on them, it was implied. There was always the feeling that the pastor's children had to be perfect. Look better, act better . . . be better. The strain was hard on Cheryl, but it had finally been too much for Matt. He began acting out when he was twelve, and it had caused great concern for her parents. Responsibility for the fallout seemed to land mostly at their mother's feet since her father was seen as too busy pastoring to spend much time disciplining his children. As time went on, Cheryl's mother seemed to take Matt's actions personally. As if somehow his rebellion was her fault.

"Here you go," she said, handing Matt his cup of cocoa. "Now tell me about this new job."

"Well, it's not all that new," he said after a quick sip of the hot mixture. "It's something I've been working on for a while." He put his cup down and stared at it. "About four years ago a friend of mine introduced me to his sister. Nicki had been living in Los Angeles, working for a mortgage banking company. She worked long hours, and she had two small dogs. Because it was hard to get home during the day, a friend of hers told her about a gal she'd hired to go by her house and feed and walk her dogs during the day. Nicki thought it sounded like a good idea, so she hired her too. Unfortunately, the dog sitter went through their personal papers, got their social security numbers, credit card and bank information, and cleaned them both out—along with several other clients. She disappeared but not before stealing Nicki's purebred Yorkies and selling them."

"Oh my." Cheryl looked down at Beau who had curled up by her feet.

"The dogs were found and returned," Matt said quickly. "But fixing her credit and getting her money back was much tougher. Her situation gave me the idea of creating a clearinghouse. You know, a company you can call that will investigate anyone you might want to hire, like housekeepers, babysitters, nannies, house sitters, you know…not companies. Just individuals who could end up with access to your home and personal information. You find the people, but we check them out." He shook his head. "People are so busy they don't take the time to look closely at the people they hire. For a fee, we do that. It seems to be working. I now have twenty investigators working for me, and we've actually been instrumental in catching over sixty crooks with outstanding warrants. People who would have ripped someone off if we hadn't found them."

Cheryl stared at her brother with her mouth open. "I...I don't know what to say. That's just...amazing, Matt."

He smiled at her. "I think it is. I really feel like we're helping people."

"I'm sorry about Nicki though. I hope she was able to get her credit cleaned up."

Matt nodded. "We got it taken care of."

"Your company does that too?"

He shook his head. "No, I helped her." He looked at Cheryl, a grin on his face. "I couldn't allow my fiancée to have bad credit."

Cheryl gasped. "Fiancée? Matt! Wow, when you share news, you go all the way."

"She's wonderful, Cheryl. You'll love her. She's the one who got me back into church." He took a deep breath before saying, "Actually, that's not the most important part. She helped me to see that God wasn't disappointed in me. That I wasn't too big a mess for Him." He put his hands around his cup. "Going back to church wasn't as important as being able to believe I was actually worth something to God. That He had a plan for me."

"Oh, Matt, I'm so glad. When do I get to meet this wonder woman who snared my handsome brother?"

He smiled. "Soon. First I want to tell Mom and Dad about her. We'll take it from there."

Cheryl noticed the hesitation in his voice. "You're afraid they won't approve?"

"I don't know." He sighed. "There's no reason they shouldn't, but I guess it's just so important—"

"You don't want to see *the look*?"

He nodded. Cheryl knew that look. It didn't always come with negative words, but it spoke volumes. Although Cheryl had seen it a few times, it was usually reserved for Matt. She suddenly felt very protective of her brother.

"Do you want me to talk to them first?"

"No."

Matt's sharp response surprised her. "I'm not trying to take over, I just thought—"

"You'd smooth the way? Ask them to be nice?"

She nodded slowly. "I guess so. Sorry."

"You've covered for me so many times, Skeeter. Tried to make things better. I appreciate it. I really do. But I think it's time for me to stand up for myself, don't you?"

"I guess I do." She patted her brother's arm. "I want you to know how proud I am of you. Very proud."

"Thanks. That means more than I can say."

They finished their hot chocolate and headed to bed. Once Cheryl had shut the door to her room, she slumped down in the rocking chair in the corner. Her emotions were swinging from one extreme to the other. Joy for her brother's business success and the new love in his life, concern her parents would say something to hurt him, and uncertainty about contacting Chief Twitchell about the missing purse and valise.

As she prepared for bed, she prayed for Matt and her parents. Would tomorrow bring healing? Or would the rift that divided them grow even wider?

Chapter Seventeen

I hope the police find your missing things," Levi said.

He and Cheryl stood in the corner of the Swiss Miss on Monday morning, looking at the new cooler. Levi, Seth, and Eli had carried it into the shop, and Chuck hooked it up before it was time for Cheryl to open for business. Seth and Eli took off right after they'd brought the cooler in, but Naomi and Levi had stayed to watch Chuck get it going.

"Ach, I do too," Naomi said, frowning. "It does not feel good when you do not know who to trust."

Cheryl sighed. "You're right about that."

"I do not know Chuck Watson well," Levi said, "but people in town speak highly of him. I would be surprised if he stole from you."

"I don't think he had anything to do with it," Cheryl said. "When I stopped by to talk to Chief Twitchell this morning, he took my information and said he'd see what he could do. I don't know if there's much of a chance of recovering anything, but at least I know I've done all I can do."

"Will he question anyone?" Naomi asked.

"Not right away. First he plans to check pawnshops in the area for the coin. Hopefully they'll find it, and we'll be able to figure out who took it before anyone I know becomes a suspect." Cheryl picked up the cakes and pies Naomi had brought in and put them inside the new cooler. Then she closed the glass door and smiled. "That looks so nice. Maybe I'll be able to keep some of your food in stock now. I'll find out after we open, I guess."

Naomi chuckled. "I am afraid your customers will have to be satisfied. I do not believe I can bake any more than I am now."

Cheryl put her arm around her friend and gave her a quick squeeze. "Don't work too hard, Naomi. This should be fun. Not stressful."

"I do not wish to interrupt, Maam," Levi said, "but if you want to get your jams and jellies to Yoder's in time, we must leave now."

"Oh my. You are right, Son. I was not watching the time." Naomi patted Cheryl's shoulder. "I must scoot. I stopped by Maybelline's house this morning and asked if we could join her for lunch today. She is anxious to meet you. I am sure she can answer some of your questions about Ellen Streeter."

"That's great," Cheryl said. "Can you pick me up?"

"I will be here around noon," she said. "You will like Maybelline. She is a very resilient woman."

"I look forward to getting to know her."

After Naomi and Levi left, Cheryl went about her usual preparations before opening the shop. But her mind was still on the meeting she'd had with Chief Twitchell before coming to work.

"I have a hard time understandin' how somethin' can be stolen from your shop since you have that new alarm," the chief had said. "Are you tryin' to tell me it only goes off when nothin's wrong?"

The chief's normally deep voice had risen several notes, giving Cheryl a clear insight into the man's frustration. She'd explained that the alarm was off because Chuck was in the building working, but the chief didn't seem impressed.

"Maybe you need another lesson on using that thing," he'd said, frowning at her.

Cheryl had graciously denied his offer and asked him to let her know if Ellen's items showed up, but Chief Twitchell didn't seem too hopeful.

"I'll check pawnshops in the area about the coin, but I doubt you'll see the other stuff again. The thief probably went through everything and tossed whatever he couldn't sell. That's what usually happens in these kinda cases."

As she'd suspected, Twitchell asked who'd known about the coin. The list wasn't very long. Chuck, Matt, her...and Amos Streeter. She told the chief about going over to the Streeters' house and why.

"Any of these folks could have told someone else about the coin, right?"

"Except for Matt, I guess so. And I'm certain Matt had nothing to do with it." She tried to keep her voice casual, not wanting to sound defensive about her brother.

Twitchell hadn't said anything in response, but he'd raised his eyebrows and studied her for a moment before going back to taking notes.

Cheryl was relieved to get her trip to the police station out of the way. Although she wanted the coin back, she was still a little afraid to find out who took it. Could it really be someone she knew? All she could do was hope it wasn't.

As usual, she unlocked the door at nine and turned the Open sign over at ten. The morning went by so quickly, Cheryl was surprised when Naomi and Esther walked through the front door.

"Is it noon already?" she said to the women.

"Ach, it is just a little early," Naomi said. "Esther wanted to see the new cooler before she starts to work."

"Oh, Cheryl." Esther gazed up at the wall behind the counter where Cheryl had hung the beautiful cross-stitched picture of the Swiss Miss.

"A place of honor," Cheryl said with a smile. "Doesn't it add something wonderful to the shop?"

Naomi sniffed and lifted her apron so she could dab at her wet eyes. "It is quite lovely, and it looks so nice in the spot you've chosen."

"I am so glad you like it," Esther said, her voice choking with emotion.

"I absolutely love it," Cheryl said. "I intend to take a picture and send it to Mitzi. She'll love it too. Thank you again, Esther."

The girl didn't say anything, just nodded, but Cheryl could tell she was pleased.

"Let's go see the new cooler," Cheryl said. She led them over to the corner where the new appliance sat, full of goodies.

"It is so big," Esther said softly.

Cheryl smiled. "Yes, it is. Now I'll have plenty of room for all the food you bring me. I hope Mitzi will like it."

"I am certain she will be very pleased, Cheryl," Naomi said. "You have done such a wonderful job with the shop. I know Mitzi is proud of you."

"Thank you. I hope so." Her aunt had always made her feel special, and she didn't want to let her down. Cheryl smiled at Naomi. "I need to take care of a couple of things, and then we'll go."

"I will wait in the buggy," Naomi replied. "I made lunch for us . . . and for Maybelline."

"Sounds great."

Cheryl went to the office and made a couple of notes. Then she gave Esther some instructions about orders that might be picked up while she was gone. When she got outside, she found Naomi sitting in the buggy, their horse, Sugar, in harness. Cheryl stopped to stroke her face before climbing in beside her friend.

"Did you like Levi's gift to you?" Naomi asked once Cheryl was seated next to her.

Cheryl smiled. "I still can't believe it. It's a dream come true."

Naomi flicked the reins, and Sugar began to trot down the street. "I am glad. He came to us before bringing Ranger home. He wanted to be sure it would be appropriate. Seth and I both approved. Please come by anytime to ride him. You know where we keep the tack. Just make sure you close the gate to the corral. And you might let us know when you take him so no one will think he got out."

"I'll do that." Cheryl could hardly wait take Ranger out for a ride, but with her parents in town, she wasn't sure when she'd be able to find the time.

As if reading her mind, Naomi said, "How long do your folks plan to stay in Sugarcreek?"

Cheryl sighed. "I honestly don't know. Matt and I are having dinner with them tonight. Maybe they'll tell us then."

Naomi was silent for a moment, and Cheryl looked at her with concern. Although there was a nip in the air, the weather was mild and the steady clip-clop of Sugar's feet made Cheryl feel relaxed until she saw the expression on Naomi's face.

"Is something wrong?" she asked.

"I do not wish to interfere with parents and their children."

Cheryl chuckled. "Interfere. Please. I'll take any help I can get."

"I have been wondering if your mother thinks you no longer need her."

Surprised, Cheryl frowned at her friend. "What do you mean?"

Naomi turned to look at Cheryl. "You do not seek your mother's advice very often, ain't so?"

Cheryl thought for a moment. "I have. Many times."

"But since you moved to Sugarcreek?"

Cheryl contemplated Naomi's question. "I . . . I guess not much."

"And how was this move presented to her?"

Cheryl sighed. "My father has already told me they thought my time here was temporary. They're afraid I'll end up staying for good, and they don't see a future for me here. They're concerned I'll never get married if I live in a town this small."

"What did your mother say when you talked to her about this?"

Cheryl frowned at her. "I can't talk to her about Sugarcreek."

Naomi was silent for a moment. "May I ask how you know she does not want to listen to you?"

Cheryl searched for a response to her friend's question, but couldn't seem to find one. "I...I don't know. I guess I haven't really tried talking to her about it."

Naomi nodded. "But you have talked to Mitzi about your life? Your future?"

"Yeah," Cheryl said slowly.

Naomi smiled. "I am not an expert in these matters, Cheryl. All I can tell you is that when children do not seem to need their mothers, when they no longer seek their counsel, mothers begin to feel useless." She shook her head. "For someone like me, a woman who does not have the kind of pressure your mother does, perhaps it is even more important. Being a wife and mother is everything I am. Feeling as if I can no longer fulfill those roles would cause me great pain."

Cheryl put her hand on the older woman's arm. "Oh, Naomi, you are so much more than just a wife and mother. You are one of the most talented women I've ever met. You can do anything. I wish I could be more like you."

"Oh, my dear friend, I know you are speaking out of a good heart. But I do not see myself as *just* a wife and mother. Ach, those roles mean more to me than anything else in life. I believe I am called to be Seth's wife—and to be a mother to his children. If I do my job well, there will be generations of our family who will serve the Lord. What greater calling is there?"

"I…I hadn't thought about it like that. You really think my mother feels the same way?"

"I cannot say she sees this calling in the exact manner, but I am fairly certain she feels she has failed you and you have put Mitzi in her place." Naomi smiled at her. "I have found that many times people criticize others as a way to deflect their own insecurity. I do not pretend to speak for Gott in this situation, but as a mother, I believe I am speaking the truth."

As they continued their journey to Maybelline's, Cheryl turned Naomi's words over in her mind. She thought about the close relationship she had with her aunt and the times she'd gone to her for counseling. Many times she'd mentioned Mitzi in front of her mother. Now she was in Sugarcreek running the Swiss Miss, once again following in Mitzi's footsteps. Was it true? Did her mother feel resentful of their friendship? Could she feel Cheryl had rejected her? And what about Matt? Did she believe his leaving home was also rejection? Suddenly, her mother's change in attitude began to make sense. It wasn't just that she thought Cheryl was making a mistake, she felt her daughter didn't value her anymore. And that she'd replaced her with Mitzi.

"Oh my," she said quietly. "I think you're right. I . . . I never saw it."

"Most children never do. For a parent, feeling you are not needed anymore is . . . terrible."

"But your children *do* need you," Cheryl said, frowning. "You talk as if you've felt that pain. How is that possible?"

"When Sarah left us, I felt rejection. She abandoned our beliefs and our values. I could have faced that. As I have said, I do not want my children to believe in the Amish way because I do. But she did not talk to me about her choice. She just left. The real pain came from that. She did not need me. She did not seek my counsel."

"Even though Sarah isn't your biological child?"

Naomi nodded. "In a way, it felt even worse. It was my job to fill the role of the mother she lost. When she abandoned us, I felt she had turned her back on me as a person—and as a mother. I felt I had failed Seth as well."

"Naomi, I'm sure Seth didn't see it that way at all."

She offered Cheryl a tight smile. "No, he did not. But still, I watched him suffer, and I felt responsible. It was a very difficult time."

"And then Sarah came back."

Naomi's face relaxed. "Ja, Sarah came back. Even though she has chosen to live her own life, at least now we have a connection to her. Gott is good."

Cheryl didn't say anything else until they pulled up to a large Victorian house on the west side of Sugarcreek. Naomi got out of the carriage and tied Sugar up to the white wooden fence that encircled the front yard.

Cheryl climbed down while Naomi went to the back of the buggy to retrieve a large woven picnic basket. As they walked toward the gate, Cheryl reached out and grabbed her arm.

"Thank you, Naomi. You've given me something to consider. I think I see what I need to do to repair my relationship with my mother. Unfortunately, I'm not sure Matt's situation will be as simple."

"Do not rule Gott out. He loves Matt, and He wants your family to be whole. Gott is in the business of second chances, ain't so?"

Cheryl watched as Naomi opened the gate and made her way toward the front door.

"Ain't so?" she muttered under her breath.

CHAPTER EIGHTEEN

Maybelline's house was lovely inside. Antique furniture adorned the front sitting room, and a huge fireplace reigned as the centerpiece of the spacious living room. Although the furnishings were old, they were well maintained. Cheryl could smell lemon oil. The wood floors shone, and the walls looked freshly painted. Cheryl was pretty sure Maybelline wasn't responsible for the upkeep of her home. Its condition pointed to friends who obviously cared for her and made sure her surroundings were cared for even though the owner of the house would never see them.

"Maybelline, I am here," Naomi called out. "And Cheryl has come with me."

A door on the side of the room opened, and a tall, stately woman with a wide smile stepped inside. "So I get to meet your friend Cheryl today? I've been looking forward to it."

If Cheryl hadn't known Maybelline was blind, she wouldn't have guessed it. She could have almost sworn the woman looked right at her, but as she approached, Cheryl realized she was gazing just a little bit past her.

Naomi stepped forward and took Maybelline's outstretched hand. She guided her closer to Cheryl. "Maybelline, this is Cheryl."

Cheryl reached out to grasp the woman's other hand. "I'm so glad to meet you, Maybelline. Thank you for allowing me to come to your home. It's lovely."

Maybelline's wonderful smile widened. "It is, isn't it? I love it here." She removed her hand from Cheryl's and waved toward two chairs and a couch placed several feet away from the fireplace. Cheryl sat in one chair while Maybelline took the other. Except for lightly touching the furniture when she moved, again, it was almost impossible to tell she couldn't see.

"I will go into the kitchen and set out our lunch," Naomi said with a smile. "You two visit. I will let you know when everything is ready."

"Thank you, Naomi," Maybelline said softly. She turned her head toward Cheryl. "I understand you have some questions about Ellen Streeter? Would you mind telling me why you're interested in her?"

Cheryl slowly recounted the find inside the laundry chute, trying not to leave out any details.

"So you found her coin?" Maybelline said when Cheryl finished. She smiled. "Her father gave her that. Told her to keep it safe. It was worth quite a bit back then, but he knew it would grow in value. It was his way of making sure she would always have a way to leave Bill if she needed to. She kept it secret. I only know because I overheard her talking to my mother about it. Mom was her only friend."

"I'm very concerned about Ellen," Cheryl said. "I have no idea where she is. If she's even alive. I wanted to give her things back to her. Especially the coin. But now someone has taken them. I wanted to talk to you in case you have some kind of insight. Is there something you know about Ellen that might help me?"

A frown deepened the fine lines around Maybelline's sightless eyes. "The night Bill died has always bothered me. Not just because of his death, but because I heard things that didn't make sense. I asked my mother about them the next day, but she told me I must have been mistaken." She shook her head slowly. "I think she knew...something. Something she wanted to keep secret."

Naomi came back into the room and put a cup of coffee on a small table next to Maybelline. Then she took her hand and slowly guided it to the cup handle.

"Thank you, dear Naomi." She picked up the cup and took a sip. "Naomi knows how much I love my coffee."

Naomi looked at Cheryl. "Would you also like some kaffee?"

Cheryl shook her head. "I'll wait until we eat. Thank you."

Naomi nodded and left the room again.

"What was it that bothered you that night?" Cheryl asked.

Maybelline set her cup down before reaching up and brushing back a tendril of silver hair that had fallen across her cheek. Her long, graying hair was swept upward and held loosely by a lovely jeweled comb. Cheryl marveled at her graceful presence. She was a handsome woman who must have been strikingly beautiful when she was younger. Cheryl couldn't help but wonder why she wasn't married. Surely it wasn't because she was blind. Had all the men she'd met been so shallow?

"I remember that I couldn't sleep that night," she said softly. "It was hot so I opened my window. I remember there was a light breeze that drifted through my room from time to time. It was so refreshing." She smiled. "Our house had air conditioning, but I'd pushed and prodded my mother for the attic room where there was no vent. I had an electric fan, but I hated the noise. I wanted to listen to the sounds of the night through my window." She laughed lightly. "I'm sorry. I drift away from time to time. The older I get, the more I think about the past."

She reached down and adjusted her skirt. She wore a lovely dark blue dress with white lace accents. The satiny material accented her lithe body. For a woman her age, she was in remarkable physical shape. There was a confidence that exuded from her. Cheryl found herself feeling slightly envious of this older, blind woman.

"That night, I heard a car arrive at Bill and Ellen's house. A little later, a car left. And then a couple of hours later, a car arrived—about fifteen minutes before the police showed up. The story was that Amos came over to the house to see his brother and found Bill at the bottom of the stairs. According to him, Ellen had left Bill a week earlier. She wasn't anywhere near Sugarcreek when her husband died." Maybelline took a deep breath before saying, "But I heard her talking to my mother two days before Bill's accident. Mom denied it, but I have excellent hearing. My mother was a godly, honest woman, but she lied to me, Cheryl. As far as I know, it was the only time she ever lied."

"So you think Ellen was there when Bill died? And that she left before the police came?"

"I checked with another neighbor. He told me that Bill and Ellen's car was there when the police arrived. So was Amos's car. If Ellen left, how in the world did she leave without a vehicle? And who came and left that night? Something else went on. Something the police never looked into." She sighed. "The police chief back then was a friend of Amos's. I'm not saying he covered up anything, but Bill's death was quickly ruled an accident, and the case was closed. A short time later Amos sold his house—and Bill's—and moved away." She clasped her hands together, her long slender fingers intertwined. "I've never shared that story before. I knew my mother didn't want me to, but what harm can it do now? I think the truth should come out, don't you? Isn't it about time?"

Cheryl nodded before remembering that Maybelline couldn't see her. "Did Naomi tell you about the letter I found in the purse?"

Maybelline shook her head slowly. "Naomi didn't tell me anything about what you'd found, Cheryl. She only told me you're working in the shop that used to be Bill and Ellen's home, and that you wanted to ask me a few questions."

Cheryl repeated what she could remember from the letter. "She was asking for a ride to the bus station. Maybe that's why Bill and Ellen's car was still there."

"I don't believe there was a bus stop in Sugarcreek back then," Maybelline said. "Ellen would have had to get to Canton, and Bill never allowed her out of the house. My mother was the only person she ever talked to, and that was only when Bill was gone. And Ellen's fear of her husband kept those visits to a minimum. She was always afraid he'd come home and catch her talking to Mom, and she didn't want to lose contact with the only person in her life besides Bill."

"Could your mother have driven her to Canton?"

Maybelline shook her head with conviction. "No. I would know. She would have taken me with her or called my grandmother to stay with me. She would never have left me alone."

Cheryl thought for a moment. "What about Amos?"

"I don't think so. He did come by from time to time to see Bill. The brothers weren't that close, but Amos did stay in contact with him. Blood is thicker than water, I guess. Amos didn't care much for Ellen though. Wouldn't have anything to do with her. The few times he was around her, my mother said he was quite rude. He told Mom once that he blamed Ellen for his brother's bad temper. That Bill should never have married her. He certainly wasn't the man Ellen was in love with." She shrugged. "Remember that anyone could have come by the house when Bill was gone. When I said Mom was the only person she talked to, I meant as a friend. There were delivery men, men with the utility companies, even men from the local church. Any of them could have stopped by when Bill wasn't home, I guess. No one in particular stands out though."

"Well, that doesn't narrow it down much, does it?"

Maybelline smiled. "I'm sorry. I don't think I'm helping you much. If Mom were still alive, we could ask her. She could probably fill in the blanks. If Ellen was in love with another man, Mom probably knew about it, but she wouldn't have told anyone."

Cheryl sighed. "So the night Bill died, someone came to the house. Then they left for a while and came back. After that, someone, probably this same person, called the police."

"I can't say for certain that the car that left is the same car that came back," Maybelline said, "although I was sure about it that night. They say when you lose one of your senses, the others are heightened. There is some truth to that, but now, many years later, I just can't be positive. I assume the last car to arrive belonged to Amos since he's the one who called the police. Mom said Amos was there when the police arrived, and he was pretty upset."

Cheryl turned Maybelline's information over in her mind. Frankly, it didn't tell her anything useful. "So Ellen was planning to leave Bill," she said softly to herself, trying to put the pieces together. "Bill must have figured out her plan and taken her purse and valise. He put them in the laundry chute and covered them up thinking she wouldn't leave without her identification and clothes. But she left anyway, probably to meet another man, and Bill fell down the stairs and died." She looked over at Maybelline. "Quite a coincidence, isn't it? Maybe the simple truth is that Ellen killed Bill before she left town."

"I thought of that," Maybelline said. "But Ellen just wasn't the sort of person to do something like that." She shook her head. "I know people say that all the time, but I truly believe it. She was such a gentle soul. Like an injured bird. Wanting to fly away but not trusting her wings. I just can't see her killing her husband."

"People sometimes surprise us," Cheryl said.

"That's true, but if Amos had suspected her of something like that, he would have made a terrible fuss. Insisted the police find her. As I said, he didn't do that. He must have believed Bill's death was an accident."

"But he said Ellen left a week before Bill died. You heard her talking to your mother two days before the . . . accident. I assume since she didn't admit that to you, she never told the police either?"

"No, she never told them." Maybelline rubbed her hands together as if she were cold. "My mother was a good woman, Cheryl. For whatever reason she kept that information to herself, I'm confident she did it for the right reasons. When Bill told the police that Ellen was gone, I'm sure he believed it too." Maybelline cocked her head and frowned. "Naomi said you talked to Amos about your discovery?"

"Yes. I took the purse and valise over there, hoping he'd know where Ellen was. To be honest, I've been worried Ellen might be dead. In fact, I've been afraid she might be buried somewhere on the shop's property. But Amos told me she was alive. That she'd called him when she found out about Bill." Cheryl sighed. "Frankly, he was pretty rude. Didn't want anything to do with me. Since he said he didn't know where Ellen was, I decided not to leave her things with him."

"Did you believe him? I mean about Ellen being alive?"

"To be honest, I haven't known what to believe. I felt he lied to me, but I'm not sure why. When I left I wasn't convinced either way."

"Mom never mentioned anything about Ellen calling. Of course, he wouldn't tell my mother something like that. He didn't like people sticking their nose in his business."

Cheryl chuckled. "He hasn't changed much. He told me the very same thing."

Maybelline stared off into space as if she was actually seeing something. "But why would he lie? Why did Mother lie?"

"Maybe he didn't," Cheryl said. "I mean, maybe Ellen left a week earlier but came by the day she talked to your mother so she could get some of her things. Amos might not have known anything about it. You said they weren't close."

"Of course that's possible." Although Maybelline voiced her agreement with Cheryl's conclusion, her expression showed doubt.

"Lunch is ready."

Cheryl jumped, not realizing Naomi had come back into the room. She went over to Maybelline who stood up and put her hand lightly on Naomi's shoulder. As Naomi made her way toward the kitchen, Maybelline stayed by her side. They hadn't quite reached the doorway when Maybelline stopped.

"Naomi, I want to show Cheryl something in the secretary."

Naomi led Maybelline over to a large cherry secretary desk with carved legs and many drawers. Maybelline reached out and found the drawer she wanted, sliding it open and reaching inside. She pulled out a lovely embroidered handkerchief. She held it out, and Cheryl took it from her hand. It was edged with lilacs.

"This is just like the handkerchief in Ellen's purse," she said.

Maybelline nodded. "Ellen made it for Mom. She was so talented. And she loved lilacs."

"It's beautiful," Cheryl said. As she held the handkerchief, she felt a connection to Ellen. It made her feel even worse about losing her coin. She wanted so much to find it and get it back to her. Knowing that might not be possible made her feel sad.

"Thank you for showing this to me," Cheryl said. She gave it back to Maybelline who placed it back in the secretary. It obviously held great meaning to her.

Maybelline's kitchen was modern, spacious, and lovely. The walls were painted a dusky blue, the cabinets and the crown molding a sparkling white.

"Your house is gorgeous," Cheryl said. "So beautifully decorated."

"You're wondering why a blind lady has such a lovely home?" Maybelline asked with a smile.

"Uh, no. I mean..."

Maybelline laughed while Naomi grinned at Cheryl.

"Sometimes it is good enough to know we are surrounded by beauty even if we cannot see it with our eyes," Naomi said. "Maybelline sees her home in her heart. She knows it is beautiful, and it makes her happy."

"My friends take good care of me," Maybelline said quietly. "They clean my house, and when something is broken, they fix it."

"We do what we can," Naomi said, "but most of the painting and the upkeep is done by your friend Chuck."

"Chuck? Wow. He's a surprising man."

"Yes," Maybelline said. "He is."

The tone of her voice caught Cheryl's attention, and she looked at Naomi who shook her head and put her finger on her lips.

Cheryl was quiet as Naomi served them iced tea. The information about cars coming and going the night Bill died was interesting, but it didn't bring her any closer to the truth. Nor did Maybelline hearing Ellen a couple of days before the accident. She could have come back to get more of her things while Bill was out of the house. Maybe she was looking for her purse and her valise. Cheryl would never know. Perhaps the truth was simple. Ellen Streeter made plans to leave an abusive husband who hid her things inside an old laundry chute, hoping it would keep her from running away. Not long after she left, the husband had an accident and died. It was possible there was nothing more to it and Cheryl had been imagining some kind of dark conspiracy. The truth was, she'd reached a dead end. Now she couldn't even return the purse and valise even if Ellen was alive. In reality, there was nothing else to do. The best decision she could make was to focus on her family situation and let Ellen Streeter go, just like her belongings. Whoever took them could end up being an unsolved mystery as well.

The decision to give up trying to find the truth about Ellen should have brought her some peace, but she still felt vaguely unsettled. As if there was something important she'd missed.

Cheryl tried to concentrate on Naomi and Maybelline's conversation, but that strange feeling just wouldn't go away.

CHAPTER NINETEEN

"Did talking to Maybelline give you any new insight?"

Naomi's gentle voice nudged Cheryl from her troubled thoughts.

"I don't think so," she said. "Maybelline told me what she heard the night Bill died, but it didn't help. And to be honest, I'm beginning to think solving a mystery that happened over forty years ago is almost impossible. The trail is cold, and people's memories have faded." She shrugged. "I was afraid Ellen had been murdered. That her body might be buried somewhere in Sugarcreek. Maybe even somewhere on the shop's property. But now I'm beginning to believe she's alive. Amos said he talked to her a week after Bill died, and Maybelline heard Ellen talking to her mother two days before the accident. I wasn't sure I believed Amos when he said he'd talked to Ellen, but I can't see any reason he would lie. I guess I've been letting my imagination run away with me."

"Levi told me you asked him to search your basement for . . . a grave?"

Cheryl turned to look at Naomi. "I know. I'm sorry. The idea that she might be . . . still in the shop . . ."

Naomi held her hand up. "I understand. Levi told us about it at dinner." She shook her head. "The younger children found it extremely amusing."

"I'm sure you and Seth didn't think it was funny."

She watched Naomi bite her lip. Then her lips began to twitch.

"Are you...laughing?" Cheryl asked, amused by her Amish friend.

Naomi snorted, covering her mouth with her hand. "I...I must confess that we all laughed. The idea of a woman dying is not amusing, but the look on Levi's face when he told us about poking around in your basement..."

Cheryl couldn't help but giggle as she remembered his expression. Both women broke out in laughter.

"Poor Levi," Cheryl said, wiping her eyes. "I didn't mean to put him through that. I was really worried."

"I know," Naomi said. "Levi is a hard worker, but sometimes I think he is too serious. You have brought some much-needed excitement into his life." She smiled at Cheryl. "And to mine as well."

"You've brought much more to me," Cheryl said in a low voice. "You've helped me to see things more clearly." She reached over and hugged Naomi's arm. "I intend to take your advice about my mother seriously. Seems as if my family hasn't been very good at communicating."

Naomi patted Cheryl's leg. "Your parents love you very much. Gott will turn this around for your good. You wait and see."

"Thank you."

"So it is final? You are no longer looking for Ellen?"

"I have no idea where to look now, and even if I found her, I have nothing to give her. It's definitely time to move on."

"But what about the theft?" Naomi asked.

"Hopefully, Chief Twitchell will find the coin. I'm sure the rest of Ellen's things are gone for good." She rubbed her forehead with her fingers. "I should have kept that coin in the safe. It really never occurred to me that someone would take it."

"We will pray Chief Twitchell finds it."

"If he does, I don't know what I'll do with it. I can't keep it."

"Gott will work it out. Do not fret."

"I've been wondering about Lydia," Cheryl said, changing the subject. "Have you heard from her?"

"Ja. She called Marion again. She says Lydia is definitely not happy in her new home. The world is overwhelming to her. This happens many times to children who go out from our communities. They do not feel safe in a world so full of confusion and noise. We are praying she will return to us."

Cheryl quietly considered what Naomi said. She felt safer in Sugarcreek too. She'd lived in the big city, and it was noisy and full of pressures she didn't feel anymore.

"You know," Naomi said suddenly, "I realize people think the Amish have removed themselves from the world. That we are not spreading the Word of Gott as those who live outside our borders do. But I do not believe this to be true. We are an example of what can happen when you take control of the priorities in your life. How you can make faith and family the most important things. It is possible to silence the confusion of the world and find peace."

Naomi rarely spoke passionately about her faith, and Cheryl was touched. "I understand," she said gently. And she did. Cheryl might not ever agree with all the tenants of the Amish faith, but she certainly saw the beauty in their lives.

"By the way," she said, "what's the deal with Maybelline and Chuck?"

"It is a sad story. When Maybelline and Chuck were younger, they were in love. In fact, they were planning to be married. But as their wedding day drew nearer, Maybelline became afraid. Afraid that life with her would be unfair to Chuck. That he would not be happy taking care of a blind woman. So she asked a friend of hers, a young man who worked in the local saddle and tack store, to pretend that they had fallen in love with each other." She shook her head. "He did as she asked, and Maybelline broke off the engagement. Chuck was heartbroken, but Maybelline was convinced she did the right thing. Eventually, the young man moved away and married someone else. Unfortunately, the damage was done."

"I don't understand. You said Chuck works on Maybelline's house."

Naomi looked sideways at Cheryl. "Ja, he helps her all he can. He still loves her, and she still loves him. To tell you the truth, recently there seems to have been a change of heart in Maybelline."

Cheryl frowned in confusion. "What kind of change?"

"As she nears the latter part of her life, I believe she has begun to regret her actions. Now she realizes she turned love away. A love that would have given them both much happiness."

"Well, I wouldn't call Chuck *happy*. I don't think I've ever seen him smile."

Naomi nodded. "I believe his broken heart has never mended."

Cheryl sighed in exasperation. "So why doesn't Maybelline tell him how she feels?"

"Would you be willing to tell someone you still love them after thirty years? How can she be sure he still has feelings for her?"

Cheryl made a snorting noise. "Uh, he spends all his extra time helping her. Isn't that kind of a clue?"

"Maybe. Maybe not."

"Why don't you talk to him?"

Naomi was quiet for a moment. "Maybelline asked me not to tell Chuck about her regret. So I cannot speak with him. As far as I know, I am the only person who knows how she feels."

"No you're not. Now I know."

Naomi didn't respond, but a small smile played on her lips. "As I said, Cheryl, Maybelline asked *me* to keep her secret from Chuck."

Cheryl stared at her. "You're just a little bit sneaky, aren't you?"

Naomi gave her a disapproving look. "Why, Cheryl Cooper. You know the Amish are not crafty people. How can you say something like that to me?" She sniffed. "Besides, I like the word *shrewd* better than *sneaky*."

Cheryl laughed. "All right. I'm sorry. You're very shrewd. And very big-hearted."

"I am sure I have no idea what you mean."

Sugar turned the corner on to Main Street, and Cheryl noticed a police car in front of the Swiss Miss.

"I wonder what that's about," she said.

"Perhaps Chief Twitchell has found Ellen's belongings." Naomi's voice was tinged with excitement, but Cheryl suddenly felt ill.

Naomi pulled up in front of the shop, and Cheryl jumped out, grabbing the reins and looping them over the hitching post. She waited for Naomi to get down, and the two women hurried up the steps to the shop. When Cheryl opened the door, she found the chief standing near the counter, talking to Esther.

"Good news, Miss Cooper," he said as she walked in. "We found your coin."

Cheryl blinked in surprise. "But I just told you about it this morning."

The chief stared at her with an amused look on his long face. "Sometimes the law moves slowly, but other times we hit it out of the park." He pulled a small notebook from his pocket. "A man sold the coin to a pawnbroker in Akron. A place called WeBuyEm Pawn and Loan."

Cheryl took a deep breath and looked at Naomi who put her arm around Cheryl. "D ... Did the pawnbroker get a name?"

"He did, but we've looked it up. It's bogus."

Cheryl felt relief flow through her body. Even though she was curious to know who broke into her store, the truth could be much worse than not knowing.

"But we got 'em," Twitchell said with a smile. He flipped through several pages of his notebook until he found what he was looking for. Cheryl watched as he removed something. "Got a picture of him. Wondered if you recognize the guy?"

The relief she'd just felt vanished as the tall, lanky law man walked toward her, the picture in his outstretched hand. He held it out to her and she took it, but she waited a few seconds before lifting it up so she could see it. When she finally gazed at the rather grainy photo, she let out the breath she didn't even realize she'd been holding. "I don't know this man," she said. "I've never seen him before." She tried to hand the photo back, but the chief waved it off.

"You keep that. Just in case he comes into the shop. I have other copies in my car. I'm gonna spread them around town. Maybe someone else will recognize him." The chief shrugged. "If he's from outta town, there ain't much I can do. But we'll keep tryin'."

"Thanks, Chief. And what about the other things? The purse and the valise? I don't suppose he brought those in as well."

Twitchell shook his head. "Nope. Sorry."

Cheryl nodded. "I'm not surprised, I guess, but it makes me sad to think of Ellen's personal belongings tossed in the trash."

"What will happen to the coin?" Naomi asked.

"For now, it's evidence. At some point we can probably release it, but I can't guarantee that. We'll need to look for the actual owner before we can give it back to Mitzi Porter."

"I hope you have better luck than I did," Cheryl said. "Thank you, Chief."

When he left, Cheryl looked at the photo again. "You don't recognize this guy, do you?"

Naomi shook her head. "I am sorry. I do not." She looked over at Esther who'd been listening to the conversation with Twitchell. "Do you recognize him, Daughter?"

Esther came over and peered carefully at the picture. "No, Maam. I do not remember seeing him in the store." She frowned. "How did this man know about the coin? If he is not a regular in our shop, he must have heard about it some other way."

"You're right, Esther," Cheryl said. "I should have thought of that. How *did* he hear about it?"

"Someone who knew must have told him," Naomi said. "Or he was in the shop when the coin was discussed."

Cheryl walked quickly to her office, put her purse inside the door, and then returned to sit on the stool behind the counter. "I can only remember a couple of times when the coin was mentioned out loud. Once was with Chuck, but the store was closed. He and I were the only ones here. The other time was when Chuck told me he'd checked on the value of the coin."

"Was anyone else in the store then? Someone who might have overheard you?"

Cheryl tried to pull up the memory of the conversation with Chuck. "I know there were a couple of people, but I can't..." She snapped her fingers. "Janie Henderson was here. She bought a coconut cake."

"She would not steal from you," Naomi said.

"No, she wouldn't." Cheryl's forehead wrinkled as she tried to recall who else was in the store. "I'm pretty sure there was someone else, but I just can't remember who it was."

"Perhaps you could look through your receipts," Esther suggested. "If they bought something, there will be a record."

"You're right. Thanks, Esther. I'll check."

"I must go," Naomi said. "I need to go to the fabric store. Esther and Elizabeth need new dresses, and Levi must have new shirts. He is beginning to fray around the edges."

Esther put her hand to her mouth and giggled. "Oh, Maam," she said, her voice quivering, "I believe you mean his shirts are fraying around the edges."

Naomi's eyes widened, and then she laughed. "You must not tell your brother what I said. He will be embarrassed."

"Why would he be embarrassed? It is just us. Cheryl is like family."

"Perhaps you are right, Daughter, but I do not think he will be happy with the way I have described him."

Cheryl, who'd laughed along with the women, said, "I don't know if we can keep this to ourselves. It would be too much fun to tease him."

"Especially for his sister," Naomi said, shaking her finger at Esther. "You and Elizabeth are skilled in torturing your brother."

Cheryl noticed Esther's grin and the glint in her eye. Sisters and brothers were the same no matter their background. She and Matt used to tease each other mercilessly when they were younger. The memory made her smile. She had every reason to hope they would have that easy kind of relationship again. Any slight doubt she'd had about Matt taking the coin was finally gone. It was as if a huge weight had been lifted from her shoulders.

After Naomi left, Cheryl and Esther spent a rather slow afternoon. A little before two o'clock, Cheryl took some time to go through the store's receipts from Thursday. Although during the busy tourist season there were many customers she didn't know, on that day every purchase was made by her regular patrons. If the man in the photo was in the store, he hadn't purchased anything. Just another dead end.

When Naomi came back at three, Cheryl didn't have time to talk to her. A charter bus had come into town and visitors filled the shop. Esther worked a little longer than usual, helping Cheryl to catch up. She and Naomi finally left a little after three thirty.

Matt called about four. Their folks were coming over to Mitzi's tonight, and Matt was in charge of picking up dinner. She'd told him to go to the Honey Bee Café for sandwiches, wraps, and broccoli cheese soup. She was relieved to find that he'd gotten to the café before it closed. Cheryl was bringing home dessert. With such a great assortment, it was hard to pick, but she finally settled on Naomi's caramel pie and a coconut cream pie made by another local baker.

It was almost five when the door of the shop burst open, and Chuck Watson rushed in. His face was red, and his eyes were wide. He shoved a photograph across the counter toward Cheryl.

"Is this really the man who stole your coin?" he sputtered.

Cheryl nodded, startled by his demeanor.

At her response, Chuck slumped against the counter. "It's my fault," he muttered. "All my fault. I'm responsible for the theft of your coin."

CHAPTER TWENTY

After some coaxing, Chuck finally calmed down. Cheryl took him to the office and made him sit down while she got him a cup of water. She'd never seen the big man so emotional. After gulping all the water in one swallow, he set the cup down and took several slow, deep breaths as if trying to regain his composure.

"What's going on, Chuck?" Cheryl asked softly.

"Sorry I got so upset," he said, rubbing his face. "I just couldn't believe it when I saw the picture. It was up on the bulletin board in Yoder's. I called the police chief to ask him why he wanted to know who this was. That's when he told me about the coin."

"So you know this man?"

"Remember when I told you I'd checked with an expert about its value?"

Cheryl nodded.

"That's him." Chuck jabbed the picture with one of his oversized fingers. "He lives in Akron. We're not friends or anything. I met him at a coin collectors' convention a couple of years ago. Since then we've just e-mailed each other about different coins."

Cheryl had been so focused on people she knew, she'd never considered the expert he'd gone to for confirmation.

"So you gave Chief Twitchell his name and how to contact him?"

Chuck's face had been crimson when he'd entered the shop. Now the color in his face drained away, leaving him a pasty white. "I...I think I hung up on him. I was so angry I forgot to give him any information."

"Maybe you should talk to him," she said gently. "I'm sure he would like to hear from you."

Chuck nodded and stood up. "I want you to know how sorry I am," he said. "If I'd thought he was capable of something like this—"

"I know that, Chuck," Cheryl said. "Please don't worry about it. Sometimes people let us down. To be honest, I'm glad it was someone I don't know. That would have been hard to take."

"I understand," he said quickly. "It's a hard thing to get over."

Cheryl took a deep breath and prayed that God would give her the right words. "Chuck, I heard a story today. It's a story about a young man and a young woman who were in love. In fact, they planned to be married."

"What are you talking about?" Chuck glared at her. "I don't know where you're going with this, but if you—"

"Let me finish, please. You can storm out of here after I'm done."

Cheryl was certain he was going to walk out, but miraculously, he stayed where he was, his expression almost menacing.

"Anyway, the young woman had a problem. A problem she was afraid might ruin the young man's life. So she lied. She told him she was in love with someone else. But she wasn't. In fact, I don't believe she ever loved anyone else her entire life. She never said anything, though, because she was still convinced she'd done the best thing for the man she loved." Cheryl's heart pounded in her chest. Was she doing the right thing? Had she stepped into something so personal that Chuck would never forgive her? Summoning all her courage, she continued. "But lately she's started to think she made a mistake. That their love was so strong, maybe being apart actually hurt this man more than being together and facing the problem she was so afraid of. In fact, I think more than anything, she wants another chance at love."

Chuck didn't say a word, but the look in his eyes made Cheryl gulp. "This is a story only one other person knows. A person who couldn't tell it to you because she was asked not to. So she told me, but I couldn't keep it to myself. I hope I've done the right thing. If I haven't, I pray you'll forgive me." She searched his face. "This story is only for you. I have no intention of ever telling it to anyone else."

Chuck put his large hand on her shoulder. "Thank you." It was the only thing he said before he turned and strode out of the shop.

As the door closed behind him, Cheryl felt a peace come over her. Interfering in another person's life was scary, but this time it felt right. Cheryl had a deep sense that life would soon be changing for Maybelline and Chuck.

"Please, God," she prayed silently. "Give Chuck and Maybelline the courage to be honest and face their feelings. If it's Your will for them to be together, I know You'll help them find a way to bridge the years they spent apart. Bless them abundantly, Lord. And thanks." Suddenly remembering supper with her folks, she glanced at her watch. It was ten minutes after five.

"Sugar and grits," she murmured. After making a quick call to tell Matt why she was running late, she locked the front door and turned the sign over. Then she quickly counted out the money and the receipts, locked them up, and grabbed her purse. She stood in front of the alarm box for several seconds, trying to get enough courage to turn it on. "Please, please help me not to set this thing off again," she whispered to God. She quickly entered the code and scooted out the door before her allotted sixty seconds.

She got all the way to the car before realizing she'd left the desserts for dinner on the counter. "Sugar and grits," she said again through clenched teeth. She hurried up the stairs to the front door, unlocked it, and was almost to the counter before the alarm started blaring. Panicked, she ran over to the box and tried to disarm it. It took her three tries before the screeching finally stopped. Cheryl grabbed her cell phone out of her purse and called the police station.

"Sugarcreek Police Station." Delores always sounded bored when she answered the phone, but she was always nice to Cheryl— even when she set off the alarm accidentally. Cheryl prayed Delores could catch the chief before he or one of his officers was sent to the shop.

"Delores," she said, "I did it again."

"I know, honey. I told the chief to wait a few minutes so you'd have a chance to call. I'll let him know everything's okay."

Cheryl breathed a sigh of relief. "Thanks."

"I guess you're going to start setting that thing again?" The tone in Delores's voice was a cross between a question and a plea.

"Yeah, I guess so. I'm sorry."

"I am too, honey."

"Delores, before you hang up…did Chuck Watson come down to the station?"

"Yep, he's in there with the chief now." She snickered into the phone. "Seems he called the chief and told him he knew who took your coin, then he hung up. I thought the chief was gonna burst an artery."

"Well, at least I'm not the only one driving him crazy today."

Delores laughed. "No, honey. You're not."

She thanked Delores and said good-bye. This time she got the desserts, set the alarm, and locked the front door without incident. By the time she got home it was almost five thirty. She parked her car, put her purse over her shoulder, and carefully picked up the pies. As she walked up the steps to the porch, Matt opened the door.

"Let me help you," he said, taking the boxes from her arms.

"Thanks." When she came into the living room, her parents were sitting on the couch. "Sorry to be late. Something came up."

"Not a problem," her father said. He got up and hugged her. "What can I do to help?"

Cheryl looked over at her mother who sat quietly on the couch, looking unhappy.

"Why don't you make sure everyone has something to drink, Daddy?" she said. "I'll start heating up the soup."

"I took the wraps and sandwiches out of the fridge so they wouldn't be cold," Matt said. "I would have heated up the soup, but I wasn't sure when you'd be here."

"Thanks, Matt." Cheryl headed to the kitchen, poured the delicious soup from the café into a bowl, and stuck it in the microwave. While her father got out glasses and filled them with ice, Matt put the food on a platter so people could pick what they wanted. The Honey Bee made awesome sandwiches and wraps. Cheryl's favorite hummus wrap was one of the choices. She grabbed some chips and put them in a large bowl. Within a few minutes, they'd assembled a delicious-looking buffet.

When her father went into the living room to see what her mother wanted to drink, Cheryl leaned in close to her brother. "Where's Beau?" she whispered. Matt and Beau had bonded and seemed to enjoy each other's company. Matt took time to play with him, something Cheryl didn't get to do as often as she'd like.

"I put him in your bedroom."

"I hope you put his litter box in there too."

Matt chuckled. "Of course, Skeeter. And I fed him. He's good. We played so much today, he's worn out. He'll probably sleep the entire time the folks are here."

Cheryl was grateful to her brother for his kindness to Beau. He was more than just a pet. He was family. She felt tears spring to her eyes.

"Oh brother," Matt said when he saw her show of emotion. "You're in love with a cat."

"I am not." She smiled and wiped away a tear. "Okay, maybe I am. He means a lot to me."

Matt reached over and patted her shoulder. "It's okay. I understand."

Her dad came back into the kitchen. "Your mother wants iced tea. How about you two?"

Cheryl opened the refrigerator and took out a large pitcher of tea. It was a special blend of black tea with orange zest, cinnamon, cloves, and cardamon. Cheryl brewed it herself. She loved the spicy flavor, especially since it was decaffeinated. She and Matt both chose a glass of the delicious tea.

While Matt and her father helped her, Cheryl's mother stayed where she was in the living room, gazing out the window. Cheryl stared down at the tray of sandwiches. It looked great, but without saying a word to her father or her brother, she scooted things around until it was a jumbled mess.

"Momma, could you help me, please?" she called out. "I'm trying to make this platter look nice, but I just can't do it. You were always so good with this kind of thing."

With a big sigh, her mother stood up and came into the kitchen. "Goodness gracious, Cheryl," she said. "What did you do? Stand back and throw the food on the plate?" She quickly cleaned up the platter until everything looked even better than it had when Cheryl arranged it.

"Wow," Cheryl said to her mother, "you really do have a way of making everything look just right."

"Your mother oversees all of our church suppers," her father said, pride evident in his voice. "She's also asked to plan almost all the weddings in the church."

"You could have been a party planner or an interior decorator," Cheryl said with a smile. "Thanks for helping. I couldn't have ever made it look this nice."

"You're welcome," Ginny said.

Although her mother didn't actually smile, Cheryl was pretty sure the corners of her mouth turned up a bit.

Cheryl got some plates and silverware and put them on the counter behind them. "Why doesn't everyone help themselves? Then take your plate to the table."

Within a few minutes, the family was sitting around the table. After her father prayed, they started to eat. Cheryl's mom complimented her on the choice of food. Cheryl was relieved to see that her mom was in a better mood. As Cheryl chewed her hummus wrap, she thought again about what Naomi had said. When her folks left, Cheryl intended to talk to Matt. Maybe they could make an effort to let their parents know they were appreciated—and needed. The solution seemed so simple. Why hadn't it occurred to her before? She remembered something Mitzi had told her once. "Sometimes we're too close to a problem to get the whole picture," she'd said. "It's like looking at a beautiful painting. You can't stand next to it, you have to step back to take in the whole thing." Maybe that was it. Cheryl and Matt were too close. It had taken someone like Naomi to give her "the whole picture."

Conversation during supper was relaxed and congenial. Once they finished, Cheryl suggested they take their desserts into the living room.

"Anyone want coffee with their dessert? I have a really good decaf."

Her mother's eyebrows went up. "I've tried all kind of decaf coffees," she said, "but I've never found one that tasted anything close to the real thing."

Cheryl smiled. "You might be surprised. Kathy Snyder at the Honey Bee told me about this coffee. It's great."

Everyone elected to try a cup, so while Matt cut the pies, she put a pot on to brew.

"How do you think it's going?" Matt whispered once their parents were in the living room.

"I think it's going great," Cheryl said. "What do you think?"

Matt was silent for a moment. "Look," he said finally. "I have no idea how much longer the folks will be in town, but I think..." He gazed into his sister's eyes. "I think we need to talk. As a family, I mean."

Matt's words sent a feeling of apprehension through her. "What do you mean? Talk about what?"

Her brother stared at her like he'd just discovered she was an alien from another planet. "About what? Are you serious? Wouldn't you like to clear the air? Try to fix...us?" He stopped cutting the caramel pie and shook his head. "I know you hate confrontation, sis, but I don't know when we'll see each other again. I don't want to let this chance pass us by. Do you?"

Cheryl was silent for a moment. She quickly shared with him what Naomi had told her. "Please, Matt. I'm afraid if we start telling Mom and Dad why we think they're wrong, they'll just take it as more rejection. I think it's the wrong move."

Matt scooped a big slice of coconut cream pie on to a dessert plate. "So what do you propose?"

Breathing a sigh of relief, Cheryl thought for a moment. "I think we should make them...more important in our lives. Let them know they're appreciated. Make sure they understand how much we respect them."

"I do appreciate them, sis. And I respect them immensely." He shook his head slowly. "I saw what you did with the sandwiches, and Mom loved that you asked for her help. But my problems with them are too deep to be solved by some sandwiches on a platter."

"Please, Matt. Follow my lead out there. If it doesn't work..."

Her brother looked dubious. "A few niceties won't solve problems that have built up over the years."

"You might be right, but first let's try it my way, okay?"

Matt sighed. "All right, Cheryl, but I think you're hiding from the problem. Just like you always have."

While Matt carried the dessert plates out to the living room, Cheryl waited for the coffee to finish brewing. Was he right? Was she trying to put a small bandage on a deep wound, hoping it would heal on its own?

Chapter Twenty-One

The next morning, Cheryl got to the shop a little later than usual. The night before had passed pleasantly. Her father had finally asked Matt about his new job, and both of her parents seemed interested in what he had to say. He also told them about Nicki. They both seemed happiest to find out Matt was back in church. Even though it had been an enjoyable evening, Cheryl felt like someone who was waiting for a storm to arrive. As if forecasters had announced it was coming, but it just hadn't hit yet. Matt's problems with their parents had been building for a long time. Maybe he was right, and there wasn't any fast fix.

A little after ten, the phone rang and Cheryl answered.

"Cheryl, this is your father. Your mother and I would like to have lunch with you and Matt today. We want to talk to you. Can you meet us at the Honey Bee? At noon?"

"Sure, Daddy. I mean, I can meet you. Have you talked to Matt?"

"No, I haven't called him yet. I wanted to check with you first."

"I can be there. I'll see you at noon."

"Good. Thank you."

Cheryl heard a click in her ear, and that was it. Her father had been oddly businesslike. Was this what she'd felt uneasy about? She wanted to call Matt and warn him, but she decided not to.

"Don't try to make something out of this that isn't there," she said to herself. "You shouldn't automatically assume something's wrong."

Just then the bell over the door jingled and the Vogel brothers came in to play checkers. Cheryl greeted them and got them coffee. The next hour was pretty busy, and she didn't have much time to think about her father's phone call.

A little before twelve, Naomi and Esther came through the front door. Cheryl noticed immediately that they both looked excited.

"What's going on?" Cheryl asked as they approached.

"Ach, Cheryl," Naomi said. "Marion Berryhill received another call from Lydia. She is coming home."

"Oh, I'm so glad to hear that."

"She decided the world outside is not for her," Esther said with a smile. "She wants to join the church—like me."

"So you'll both join the Amish church?"

Naomi and Esther nodded simultaneously. They reminded Cheryl of two bobblehead Amish dolls. She couldn't help but smile at them.

"It is not because she is afraid to live in the world," Naomi said. "It is because she believes life here is what Gott wants for her. It is what we have hoped for."

Cheryl gave her friend a hug. Christian parents were the same everywhere. They wanted their children to follow God, be safe, be happy, and find fulfillment. Even though she still had problems with rumspringa, at least now she could see the reason for it. In Lydia's case it had worked. Lydia was coming home because she wanted to. And she'd decided to be Amish. "When will she arrive?" she asked.

"She will get to Canton on Wednesday. Her parents will pick her up at the bus station."

"Marion said she mentioned you when she called," Esther said with a shy smile on her face.

"She mentioned me?"

Naomi nodded. "I believe she would like to come back to work. If you will have her."

"Of course she can come back," Cheryl said. "Truth be told, I hate doing inventory, and Lydia's great at it. Besides, I miss her."

"I do too," Esther said, blinking away tears.

Cheryl reached over and grabbed Esther's hands. "Why don't we plan a little welcome-back party for her?"

"She would like that. Thank you, Cheryl."

Cheryl let go of Esther's hands and glanced up at the clock on the wall. "I've got to get going. I'm meeting my folks across the street."

"Go," Esther said, grabbing her apron from behind the counter. "I am ready to work."

"And I will see you later," Naomi said with a smile. "I want to visit Lydia's parents. We have something to celebrate."

"Please tell them how happy I am for them, will you?" Cheryl said.

"I will be glad to do so."

Naomi hurried out of the shop and got into her buggy while Cheryl got her purse and gave Esther a few quick instructions. Then she stepped outside on the porch. The morning seemed to be turning colder, and she wished she'd grabbed her jacket. As she crossed the street and approached the restaurant, she noticed her parents sitting at one of the tables on the porch. Matt was already with them.

"Sorry to keep you waiting," she said once she neared them. "We should get inside. It fills up fast at lunchtime."

"We'd rather sit out here," her mother said. "We won't be staying for lunch." She pointed to an empty chair and pushed a Styrofoam cup toward Cheryl.

Confused and chilly, Cheryl sat down slowly. "I don't understand."

"I think we're about to," Matt said in a low voice, shooting a look at his sister that alarmed her.

"Your mother and I love you both very much," her father said slowly, "but we have a few things we feel we must say. This will be the only time we'll bring these topics up. For our own future as a family, it wouldn't be good to talk about them anymore after today."

"What do you mean, Daddy?" Cheryl felt a twinge of frustration. Last night had been fun and relaxed. Today she felt she was being ambushed.

He didn't answer her, just looked at Cheryl's mother.

"Your father and I raised you both to be responsible people," she said, her Southern accent more pronounced than usual. "To make good decisions. Of course we hoped you'd be interested in ministry, but we realize not everyone is called to it. We decided that whatever you wanted to do was fine—as long as it was stable and had a future. You're both very bright, and we expected great things from you."

Her dad cleared his throat. "When you went to college, Cheryl, and majored in business, we were satisfied with your choice. You got good grades and showed wonderful potential. Then you started working at the bank, and you got engaged. We felt your life was on track."

"And now you're here." The distaste in her mother's voice was clear. "You broke your engagement, and you're running an insignificant shop in Sugarcreek. There's no future in it. Even if your aunt decides to stay overseas and this temporary situation becomes permanent, you'll never do more than what you're doing right now. You've made friends with...Amish people, and that's fine. As long as you don't throw away everything we've taught you—or become involved in a religion that could lead you away from the grace of God. We're also very concerned about your relationship with the Millers and feel you probably shouldn't be so close to them."

Cheryl could only stare at her mother in amazement. She wanted to respond, but it was as if she'd been struck dumb. Her brain searched for words to counter her mother's opinions, but she couldn't seem to find them.

"I think you're wrong, Mom," Matt said. "You—"

"Be quiet, Matt," Cheryl's father said. "Let us finish, please. Give us enough respect to allow us to say what we feel needs to be said." He looked at Cheryl. "I don't necessarily agree with your mother about your situation, honey. I understand why you like it here. Even though I chose to leave, it's a charming place. And I think you're doing a wonderful job with your aunt's shop. But I must admit I'm concerned too. What if Mitzi comes back? What will you do then? Just work for her? Is that really all you want to do with your life?"

"No, I guess not," Cheryl said slowly. "I haven't really thought that far ahead."

"No, you haven't," her mother snapped. "And that's the problem. You're not thinking. Instead you're wasting time in this place, throwing your life away."

"That's unfair," Matt said, his voice a little stronger this time.

"Unfair?" his mother interjected angrily. "I'll tell you what's unfair. A son who rejects his parents and takes off without telling them where he is. Who only contacts them when he wants money. Do you know how many nights I lay in bed wondering if you were okay? If you were even alive? *That's* unfair."

"I realize that, Mom, and I'm sorry. I really am. That's one reason I came here. I wanted to let you know I was doing better. And try to fix things—"

"Fix things?" Cheryl's father's words were spoken like bullets fired from a gun. "You think showing up and peddling a story about some silly business you've supposedly started—"

"It's not silly—"

"Oh, Matt, please." His father shook his head. "I'm sorry, son, but you don't know how to run a business. And you supposedly intend to spend your life like some kind of TV detective? I'm sure you think it's exciting, but we hoped someday you'd grow up and get a real job. I guess it was too much to ask for."

Cheryl's mother stared at her son. "And now you have a fiancée? Someone we've never met? That's just like you, Matthew. Cutting us out again. As if we didn't spend the best years of our lives raising you to be a responsible person."

Matt looked as if he'd been slapped, and something rose up inside of Cheryl. "All right, that's enough." She turned to her mother. "You know what? Naomi and I were just talking about a young Amish girl who left town because she thought she might want something different than the life her parents had chosen for her. You think rumspringa is silly, and maybe in some ways it's not a good idea. I don't really know anymore. But I will tell you that Naomi sees it as an opportunity for young people to choose who they want to be. To find their place in the world. Of course, their parents hope it will be with them. That they will choose the Amish church. But they don't want their children to join the church because they're afraid. They want them to listen to God and find their own calling." She turned her attention to her father. "And that is exactly what I've done. I left the bank because I was miserable there. I appreciated the job, but it didn't make me happy. Now I'm happy." She turned to look at her mother. "And I don't think the shop is insignificant. I think it's awesome." She took a deep breath.

"By the way, I didn't break my engagement. Lance did. Yes, he tried to get me back, but by the time he showed up, I realized I didn't want to marry a selfish, self-involved man. I wanted someone special. Someone like..." She realized with a start that she'd started to say Levi's name. She shook her head. "And let's talk about grace, okay? By watching the Millers, I've learned more about grace than I ever learned all the years I sat in church."

"Are you finished, Cheryl?" her mother said softly.

"As a matter of fact, I'm not," she said. "Matt left home because he was afraid he couldn't live up to what you both wanted. Being a preacher's kid is more pressure than you can imagine. Everyone watches you. Some people wait for you to mess up. The fear of letting you down was so overwhelming to him he decided being alone was better." Cheryl swiped away the tears that ran down her face. "I think what he's accomplished is incredible. He came here hoping he might finally make you proud, but you're not giving him a chance. All you see are his past failures." She turned to her brother and gazed into his eyes. "Well, I'm proud of you, Matt. Incredibly proud. And I'm also proud to call you my brother."

She stood up. She wasn't sure if it was the sharp wind that made her shiver or if it was the way she'd just addressed her parents. "I love you both, and I'm sorry if I ever made you feel as if I didn't need you. I do, and so does Matt. You taught us so much. You planted God in our lives. You taught us to be honest. To work hard. To reach out to people who need help. To be generous." She shook her head. "If I stood here all day, I couldn't thank you for all the wonderful things you gave us. If not for the both of you, Matt and I might be completely lost. Different people. People without hope. Without faith." She wiped her cheeks again, aware for the first time that people going into the café could hear her, but she couldn't care about that now. "Thank you, Daddy. And thank you, Momma. I hope you'll listen to what I've said and consider it. And I hope you'll stay a couple more days instead of leaving after . . . this. But I have to get back to my life. The wonderful life God's given me. I'm so blessed to be in Sugarcreek, and I'm blessed to have a best friend who happens to be Amish. I'm also blessed to be considered part of a family that loves each other so much. That believes in each other. Someday when I do get married, I want to have a family that combines the wonderful attributes I see in the Millers with all the wonderful things you've taught me. If I can do that, I'll have accomplished something incredible. Just like you have."

Cheryl turned and hurried down the stairs. Then she strode quickly across the street and into the Swiss Miss. Esther was talking to a customer and stared at her with concern as she headed to her office. Once inside, she closed the door and slumped down in the chair behind her desk. She reached into a desk drawer and pulled out a tissue, wiping her face and trying to calm herself. She'd never talked to her parents like that before. Cheryl loved her mother and father, but she had to stop trying to please them. All she could do was pray they'd find a way to accept her decisions, even if they didn't agree with them. She was more certain that she belonged in Sugarcreek—at least for now—than she'd ever been sure of anything else in her life.

She heard a knock on the door, and it opened slowly. Esther poked her head inside the office. "Are you all right? Can I help you?"

Cheryl shook her head. "Just family drama, Esther. Nothing you can do."

Esther slipped past the door and stood in front of Cheryl's desk. "All families have…*drama*, Cheryl. When Sarah left…" Esther shook her head and looked down at the floor. "I hope you do not mind me saying this, but I have found that families cannot exist without forgiveness."

"Sometimes it's hard to forgive," Cheryl said, her voice shaking. "Especially when the people who are supposed to love you are the ones who hurt you."

Esther raised her face and gazed intently at Cheryl. "But when it is easy to forgive, what does that mean? I know I am young and have much to learn, but I have discovered that real forgiveness happens when you do not have the strength to do it. When you must ask Gott to help you. He is the one who knows all about forgiveness. He forgave all of us when it made no sense, ain't so?"

Cheryl wiped her face once more and smiled at the young Amish girl. "It *is* so, Esther. It is certainly so. Thank you."

Esther nodded and left the room, slowly closing the door behind her.

Cheryl put her face in her hands and began to pray.

Chapter Twenty-Two

After spending some time talking to God, Cheryl got out the receipts and tried to work. Although she made every attempt to concentrate, her words to her parents kept ringing in her ear. Finally she pushed the receipts away and bowed her head once again. "God, if I was disrespectful, I'm sorry. Please forgive me. I love my parents, and I don't want to lose them. If I need to apologize, I will. Help me to forgive them. I know they think they're right. That they're trying to help us."

For the first time since she'd left the Honey Bee, she began to feel some peace. Before she had a chance to pray any more, a knock came at the door.

"Come in," she said.

Esther opened the door and put a small bag on her desk. "I was concerned that you did not have time to eat lunch," she said. "I went across the street and got you a sandwich."

As if on cue, Cheryl's stomach growled. "Thank you. Your assumption was correct. I'm starving." She reached for her purse so she could reimburse Esther.

"No, Cheryl. This is a gift. Please."

Once again Cheryl felt tears in her eyes, but she blinked them away. There had been enough tears for one day.

"Thank you, Esther. I truly appreciate it."

The door opened again, and Matt came in. He was holding a bag that looked similar to Esther's. He grinned when he saw the other sack.

"I guess bringing you lunch is a popular choice today."

Cheryl laughed. "Well, I am pretty hungry."

Esther smiled at both of them. "I will go back to work now. Please eat something."

"Thank you again, Esther," Cheryl said.

"You are quite welcome." With that she left, closing the door behind her.

Matt sat down in one of the chairs in front of the desk and opened the bag. Inside were two hummus wraps and some cookies. Cheryl recognized the Honey Bee's oatmeal walnut chocolate chip cookies. "I'll put my wrap in the fridge and eat it later," she told her brother. "Esther's sandwich is hot."

"I can certainly eat some of these cookies if you have too much food," Matt said.

"Gee, thanks, but I don't think that will be necessary." She opened the Styrofoam container that held the sandwich Esther had given her. It was a turkey bacon avocado melt.

"Wow, that looks good," Matt said. "If you need any help—"

"Forget it, brother," Cheryl said. "Blood may be thicker than water, but when it comes to food from the Honey Bee, all bets are off."

Matt laughed and took a bite of his wrap. "I suppose you'd like to know what happened after you stormed off?"

Cheryl shook her head. "I don't think I do. Maybe it would be best if we don't talk about it."

"I think you're wrong, Cheryl." Matt put his wrap down. "I've been your brother for a long time. Well, all my life, but I've never seen you talk to our folks like that."

"I know. I'm so ashamed. I try so hard to control my temper. I've been doing pretty good...until now that is."

"Skeeter, that wasn't temper. That was...well, it was the truth. Being emotional about something doesn't mean what you're saying is wrong. Remember that Jesus wasn't always mild-mannered."

Cheryl snorted. "Our pastor parents are hardly similar to the money changers in the temple."

"I'm not talking about that." He frowned. "He forgave the woman caught in adultery. But He also told her not to sin again. He showed His love, Cheryl. But He also told her the truth. What you said today was...true."

"I don't know. Maybe." Cheryl sighed. "I love them, Matt. They really are great parents. I wanted them to know that. We're blessed to have them. But they need to forgive you, Matt. And they need to let both of us learn to follow God's voice. Isn't that more important than doing everything your parents want?"

Matt took a bite of his wrap, chewed it up, and swallowed it. "Yes, of course it is, Cheryl. Mom and Dad know that."

"That's not what it sounded like to me."

Matt took another bite and watched his sister as he chewed.

Cheryl put her sandwich down and shook her finger at him. "Okay, tell me what happened after I left. Was it awful?"

Matt smiled and shook his head. "You spoke your piece, so I spoke mine. Basically, I said the same thing you did. Except I told them how much money my *silly* business brings in. Then I gave them a check I've been carrying around with me since I got here. Enough to pay them back for everything they loaned me—with interest. I also told them how incredible I think you are."

Cheryl gave him a small smile. "Thanks for that, but I'm pretty sure Mom doesn't agree. I suppose we won't hear from them for a while."

Matt shrugged. "Not until tonight when they come over for dinner."

"Wh...what?"

Matt laughed as he looked at his sister. "Don't look so shocked. I have no idea what they plan to say. It might be more of the same. I hope not. But if it is, we'll deal with it. Together."

Cheryl didn't say anything, just quietly ate her sandwich. One confrontation with her parents was enough. Why in the world did they want to come over tonight? What possible good would it do?

"I can't believe you told them it was okay," Cheryl said. "Haven't we been through enough?"

Matt seemed to study her for a moment. "No, we haven't been through enough because our family is still fractured. God wants to heal it, and we need to hang in there until He does what He wants to do."

Cheryl sighed deeply. "It was much easier to win arguments with you when you weren't so...spiritual."

Matt's hearty laugh made her feel better. They were just finishing their lunch when another knock came at the door. It was Esther.

"I am sorry to bother you again," she said, "but Chief Twitchell is here and wants to see you."

Cheryl gathered together the boxes and napkins from their lunch and put them in the trash. "I'll be right there, Esther." She nodded at Matt. "Can you hang around for a while?"

"As long as the chief isn't here to arrest me."

Cheryl grinned. "Unless there's something you're not telling me, I think you're safe."

She went into the shop and found Chief Twitchell talking to Janie Henderson who'd come to pick up her monthly order of apple butter and strawberry jam.

Janie greeted Cheryl. "So were you surprised to get Ranger as a birthday gift?" she asked.

"Surprised and thrilled," Cheryl answered. "He's a beautiful horse. I plan to go over to the Millers' this week and ride him."

"Levi was so excited to give him to you. He obviously cares for you a great deal."

Cheryl smiled. "We're very good friends. It was a wonderful thing to do."

"If you need any help with him, let me know, okay? I'd be happy to do whatever I can."

"Thanks, Janie. I really appreciate that."

Janie said good-bye to the chief and took her selections to the cash register.

Cheryl turned her attention to Twitchell.

"I wanted you to know that the guy who stole your coin, Barry Atchison, has been charged with theft. The police in Akron will hold the coin in evidence for a while, but you should get it back soon. Atchison pleaded guilty, so after he's sentenced, the coin will be returned."

"I thought you said that you'd try to find the real owner, Ellen Streeter," Cheryl said. "I have no idea where she is or how to find her."

He shrugged. "Sorry, not my jurisdiction. Akron doesn't care. As far as they're concerned, it was stolen from you, and it'll come back to you. You'll have to figure out what happens after that."

"Okay." Although Cheryl still didn't know what to do with the coin, at least she'd know where it was in case Ellen showed up someday.

The chief turned and headed toward the front door, but all of a sudden he stopped, snapped his fingers, and came back over to the counter. "I almost forgot to tell you," he said. "Not sure it means much, but Atchison said he took the coin out of the purse Friday night. He says he didn't take the purse or the other bag. Left 'em in your drawer."

"I don't understand," Cheryl said, frowning. "Everything was gone. That can't be right."

He shrugged. "Don't know what to say. Can't see why the guy would lie. The coin seems to be the only thing worth much."

"It was."

"Unless he's not tellin' the truth, it sounds to me like you had two robberies. Atchison was first, and then someone else came in later and took the rest of it."

"But why?"

"I have no idea." The chief took a notepad out of his pocket, flipped through it, and then tore a sheet out. "Here's all the stuff you mentioned that was in those bags. If you decide there might be some other valuable item you forgot about, let me know. Maybe Atchison is holdin' on to it and thinks we won't suspect him if he says he only snatched the coin. If you come up with something else, give me a call."

Cheryl nodded absentmindedly. "Sure. Okay."

"Well, that's odd," Matt said. He stood in the office doorway and had obviously heard her conversation with the chief.

"I know. It doesn't make any sense."

"Well, I'm going to leave it to you to figure out. I've got to pack. And I'm going to pick up some snacks for tonight."

"You're leaving town?"

Matt laughed lightly. "Did you think I was going to stay in Sugarcreek forever? I've got to get back. My business doesn't run by itself."

"I know," Cheryl said. "But I don't want you to go. I'm really going to miss you."

Matt put his arm around his sister. "I'll be back to visit whenever I can. And you can come to Kansas City to see me. I'll treat you to the world's best barbecue."

Even though she felt sad, Cheryl smiled. "That sounds great."

Matt kissed her on the top of the head. "I'm not leaving until tomorrow. I'll be by your side for whatever happens tonight, Skeeter. Okay?"

Cheryl wrapped her arms around him. "Okay. I love you, Matt."

"And I love you too."

She watched him leave, grateful to have her brother back in her life. Hopefully they could find a way to bring restoration to their entire family.

A few moments later, Naomi came through the door. "I was across the street when I saw Chief Twitchell drive away. Is everything all right?"

Several customers came in the door at the same time, so Cheryl motioned for Naomi to go into the office. After Esther and Cheryl had taken care of the people in the shop, Cheryl joined Naomi. She quickly shared the chief's information.

"That certainly is strange," Naomi said, a puzzled look on her face. "Do you believe the thief lied? Why would he do that?"

"I don't know," Cheryl said with a sigh. "He's dishonest. Maybe he's covering up something else. I can't worry about it now. At least the coin has been found."

Naomi nodded, but Cheryl noticed the apprehension in her expression.

"Is something wrong, Naomi?"

At first Naomi didn't respond, she just sat down in one of the chairs in front of Cheryl's desk. "We are friends, and I do not wish to keep secrets from you."

"Secrets? I don't understand."

"I saw your mother a little while ago, and she asked to speak to me."

Cheryl sat down in the chair next to Naomi. "What? Why?"

"I do not believe I can share the details with you. She asked me not to. But I will tell you that she is concerned."

Cheryl grunted. "She's so concerned that she and my father sat Matt and me down earlier today just to make sure we realized how disappointed they are in us."

Naomi frowned at her. "And what did you say?"

Cheryl bit her lip. Would Naomi be horrified by what she'd said to her mother? She couldn't imagine Levi or Esther talking to their parents the way Cheryl had. "She said the shop was insignificant, Naomi. And my folks said Matt's new business was silly." She sighed. "Let's just say that I disagreed. I didn't mean to be disrespectful. At the time I felt some things needed to be said. In retrospect, I may have gone overboard."

Naomi nodded. "When Sarah decided to leave home, we had the same kind of conversation. We all said the things we felt 'needed to be said.' Just like you."

"Are you telling me I was wrong?"

"No." Naomi's eyes sought hers. "Nor do I believe our conversation with Sarah was wrong. We needed to speak the truth to each other." Naomi reached for Cheryl's hand. "Our mistake was that we allowed those words to be the last ones we spoke for quite some time. It is not wrong to be honest about our feelings, but once we have brought out our dirty laundry, it needs to be washed, dried, and neatly folded."

Cheryl frowned at her. "I'm sorry. I don't understand."

Naomi smiled and squeezed Cheryl's hand. "Airing our feelings is a means to an end. But unless it brings us to a place of peace, it is not finished. You and your parents are not finished."

"Is that why they want to meet with us tonight? Is that your doing?"

"I would not say that. Frankly, after your mother shared her heart, my words to her were similar to what I am telling you. I believe you all must finish your laundry until it is clean, bright, and neatly folded."

Cheryl couldn't help but laugh. "That just might be the first time anyone compared dealing with family issues to doing a load of laundry."

Naomi chuckled. "I do not know if that is true, but I do know that our discussion with Sarah ended before our conflict was resolved. Please do not do that with your family, Cheryl. You will regret it."

"Okay. I'll meet with them tonight and try to finish our laundry." Cheryl gave Naomi a hug. "You're the best friend I've ever had."

"And you are mine as well." Naomi got up from her chair and opened the door to the office. "I will be praying for you. I love you, Cheryl." She closed the door behind her.

Cheryl finished the receipts and went out into the shop. At three o'clock, Levi pulled up outside in one of the Millers' buggies and Esther left with him.

Cheryl spent the next two hours thinking about what Naomi had said and trying to figure out what she should say to her parents. She couldn't tell them what she said was wrong because she didn't believe it was. But somehow she needed to bring their discussion full circle. Use it to bring healing and restoration. Naomi was right. They weren't done. They'd aired their dirty laundry; now they needed to clean it.

"I may never see laundry the same way again," she whispered as she straightened up the shelves.

It was amazing how customers could riffle through items and then just walk away, leaving them in disarray. She was refolding a stack of embroidered dish towels when a thought struck her. She stared at the towels with her mouth open. The truth had been there all along. How could she have missed it?

Suddenly, she knew exactly what had happened to Ellen Streeter.

Chapter Twenty-Three

I understand what happened," Cheryl said. "But you need to tell me why. I can guess, but I'm not sure I have it right."

"If only Bill hadn't put those bags in the laundry chute."

The man who sat across from Cheryl looked almost sick with worry. His wife perched on the edge of their living room sofa across from them.

"First of all, I have no intention of telling anyone about Ellen," Cheryl said. "I think you should have told the truth though. You had nothing to hide. You didn't do anything wrong."

Amos Streeter's hands grasped the arm of his chair so tightly his knuckles were white. "No, but I couldn't trust anyone else to believe that. Bill spread lies all around town. Said Ellen was crazy. That he kept her inside to protect her. Of course, he was just protecting himself. Telling people she was a danger to herself so they wouldn't question their odd relationship. Then when he fell down the stairs, I was afraid they'd think she'd done it, and they'd lock her up. So I came up with a solution."

"The night Bill died, you came to the house, found out he was dead, and then you helped Ellen get away."

He nodded. "I took her to a friend in Akron until I could make other arrangements."

"Was Ellen there the night Bill died?"

He nodded slowly. "Bill knew she was trying to leave. He found her purse and the small suitcase she'd packed and hidden in the back of her closet. He was supposed to be removing the old laundry chute, so I guess he stuck her things inside the chute and walled it up so she couldn't find them. Ellen never suspected. She thought he was either hiding them or had thrown everything out.

"We had to wait a few days until he finally left the house. He said he'd be gone a couple of hours. Ellen called me, and I told her I'd pick her up and take her to the station in Canton. I don't know if Bill sensed something, but he came back early and found Ellen downstairs getting some things out of the dryer. She had another suitcase on the kitchen table. It was evident she was packing. Bill became furious. He confronted her on the stairs. He told her he'd read a letter he'd found in her purse." Amos sighed. "Ellen had forgotten the letter she'd written to me was still in her wallet. She'd never sent it because she decided she couldn't leave without telling me. Once she admitted that she planned to run away, we started planning her escape.

"Anyway, Bill accused her of having an affair and trying to run off to be with another man. He had no idea it was me. He charged down the stairs, threatening to kill her. That's when he tripped. Ellen tried to help him, but he died instantly. I arrived a few minutes after the accident. I was afraid the police would think Ellen had something to do with his death since Bill had told everyone she was mentally unbalanced. Concerned that the authorities might check the buses leaving Canton, I took her to a friend's house in Akron. By the time I'd driven back to Sugarcreek,

I came up with a new plan. Since almost no one ever saw Ellen, I decided to tell the police that she'd left a week earlier. That way she wouldn't become a suspect. And it worked. Bill's fall was ruled accidental, which it was. After taking care of the funeral, I sold my house and Bill's, and then I left Sugarcreek."

"So you were the man she loved. That hadn't occurred to me."

Amos grimaced. "I know what it sounds like. I betrayed my brother and tried to steal his wife, but it wasn't like that at all. Bill and I were family, but we were two different peas from the same pod. He was a mean human being. Had been mean ever since he was a boy. I can't explain it, and I never understood it. I did everything I could to help him, but Bill didn't want help. He liked hurting people. I think there was something wrong with him. In his mind, I mean. I would have done anything for him, but when people don't want to change, it leaves you powerless. All I could do was protect Ellen. Yes, after a while, we fell in love." He pointed a finger at Cheryl. "But we never cheated on Bill. Never. Neither one of us would ever do that."

"You would have stayed away from Sugarcreek the rest of your life, but then your sister moved here." Cheryl said it matter-of-factly. All the pieces of the puzzle were coming together. It was like Naomi said. She could step back now and see the entire picture.

"That's right. As I said before, Dorothy needs me. I'm the only family she has left. I had to come back."

Cheryl nodded. "But why did you take the purse and the valise from my office? All you had to do was tell me you knew where Ellen was. I would have given them to you."

"I panicked when you told me you found them. All I could think to do was tell you she was alive but that I had no idea where she was. I hoped you'd leave it alone. But I guess that backfired."

"Yes, it did. The way you acted only made me more suspicious."

Amos picked at a loose thread on the arm of the chair. "I decided I had to get her purse and valise back. If you didn't have anything of hers, I hoped you'd quit poking around. There'd be nothing more you could do."

"But I couldn't ignore the theft of the coin. I felt I owed it to Ellen to recover it if I could. That made it impossible for me to walk away."

Amos managed a small smile. "Impossible for you, I suspect. Not for everyone."

"You're probably right about that. So you slipped into the Swiss Miss the night Chuck was working?"

He nodded. "It was easy. The front door was open, and Chuck was on the other side of the room. He was behind a thick plastic tarp and never heard me. The door to your office was unlocked. I started looking around and found Ellen's stuff in one of your desk drawers. I grabbed them and got out of there." A deep frown caused his forehead to crease. "You really should lock things up when you're not there."

Cheryl found his comment rather ironic, but decided not to say something snarky, even though she wanted to. It was certainly true that she'd made things incredibly easy for Amos and for Mr. Atchison. That would have to change.

"So how did you figure it out?" Amos's wife asked.

Cheryl turned her head to look at the attractive older woman sitting on the couch. "Well, first of all, something Amos said kept bothering me, although I didn't know why until I put everything else together. He said he didn't know Ellen, yet he knew how important the coin was to her. What it meant. Then Maybelline told me that the only person who knew about the coin was her mother. If Ellen only told people she was close to about that coin, then didn't that mean she was close to Amos? Also, I was really bothered by the theft of the purse and valise. The coin was already gone. Was it possible that whoever took them wasn't after the coin? I mean, wouldn't they have checked to make sure it was there? If it was gone, wouldn't they have abandoned their quest and left the bags behind? And what about the money I'd left in the drawer? If the thief was after something of value, why didn't he take it? I mean, I knew it was only a possibility—that the purse and the valise were the second thief's intended targets—but it was enough to point me in the right direction. And if it wasn't about the coin, then it had to be personal. Someone who had a stake in Ellen's disappearance. I couldn't figure out who that might be until I was straightening a stack of embroidered dish towels in the store. Then I remembered the handkerchief in Ellen's purse. It was just like the one Maybelline had." Cheryl pointed at one of the pillows on the couch. "Just like these pillows. Obviously, you really love lilacs, Ellen."

Ellen Streeter smiled. "My mother grew them. When I think of them, I remember her. She was a wonderful woman. She died when I was nineteen. If she'd lived, she never would have allowed me to marry Bill. She would have seen him for who he was. I was young and ignorant, and I missed all the warning signs."

"We planted lilacs at our house in Kansas," Amos said. "We'll plant them here too." He got up and went over to sit near his wife on the couch. Then he took her hand and kissed her cheek. "I'm sorry for everything she went through with Bill," he said to Cheryl. "But if she hadn't met him, she wouldn't have met me. We've been happy together for forty years. I hope finding out the truth won't change anything."

"I have nothing to say about that," Cheryl said. "I think you should meet with Chief Twitchell and tell him the truth about Ellen. That she was there when Bill fell. I really don't think he'll reopen a forty-year-old case that was ruled an accident. I'll leave that up to you."

"I'm sorry I took those things from your shop," Amos said. "I hope you'll forgive me."

"I already have."

"We went through a lot back then," Amos said softly, "trying to find a way to be together without hurting my brother. I had to act as if I didn't like Ellen. I treated her badly in public so no one, including Bill, would suspect we were in love." He raised her hand to his lips and lightly kissed her fingers. "It hurt me to say bad things about her. I've spent many years making it up to her."

"You did that long ago," Ellen said with tears in her eyes.

"I do have a question," Cheryl said, "although I think I know the answer. Maybelline Finn's mother. Did she know what was going on?"

Ellen nodded. "Yes. She was the only person I could talk to. She knew I hadn't left a week before Bill's fall. I talked to her a day or two before it happened. The night of the accident, she saw Amos drive me away, but she never said a word. I'll always appreciate what she did for me."

"I think Maybelline would love to hear your story—if you want to share it with her. She's a wonderful woman. You'd like each other."

Ellen smiled. "She was just a child when I knew her, but she was so sweet. I'd enjoy seeing her again."

Cheryl stood up. "I'm running late for an important meeting." She turned toward the door but then remembered something. "When the coin is returned, I'll bring it to you."

"Thank you," Ellen said. "I don't care how much it's worth, but it has a lot of sentimental value. I'd be happy to have it back."

"Sure," Cheryl said. "I'm glad you two found a way to be together, but I'm sorry about the loss of your brother, Amos."

Amos looked away. "I am too," he said sadly. "The truth is, I lost him years before his accident. I wish I could have found a way to reach him. Family is so important. Bill dying before we could find a way to repair our relationship is something I'll regret the rest of my life. I wouldn't wish that on anyone."

Cheryl paused with her hand on the doorknob. "You're right," she said. "I wouldn't either."

By the time she got to the house, her parents' car was already there. Cheryl steeled herself for what was ahead. When she opened the door, she expected to find her stony-faced family sitting in silence, waiting for her. But instead, the sound of laughter met her. No one was in the living room, so she headed to the kitchen. Sure enough, her parents and Matt were gathered around the table. All of them were bent over. Cheryl got closer, trying to see what they were doing. Matt had one of Beau's toys, a long plastic stick with feathers on the end. Beau was chasing it with gusto, trying to grab the feathers before Matt quickly pulled it away. To Cheryl's amazement, her mother was giggling over the cat's antics like a schoolgirl.

"What's going on here?" Cheryl asked.

"Hi, honey," her dad said. "We're just playing with Beau. Why did you keep him locked up the other night?"

A vision of a cartoon character whose jaw dropped to the floor in surprise flashed in Cheryl's mind. "Okay..."

Matt straightened up in his chair. "Sorry, Skeeter. Beau just loves this silly feather thing. I could play with him all day."

Cheryl had an urge to go outside and come back in. Maybe this was an alternate universe where the family all liked each other.

"Come sit down, dear," her mother said. "You look tired."

"I'm so sorry to be this late. Something happened, and I couldn't get away any sooner."

"We called this meeting at the last minute," her mother said. "We're just glad you're here."

Cheryl sat down slowly at the table and looked at her brother with arched eyebrows. What in the world was going on?

"We've been talking," Matt said. "I think we were able to address some of our problems."

"Well, they may not be completely solved," her father said, "but at least we seem to understand each other a little more."

"The things you said at the Honey Bee made me think," Cheryl's mother said. "You were right about so many things. And then I got a chance to talk to Naomi. She's a very wise woman. She made me realize that I have to trust you. Dad and I raised you the best we could, and now we need to allow you to make your own decisions even though it's hard to let go." She reached over and took Cheryl's hand. "When you were a little girl, you talked all the time about growing up and getting married. Being a mommy. It was so important to you. When you moved to Sugarcreek, I assumed it was just until Mitzi returned. But then we'd talk on the phone, and I heard something in your voice. Something that didn't sound temporary at all. And it scared me. For that little girl. And for you. Sugarcreek is so small; there aren't that many eligible men here, and of the men who are single, a lot of those are Amish." She shook her head. "I started to feel like your choices would lead you down a road where your dreams would be dashed. You're thirty-one and your only serious relationship ended with a broken engagement."

"I know that, Momma. I was there. Did you think it didn't hurt me? Didn't affect me?"

"I realize it did, Cheryl. And I worried you'd be afraid to get involved again. It's as if the mother in me suddenly became protective of that little girl who dreamed of her own family. I should have prayed for you. Instead I let my fear turn into anger—at you. It was wrong, and it was stupid. If Sugarcreek is where you're supposed to be, why would I get upset? God will take care of you. He's the one who's in charge of fulfilling the desires of our hearts. Not me." She looked into Cheryl's eyes, her own eyes full of unshed tears. "Can you ever forgive me?"

Cheryl couldn't hold back the sob that escaped her throat. "Of course I can. I just don't want you to be disappointed in me."

"Oh, honey, I'm not. Your father and I are so proud of you. You're a fine young woman with wonderful friends who love you. And you were brave enough to change your life from one that wasn't working to one that is. We're glad you're happy here."

Cheryl cleared her throat and tried to rein in her emotions. "Naomi told me that somehow you might think I don't need you anymore. That's not true. So many times when I'm not sure what to do, I'll wonder what you'd do in the same situation, and I'll follow the example you've set for me. You're part of who I am, and you always will be. I'm sorry if I made you feel like I don't need you."

"Thank you, Cheryl. I have felt a little left out. I know you love your aunt. I do too. But I guess I want to be the one you turn to first. The one you're closer to."

Cheryl picked up a napkin and wiped her face. "I love you and Daddy more than anyone else in the world. And I always will."

"Good. I promise to support you and Matt more, okay?"

"I apologized to Matt," her father said, his voice low and strained. "I made his life too hard when he was growing up. I didn't want him to embarrass me. I should have been thinking much more about him—and less about my reputation." He sighed.

"Look, Snicklefritz, we've all made mistakes. Let's forgive each other and give it another try. Are you willing?"

Cheryl smiled. "I would love that, Daddy."

"I found out who Maddy was," Matt said. He looked over at his mother. "Will you tell her?"

She nodded and let out a long, shuddering sigh. "I never wanted you two to know about Maddy. Maybe I was wrong. It seems my desire to protect you didn't work. Instead, it caused Matt to feel as if I didn't want him. And that is absolutely not true."

As Cheryl steeled herself for whatever was ahead, she was greatly moved by the pain she saw in her mother's eyes.

"I had a miscarriage, honey," she said slowly. "Before you were born. I put those baby things away because I couldn't stand to get rid of them. Even though Maddy didn't get to live with us, she's still part of our family. A sister you both will meet someday. I wasn't hoping Matthew would be a girl at all. In fact, we really wanted a boy because we already had a wonderful little girl."

"When I found that box, I believed the worst," Matt said.

His mother reached over and hugged him. "You were always wanted, Matt. Always. We love you."

"I'm sorry you went through that, Momma," Cheryl said. She was still reeling under the knowledge that she had a sister.

"I am too, but it was a long time ago, and God has brought me healing. Although it still hurts, He's given me the strength I need to get through every day. And He gave me you and Matthew. I'm very grateful."

Cheryl reached for her mother's hand. "Can we start talking on Sunday afternoons again? I miss that so much."

"Absolutely. Who knows, I might get wild and even call you during the week sometime."

"Now, Ginny. Let's not get crazy," Cheryl's father said, a wry grin on his face.

"Funny, Dad," Matt said.

Cheryl's mother looked around the table. "We have a long way to go, but I know we can recover from our mistakes."

Cheryl smiled. "A very wise woman once told me that after salvation, family is God's greatest blessing. She was right."

"Was it Naomi?" her mother asked.

Cheryl shook her head.

"Mitzi?"

Once again, Cheryl shook her head.

Her mother looked confused. "I give up. Who said it?"

Cheryl leaned over and put her head on her mother's shoulder. "It was you, Momma." She tried to blink away the onslaught of tears that filled her eyes, but she was unsuccessful. "It was you," she whispered.

AUTHOR LETTER

Dear Reader,

A recent trip to Sugarcreek, Ohio, helped me to see our setting in a more realistic way. I certainly wasn't disappointed. This charming town not only lives up to the way we envisioned it, it surpassed it. The people of Sugarcreek are gracious, friendly, and fun. Many of them showed up to say hello while author Tricia Goyer, editors Susan Downs and JoAnne Simmons, and I spent some time at the wonderful Honey Bee Café on Main Street. After that we toured Heini's Cheese Chalet and took in several other sights. Even though our visit showed us we may have placed some fictional buildings in spots where they really shouldn't be, I hope we captured the essence of this wonderful place through the eyes of its people.

As you read *Simply Vanished*, I pray you will enjoy a return visit to Sugarcreek. I know I did.

God bless you all,
Nancy Mehl

ABOUT THE AUTHOR

Nancy Mehl lives in Festus, Missouri, with her husband, Norman, and their very active puggle, Watson. Nancy has authored twenty-two books in the mystery/suspense genres and is now branching out into a brand-new series based on law enforcement.

Readers can learn more about Nancy through her Web site nancymehl.com. She, along with several other popular suspense authors, is part of the Suspense Sisters (suspensesisters.blogspot.com).

MEET THE REAL PEOPLE OF SUGARCREEK

Sprinkled amid our created characters in Sugarcreek Amish Mysteries, we've fictionally depicted some of the town's real-life people and businesses. Here's a glimpse into the actual story of the Honey Bee Café.

When I started writing *Blessings in Disguise*, the first book in the series Sugarcreek Amish Mysteries, I wanted to get a feel for the town of Sugarcreek, Ohio. I began to research it online, looking for businesses, restaurants, and various points of interest. As I searched, I stumbled across a quaint new café called the Honey Bee. The exterior was charming, as was the interior. With an appealing menu and ambiance, it seemed the perfect establishment to place across the street from Swiss Miss, the gift shop where our main character, Cheryl, would spend much of her time.

I contacted the owner of the Honey Bee Café, Kathy Snyder Kimble, and asked if she would mind having her business included in the series. Not only didn't she mind, she loved the idea! She sent me several pictures of the café and its employees. I shared everything with the other authors, who all caught the vision, and the Honey Bee became a happy fixture in the series.

Our wonderful editor, Susan Downs, worked with *Guideposts* magazine to bring Kathy's story to the June 2015 issue in an article titled "The Honey Bee Café." It was so much fun to see her wonderful restaurant shared with all of the readers of *Guideposts*.

When *Blessings in Disguise* was ready for release, I traveled to Sugarcreek where I met up with Tricia Goyer, one of the other authors, Susan, and the copy editor, JoAnne Simmons. We all headed to the Honey Bee where we kicked off the series with a book signing—and cake! It was fun to finally meet Kathy in person. She was sweet, beautiful, and gracious. It was also a joy to get to know other residents who were excited about seeing their hometown become part of Sugarcreek Amish Mysteries.

Through our stories, I've fallen in love with the town and plan to travel there again someday when I can spend more time enjoying all of the wonderful shops and treasures that make up this special place. Fictional places can make compelling locations for writers to set their novels, but being able to see and encounter a real town and real people has made my experience with Sugarcreek Amish Mysteries truly unique—one I'll never forget.

Something Delicious from Our Sugarcreek Friends

Amish Caramel Pie

3 cups brown sugar

3 cups water

2 tablespoons butter

1 cup flour

3 cups milk

6 egg yolks

Boil brown sugar, water, and butter together for two or three minutes for a good strong caramel flavor. In a separate bowl, mix flour, milk, and egg yolks. Slowly stir the flour mixture into the syrup, stirring constantly until it comes to a reboil. Allow to boil for one minute and then remove from the heat. Cool five minutes and stir once. Pour into two baked pie shells. Allow pie to cool and top with whipped cream.

Read on for a sneak peek of another exciting book
in the series Sugarcreek Amish Mysteries!

A Stitch in Time
by Elizabeth Ludwig

Fat raindrops thrummed against the windows of the Swiss Miss and ran in rivulets over the sills, through crevices in the aging wooden sash, and drip, drip, dripped noisily on the worn hardwood floor. Cheryl dredged a sodden towel over the mess with her toe.

Plucking a piece of loose caulk from the edge of one of the panes, she sighed and watched it crumble between her fingers. "Definitely time for new windows."

"What was that?"

Cheryl wiped her hands on her slacks and turned toward her sixteen-year-old helper, Esther Miller. Esther was the youngest of Seth and Naomi's brood, but Cheryl often forgot that, given her aptitude with customers. In fact, all of the Miller children, from Esther to Levi, the eldest, exhibited a kind of maturity that went beyond their years. Cheryl knew it was because of the attention Seth and Naomi paid to their upbringing. She appreciated the family's closeness and was grateful they had included her in it, what with her own family living so far away. It was hard to imagine that not all that long ago she had worried that Seth didn't like her.

She pointed toward the windows. "I was just saying the seals are in bad shape. Guess I'll need to hire someone to take a look at them."

Esther shrugged. "Levi could do it. My brother is very handy with those kinds of jobs. Would you like me to ask him?"

Cheryl bit her bottom lip. She was eager to have a reason for Levi to stop by, but common sense told her she had no business being attracted to an Amish man. "I don't know, Esther. Levi's pretty busy right now helping your father with the planting. Do you think he would have time?"

"Have time?" Esther twirled the strings of her bonnet around her finger, her eyes twinkling with mischief. "*Ja*, Cheryl. For you, I think he would make time."

"Oh. Okay. Thank you, Esther." Heat rose to Cheryl's face. Was the attraction between them really that obvious? She reached for a small scrub brush and concentrated on sweeping the bits of caulk from the sash into a small dustpan.

"Cheryl?" Esther picked up the clipboard where she was recording inventory from the shelves and pressed it to her chest. "Did I say something wrong? I did not mean to embarrass you—"

"No, Esther." She gave a wave of her hand and added a small laugh for good measure. "I just…have a lot on my mind. Really, no worries."

Esther managed an uncertain smile and went back to her task. Twice she glanced up as Cheryl wove toward the back of the store to stow the brush and dustpan under the counter, and both times, she looked hastily away before Cheryl could meet her gaze.

Cheryl slid the cupboard door closed then ducked into her office. The truth be told, she knew Levi wouldn't hesitate to lend a hand at the store, but whether he *should* was another matter. After all, hadn't she chided herself more than once for allowing her thoughts to wander where they didn't belong? Did she really want to risk the pain of another failed relationship? The last one had taken her months to get over.

Sniffing, she jerked the rickety office chair from behind her desk and punched the Power button on her computer. It was slow booting up, so she took a moment to brew a cup of chamomile before returning to the desk. The chair squealed angrily as she sat and then tipped to one side, causing her to slosh hot tea over her thumb.

Puffing a harried sigh, Cheryl grabbed a tissue and swiped her cup and fingers clean. Honestly, one of these days she was going to replace that old wobbly chair with something less vocal.

Settling into the worn leather cushion, she did a quick search of her inventory folder and pulled up the most recent list. Adding the items she and Esther had recorded the day before took over an hour, but when it was done, she felt relieved and more than a little satisfied. Maybe she would finish early and could afford to take a couple of days off.

The thought brought an instant smile to her face. How long had it been since she'd allowed herself time away? Between running the store and solving mysteries with Naomi, she'd barely had a chance to relax or do any of the things she'd enjoyed before moving to Sugarcreek, such as…

She frowned. Much as she hated to admit it, her life in Columbus had been just as busy and way more stressful. She tapped the keyboard thoughtfully. So what would she do with a couple of days off?

Her gaze strayed toward her office window. Despite the rain, the weather was definitely warming, and the forecast promised sunny days ahead. Spending time outdoors was appealing, but she had never been into gardening. So what else was there?

Turning to her computer, Cheryl typed, *things to do in Ohio,* and waited while the rainbow wheel on her search engine whirled. Several links popped up but most, like the Pro Football Hall of Fame in Canton, were the touristy type activities she tended to avoid. She skipped ahead several pages until one site caught her eye.

"Blaze the trail to treasure," she read out loud. "The Great American Antique Trail."

Intrigued, Cheryl clicked on the link and studied the list of antique shops and dealers running through northern Ohio.

"Cheryl?"

"Ack!" The voice jolted her from her scrutiny of the computer screen. She pressed her hand to her chest and peered around the monitor at Naomi. "Sugar and grits. You scared me."

"I scared *you*?" Puffing out a breath that stirred the hair peeking out from under her bonnet, Naomi lowered her hands from up around her chin to scowl at Cheryl. "You scared *me*. Did you not hear me coming?" She gestured toward Cheryl's office door.

"I knocked. Twice. I even called your name." She circled to peer at the computer screen. "What were you studying so intently?"

Cheryl swiveled the screen to give Naomi a better look. "Tell me, what do you think?"

Her brows rose with surprise. "Antiques? Ja, I love them, but I had no idea you were interested. Are you looking for something in particular?"

Cheryl shook her head and pushed the screen back into place. "Not some*thing*...some*where*, as in not the Swiss Miss Gifts and Sundries Shop or Sugarcreek." She took a sip of her tea and then set the cup aside with a clink.

Naomi crossed her arms, folding wrinkles into her dark blue cape dress. "I do not understand. I thought you loved Sugarcreek. And this store—"

"No, no, I didn't mean that the way it sounded," Cheryl corrected quickly, resting her hand on Naomi's forearm. "I love being here. It's just that I've had so little time for anything fun the last few weeks, and I thought some shopping might be a nice diversion."

"*Ach*, now I understand." Naomi's brow furrowed as she leaned forward to study the Web site again. "And you are considering visiting this place?"

"Actually, it's several places." Cheryl pulled up a map with bright red pins indicating the stops. "The first stop is only a few miles from here." She paused to give Naomi a chance to look over the map and then said, "What do you think? Does it sound like fun?"

Naomi's brow furrowed, as though she were pondering an idea. She pointed toward one of the places on the map. "That place there…how far is it from Dalton?"

Cheryl looked where she pointed. "Not far, I guess. Maybe ten, fifteen miles. You grew up in Dalton, right? Is there someone you'd like to visit there?"

"Indeed." Naomi straightened and then went back around the desk to sit in one of Aunt Mitzi's chintz-covered side chairs. "A sick cousin I have been meaning to visit lives near where I grew up. That is why I stopped by today, actually. I hoped to speak to you about possibly making a trip."

Cheryl started nodding before Naomi finished speaking. This was a busy time at the Millers' farm, and if Naomi considered leaving during planting, it was important. Suddenly aware of the concern lining her friend's gaze, Cheryl pushed away from her computer. "Of course I'll take you. Is everything okay? When did you want to go?"

Her questions were as jumbled as her thoughts. Cheryl sucked in a breath and started over. "Sorry. Tell me about your cousin. Is everything okay?"

"Ja, thank *Gott*. I think she is getting better, but her blood pressure is still very high. The midwife suspected a complication from her recent childbirth—something she called postpartum pre…preeclampsia, if I am saying that right, and sent her to the hospital for treatment."

"Oh no."

Naomi nodded. "She is better now, and back at home, but with a little one to care for, I thought now might be a perfect time to pay a visit, *ain't so?*"

"Absolutely," Cheryl said. "What does Seth think?"

"He is in agreement that I should go. In fact, he suggested I speak to you."

"Okay then," Cheryl said, flipping through the pages of her desk calendar. "How does this Friday sound? I don't have anything scheduled, and if you need to extend your visit, we can easily stay overnight."

Relief smoothed the lines from Naomi's brow. "Ach, Cheryl, that would be wonderful. I confess, I hoped you might be available. Seth and the boys are so busy at the farm. I could hire a car and driver to take me, but the expense would have made it difficult."

"It's no trouble at all, except for finding someone to run the store," Cheryl said, pinching her bottom lip.

Naomi waved her hand. "That will not be a problem. If you think she is capable, Esther would be happy to manage the store. Elizabeth will help. Lydia too. And if they have any questions, Eli or Caleb can stop by."

"Well, most certainly she is capable!" Excitement built in Cheryl's chest at the prospect of spending a couple of days away from the Swiss Miss. She loved her job and was grateful that her aunt Mitzi's mission work in Papua New Guinea had opened up a much-needed opportunity outside of Columbus, but a change of scenery? That would be undeniably welcome after their long, hard winter. She quirked her eyebrow, hopeful. "Maybe we could check out a new restaurant along the way?"

A smile brightened Naomi's face. "Ja, that would be *goot*. And maybe we could sample some of the cheeses from neighboring farms?"

"Of course. And I really would like to check out a couple of those antique stores, maybe do a little shopping if we have time," Cheryl said, her enthusiasm growing. "Just this morning, I was thinking of replacing this old office chair." She gave the worn arm a pat.

"Oh, that chair." Naomi shook her head, a smile lifting the corners of her mouth. "Your aunt Mitzi used to complain about it frequently, but she never bothered getting it repaired. She always said she had more important things to worry about."

Cheryl laughed and stood along with Naomi. "That being the case, I don't think she'll mind if I replace it altogether."

"No, I do not think she will," Naomi said, her eyes twinkling merrily. When they reached the door, she paused and some of her mirth faded. "You are a goot friend, Cheryl. I am grateful for your willingness to help. I thank Gott at every remembrance of you."

The sincerity with which she spoke the words pressed gently against Cheryl's heart. She could say the same about Naomi and would have were it not for the knot clogging her throat. Instead, she squeezed Naomi's fingers and followed it with a cheerful nod.

"I'll see you Friday then. Pick you up around six a.m.?"

Naomi nodded and with a bright good-bye, slipped out the door.

Cheryl returned to her desk, her heart full. This was going to be a wonderful weekend with Naomi, despite the reason for going. She could hardly wait for Friday to come so they could enjoy a little fun—away from the stress of the store or mysteries that needed solving.

Cocking her head, she smiled at her fuzzy reflection in the dimmed computer monitor. Now, what made her think that? Sure, they'd seen more than their share of capers in recent weeks, but things had settled down now, and Sugarcreek had returned to the tranquil little town she loved.

Shrugging, she rolled her mouse across a tattered pad, rousing her computer from sleep mode. Settling into her chair, she attacked the remaining inventory eagerly. Once she got her work at the Swiss Miss out of the way, she'd be able to concentrate on how she might help with Naomi's cousin.

After that, she intended to have fun—no matter what obstacles were thrown in their way.

A NOTE FROM THE EDITORS

We hope you enjoy Sugarcreek Amish Mysteries, created by the Books and Inspirational Media Division of Guideposts, a nonprofit organization that touches millions of lives every day through products and services that inspire, encourage, help you grow in your faith, and celebrate God's love in every aspect of your daily life.

Thank you for making a difference with your purchase of this book, which helps fund our many outreach programs to military personnel, prisons, hospitals, nursing homes, and educational institutions. To learn more, visit GuidepostsFoundation.org.

We also maintain many useful and uplifting online resources. Visit Guideposts.org to read true stories of hope and inspiration, access OurPrayer network, sign up for free newsletters, download free e-books, join our Facebook community, and follow our stimulating blogs.

To learn about other Guideposts publications, including the best-selling devotional *Daily Guideposts*, go to ShopGuideposts.org, call (800) 932-2145, or write to Guideposts, PO Box 5815, Harlan, Iowa 51593.

Sign up for the Guideposts Fiction Newsletter
and stay up-to-date on the fiction you love!

You'll get sneak peeks of new releases, recommendations from other Guideposts readers, and special offers just for you . . .

And it's FREE!

Just go to Guideposts.org/newsletters today to sign up.

Find more inspiring fiction in these best-loved Guideposts series

Secrets of the Blue Hill Library
Enjoy the tingle of suspense and the joy of coming home when Anne Gibson turns her late aunt's Victorian mansion into a library and uncovers hidden secrets.

Miracles of Marble Cove

Follow four women who are drawn together to face life's challenges, support one another in faith, and experience God's amazing grace as they encounter mysterious events in the small town of Marble Cove.

Secrets of Mary's Bookshop
Delve into a cozy mystery where Mary, the owner of Mary's Mystery Bookshop, finds herself using sleuthing skills that she didn't realize she had. There are quirky characters and lots of unexpected twists and turns.

Patchwork Mysteries

Discover that life's little mysteries often have a common thread in a series where every novel contains an intriguing mystery centered around a quilt located in a beautiful New England town.

Mysteries of Silver Peak
Escape to the historic mining town of Silver Peak, Colorado, and discover how one woman's love of antiques helps her solve mysteries buried deep in the town's checkered past.

To learn more about these books,
visit ShopGuideposts.org